Mayhem in the Mitten

By
Bill Blewett

Mayhem in the Mitten

Bill Blewett

Editor: Kelsey Boldt
Assistant Editor: Barb Blewett
Associate Editors: Bryn Blewett
         Ally Blewett
Medical Advisor: Charlene Blewett R.N.
Photos: Bill Blewett
Public Domain Photographs courtesy of Pixel
History Information Courtesy of Wikipedia
Copyright © 2020 by Bill Blewett
Printed in the United States of America
ISBN 978-0-578-63148-6
First Printing, 2020
Layout: Stacey Willey
Globe Printing, www.globeprinting.net

Other books by Bill Blewett
Mayhem on the Dead River
Mayhem on the Michigamme
Mayhem in the Superior Peninsula
Mayhem on Mackinac Island
Coming soon:
Mayhem on Manasota Key (2021)
Mayhem in Northwest Michigan (2022)

Dedication

I dedicate this book to my mother-in-law, Bernice Clements. I never realized how much she meant to me until she was in heaven.

Acknowledgment

I would like to take this opportunity to thank everyone who helped write these stories. Many thanks to my family, friends, editors, and book publisher, for without all of you, this endeavor would not have been possible.

Table of Contents

Main Characters in the Book

- Bill Bennett, Retired Sheriff
- Barb Bennett, Bill Bennett's Wife
- John Baldwin, Bill Bennett's Best Friend
- Tyler Baldwin, John Baldwin's Son
- Mark Kestila, Bill Bennett's Friend
- Ben Meyer, Bill Bennett's Friend

Main Characters in Twin Killing

- Helen Bailey, Wayne Bailey's Wife
- Jeremy Bailey, Accused Murderer (Twin Brother to Wayne)
- Lisa Bailey, Jeremy Bailey's Wife
- Wayne Bailey, Accused Murderer (Twin Brother to Jeremy)
- Detective John Bullock, Saginaw Detective Sandy Howard, 1st Murdered Victim
- Inspector Dan Delton, Lead Detective
- Dimitri, Online Romance Seeker (Wayne Bailey)
- Angie Howard, Daughter of the First Slain Victim
- Mike Howard, Sandy Howard's Husband
- Amy Lipton, 3rd Murdered Victim
- Connor Lipton, Amy Lipton's Husband
- Dr. Betty Noble, Police Psychiatrist
- Officer Rich Perry, Forensic Specialist
- Tom Smith, Detective Delton's Partner
- Carrie Tonkin, 4th Intended Murder Victim's Husband
- Crystal Torres, Second Murder Victim
- Miguel Torres, Crystal Torres' Husband

Main Characters in the Diabolical Consortium
- Dr. Dan Collins, Chief Physician at Gloria Robinson's Nursing Home
- Dr. Benjamin Gayle, Member of the Consortium
- Ned Ganders, Senior Resident at a Nursing Home
- Dr. Bryn MacArthur, Member of the Consortium
- Ann Hobbes, Chief Admissions Officer at the Nursing Home
- Gloria Robinson, Sharon's Mother
- Sharon Robinson, R.N.
- Del Santos, Pimp
- Dr. Garret Willow, Member of the Consortium
- Dr. Allen Windemere, Member of the Consortium

Main Characters in Cracking the Fracking
- Mitch Avery, Foreman
- Lucy Edington, Lance Skylar's daughter
- Frank Edington, Lucy's Husband
- Steve Haskins, Kim Holland's Boyfriend
- Kim Holland, Lucy Edington's Friend and Protestor Against Fracking
- Steve Riley, State Supervisor of Wells
- Lance Skylar, Project Engineer
- Judy Skylar, Lance Skylar's widow
- Dutch Stanton, Public Relations Employee

Main Characters in Droning the Drones
- Paul Baker, Bank Robber
- Chief Brooks, Midland Police Chief
- Cal Graham, Bank Robber
- Travis Knight, Bank Robber
- Drew Payne, Bank Robber
- Nate Shaw, Bank Robber

Main Characters in Double Trouble
- Roy Bennett, Bill Bennett's Youngest Son
- Mark Dombrowski, Attorney for the Assisted Living
- Mrs. Hobbes, Assisted Living Facility Director
- Sam Jenson, Assisted Living Facility Orderly
- Chip Kendell, Assisted Living Facility Orderly
- Dr. Medford, Assisted Living Facility
- Resident Doctor
- Judge Patterson, Probate Judge
- Henry Waters, Third Party Attorney

Main Characters in Justice for the Homeless
- Sister Angelina, Co-Director of the Catholic Homeless Shelter
- Sister Kate, Co-Director of the Catholic Homeless Shelter
- Carter Rutherford, President of the Gold Investment Firm
- Herman Schuyler, CEO of the Gold Investment Firm
- Alice Simmons, Tom Simmons Wife
- Tom Simmons, Homeless Man
- Brock Van Cort, Vice-President of the Gold Investment Firm

Tri-City Introduction

The Tri-Cities include the region surrounding the cities of Saginaw, Bay City and Midland as well as the adjoining townships.

Originally, what is today Saginaw County was inhabited by the Ojibwa tribe at the time of the arrival of Euro-Americans.

French missionaries and traders first appeared in the area during the late 17th century and met the Ojibwa who inhabited the area. A trading post was built on the west bank of the Saginaw River. Soon the army established Fort Saginaw in 1822 but was abandoned by 1824. By the late 1820s, the American Fur Company was operating a post at Saginaw.

In 1853 the Ojibwa and Ottawa tribes established large hunting camps along the Saginaw River, although white settlers were beginning to establish saw mills and farms in the area.

Growth of the settlement increased during the 19th century due to the lumber industry. Saginaw was the site of numerous sawmills and served as a port for Great Lakes vessels. What is now the city of Saginaw resulted from the consolidation of the cities of East Saginaw and Saginaw City (West Side) in 1889.

The main cause for the founding and subsequent development of Saginaw was the large demand for lumber as the Americans expanded westward. A virgin growth forest principally consisting of white pine covered most of Michigan. The convenient access to transportation provided by the Saginaw River and its numerous tributaries caused a massive expansion in population and economic activity. As the trees were cut down in the region, logs were floated down the rivers to a sawmill located in Saginaw, soon loaded onto ships and later railroad cars.

Multiple settlements comprised present-day Saginaw. On one side of the river was the first settlement near the original location of Fort Saginaw. It developed into Saginaw proper, which was incorporated as a city in 1857, containing the seat of the Saginaw County government. On the other side of the river known as East Saginaw, became a village in 1855, and later, a city in 1859.

South of East Saginaw was the village of Salina. Its name relates to the salty brine that led to a growing industry of salt production in the area. Both Saginaw and East Saginaw quickly became a hub for railroad transportation in addition to ships making their way on the Saginaw River.

Lumber production peaked by the early 1870s, but had virtually disappeared by the end of the 19th century. In addition to salt production, which experienced an eventual decline as well, growing industries, such as those supporting the area's agriculture and manufacturing, developed.

Around the start of the 20th century, the auto industry spread throughout Michigan, but most notably in Detroit. General Motors and other manufacturers established foundries and other automobile-related manufacturing facilities in Saginaw. This early relationship with the auto industry would set the course for the future economic circumstances of the city

Mass production of many types of weapons and ordnances made General Motors very profitable during the Second World War.

Migration from across the country, particularly from the South, drastically increased Saginaw's population during the war years and through the 1950s. This population growth included the expanded presence of African Americans and Latinos in Saginaw. Even before the end of the war, the needs of Saginaw's growth became clear, and were met by significant investment in the city's infrastructure.

At the height of manufacturing in the 1960s and 1970s, the city and neighboring Buena Vista Township contained 12 General Motors plants. One G.M. plant employed over 5,000 people.

The manufacturing presence in Saginaw declined in the latter half of the 20th century, resulting in high unemployment throughout the city. As a result, the city's population diminished.

As a result of the increasing unemployment, Saginaw has faced increasing social problems relating to poverty. In recent years, Saginaw's crime rate has been a major area of concern for the city.

This has caused a decline in property values, which has decreased the amount of money the city government is able to raise. According to recent Bureau of Labor statistics, unemployment in Saginaw peaked in July 2009 at 23.5%. Since then, the unemployment rate has dropped to 9.0% as of April 2015

Unemployment and population loss have led to major areas of blight. In recent years, city officials, local law enforcement, and neighborhood watches have galvanized to combat this problem.

The second of our tri-cities, Bay City, became the largest community in the county and the location of the county seat of government. Most of the county's agencies and associations are located here.

Bay City, was originally known as Lower Saginaw, and fell within the boundaries of Saginaw County. On June 4, 1846, the Hampton Post Office opened in Lower Saginaw (Bay City). This helped the county seat to be placed there when the county was organized in 1857. It was at this time that the name was officially changed to Bay City.

Larger ships had difficulty navigating the shallower water near the Saginaw settlement. Because of this, many of the early pioneers moved to Lower Saginaw as it became clear its deeper waters made it a better location for the growth of industry which relied on shipping.

By 1860, Lower Saginaw (Bay City) had become a bustling community of about 2,000 people with several mills and many small businesses in operation. In 1865, the village of Bay City was incorporated. The early industrialists in the area used the Saginaw River as a convenient means to float lumber to the mills and factories and as a consequence became very wealthy

In 1873, land was settled and homes were built on property bounded by Washington, Saginaw, Ninth and Tenth Streets. This property later became the location for City Hall. During this time, Washington Avenue was primarily developed with residential homes. Businesses were concentrated along Water Street near the Saginaw River. As time passed, businesses started to expand along Washington Avenue.

Until 1905, Bay City was limited to the east bank of the Saginaw River until West Bay City was annexed. During the latter half of the 19th century Bay City was the home of many sawmills and shipbuilders. These shipbuilding companies, which ceased operations by 1975, had built naval ships for both the United States as well as the British navy.

By the late 1820s, the third city, Midland, was established as a fur trading post of the American Fur Company. Here agents purchased animal pelts from the local tribes. An independent trading post was established at this location in the late 1820s.

A study of Midland is almost an examination of one man with a vision, Herbert Dow. He founded his first company after developing a patent for extracting bromine from underground brine. Apparently, Midland was one of the few places in the United States that contained massive amounts of the chemical. Originally, thinking small, Dow sold only bleach and potassium bromide.

In 1905, German bromide producers began dumping bromides at low cost in the U.S. in an effort to prevent Dow from expanding its sales of bromides in Europe. Instead of competing directly for a market share with the German producers, Dow bought the cheap German-made bromides and shipped them back to Europe undercutting his German competitors.

From 1914-1918, during World War I, Dow Chemical supplied many war materials to our government that had previously imported from Germany. During the First World War, Dow produced magnesium for incendiary explosives, and bromine for medicines and tear gas.

By 1918, 90 percent of Dow Chemical production was geared towards the war effort. After the war, Dow continued research in magnesium, and developed refined automobile pistons that allowed more speed and better fuel efficiency in automobiles.

In the 1930s, Dow began producing plastic resins, which would become one of the corporation's major businesses. Its first plastic products were patented in 1935. Dow's production of magnesium made Dow a very valuable partner during World War II.

In the post-war era, Dow began expanding outside of North America, founding its first overseas subsidiary in Japan in 1952, and in several other nations soon thereafter. Based largely on its growing plastics business, Dow opened a consumer products division beginning with Saran Wrap in 1953. Today, Dow Chemical is worth over $68 billion.

Part I

Twin Killing

Chapter One

"Splash, splash, splash," was the sound heard as Angie Howard and her friend, Sarah Bennett, walked along the rain-soaked sidewalk. They were best friends and Angie didn't want to gloat over her great report card. She and Sarah had known each other since kindergarten.

Angie bid Sarah farewell as she turned into her driveway. She could hardly wait to show her mother her grades. All A's on her 4th grade report card. She knew her mother probably had already seen it on the school's private website, but she wanted to enjoy her mother pretending to be excited all over again. Besides a great first quarter report card, it was also Friday which meant a whole weekend to enjoy.

As she opened the door, a tall dark-haired man dressed in black, brushed past her. Angie didn't recognize him and she would have to ask her mother who he was.

"Mother, I'm home," she shouted as she entered through the kitchen doorway. No sound.

*Hm, that's unusu*al, she said to herself as she peeked into the laundry room without luck. *Where could she be?* A glance out the front window showed the garage door was still closed. Now, Angie's curiosity got the best of her. She shouted several times, but in vain.

I doubt if she's in the bedroom. She never takes a nap. Her mother, Sandy, had more energy than anyone she knew. It was going to be a waste of time but she probably better check anyway.

As Angie approached her parents' bedroom the door was closed which was very unusual. Slowly pushing the door open with ever so little pressure, Angie dropped to her knees.

Her mother was lying spread eagle on the bed; at least Angie thought it was her. The entire bed was soaked with blood and her mother's face showed a look of anguish.

Instinctively, she rushed to her mother hoping she could get a response. Grasping her hand, as if that might revive her, there was none. She started to weep incessantly, hoping it was just a bad dream.

There was a sound of a door opening and Angie heard the familiar sound of her dad, Mike, as he shouted, "Hey, anyone home?"

Angie tried to muster a retort but was unable. She continued to sob. Eventually, her dad looked in the bedroom and saw the horrible scene. He raced to his daughter's side and gasped at the sight of his wife. By now, Angie was covered in blood trying to console her mother as if that might help resuscitate her,

Mike and Angie were unable to utter a word as her father felt his wife's wrist for a pulse, but knew only too well it was futile.

The father and daughter held each other thinking this couldn't be happening. Finally, Angie's dad had the presence to retrieve his smartphone and tap in the dreaded numbers, 9-1-1.

The dispatcher asked, "Hello, what is your emergency?"

There was a quiet stillness while Angie's dad tried to gather himself. He finally responded, "There's been a murder," was all he could utter.

What is your address?" asked the dispatcher.

After relating their home address, the dispatcher asked him to stay on the line. Ignoring the request, Angie's dad dropped the phone and continued to hold his child close.

The emergency personnel soon arrived and an officer escorted the two Howards into the living room.

A uniformed officer started asking the dad and daughter standard questions, neither remembering what their responses were. It wasn't long before a plainclothes detective walked through the doorway causing the officers to become more attentive. The detective approached the grief-stricken pair and stated, "I'm Inspector Delton. Can you tell me what you saw from the beginning?"

Angie began, "I wanted to show my mom my report card. As I entered the house, a tall dark-haired man was leaving. I didn't recognize him. Once I was inside, I called for her but she didn't answer. I checked all the rooms and then I looked in her bedroom and saw her lying there."

The father reinforced Angie's account saying, "When I arrived, I saw Angie sitting next to the bed with my wife covered in blood."

The inspector asked, "Can you describe that man?"

Angie answered, "I think I can. It all happened so fast."

Looking at Angie's Dad, Inspector Delton countered, "When she feels better, we'll have someone sit down and have her give us a computer- generated sketch. That's enough for now. We'll wait for the medical examiner and he'll give us a better idea of what happened."

They could only watch as a gurney was wheeled into the room followed by the medical examiner, and others. Once the door was closed, loud mumblings could be heard inside the room. Angie slid over to her dad's side and snuggled into his arms. She thought back to happier days when the three of them enjoyed camping trips throughout the Superior Peninsula, spending countless summers at the state parks.

She remembered at one of the parks, the three of them stood in awe as they overlooked the scenic beauty of the high cliffs, mesmerized by the puffy clouds floating slowly past them. At another park, one of the lakes was so clear they could see all the fish as they polled their way across the pond on a large raft.

The most majestic view Angie would never forget was the huge Mackinac Bridge that connected the two peninsulas. She had never seen a bridge so imposing.

The three of them would never again enjoy such fun-filled times she thought as she cried herself to sleep in her father's embrace.

The father held Angie close as the gurney containing his wife was transported through the living room to the waiting ambulance. Inspector Delton approached the pair on the couch, but after contemplating it, he decided it wasn't a good time to continue his investigation.

An officer motioned for him to inspect the front door. It was apparent an intruder had forced the door ajar using a sharp object. Detective Delton pointed at the door jam and asked the police photographer to take some pictures for evidence.

Another officer caught the detective's eye and waved him into the bathroom. There in the sink was a bloody knife.

Making sure his latex gloves were secure, the detective picked up the knife and carefully slid it into an evidence bag. He walked into the kitchen and perused the room. Seeing the butcher-block knife holder on the counter, he stepped toward it and noticed there was one open slot. He scanned the kitchen table and noticed there was an empty bowl and spoon. Examining it closer, there was cereal residue in the bowl. Was it possible the murderer took time to consume a bowl of cereal after he was finished butchering Sandy Howard? Another piece of the puzzle would have to be solved. Delton called for one of the forensic team members to bag the bowl and spoon. Perhaps some DNA or fingerprints could be lifted from the items.

Returning to the bedroom, Delton noticed one forensic officer had cut a swatch from the carpet as well as the mattress, both soiled with large blood stains. Blood residue was being scraped from the wall and head board by another officer. The entire bedding was individually separated and placed into large evidence bags.

Officer Perry, the forensics expert, looked at the detective and said, "Dan, we have a boatload of fingerprints in this room. It's going to take time to dust all of them."

Inspector Delton responded, "That's fine. Take all the time you need, Rich."

With the forensics team busy in the bedroom, Inspector Delton returned to the living room and scanned the room for further evidence. His eyes fell on two wine glasses on a coffee table. He looked at the victim's husband and asked, "Did you use these?"

"No," was the reply.

Now more evidence came into play. He nodded for one of the forensics officers to bag both glasses. Inspecting the bar in the dining room, he noticed a cognac bottle on top and he said, "Don't forget to bag this bottle as well."

The officer had just finished bagging the wine glasses and nodded his head in affirmation.

Mike Howard looked at the detective and asked, "Is it okay if we go to a friend of Angies. She just lives down the street?"

Inspector Delton responded, "Certainly, we can talk later."

Mike scooped up his sleeping daughter in his arms and carried her to his vehicle. One of the officers guarding the perimeter opened the front auto door and Mike gently placed her inside. Inspector Delton watched as the Howard vehicle drove away. Now, he and his team could get to work. Detectives pulled open drawers; looked behind the furniture, sorted through books and magazines, anywhere something personal might be hidden.

Meanwhile, Detective Delton seized this opportunity to step outside and compose himself. He had been a police officer in Midland for thirty years. He had risen through the ranks and now was at the pinnacle of his profession. Retirement was an option. His wife, Midge, before she passed, had been after him to turn in his papers and drive into the sunset. But now, with this horrendous case in his lap, he couldn't retire in good conscience.

The inspector's brother worked for the huge chemical company that controlled everything in Midland. The company had recently combined its business interests with a Japanese company. Things were going to boom and his brother was going to be a part of it. His brother had promised him a security position when he retired from the police force, but he liked where he was.

Coincidentally, in the victim's office, Officer Paul Hastings, the unofficial expert on cyber technology, logged into the Howard's laptop and guessed Angie's name would be the password and bypassed the encrypted log-in. Scanning all of the emails, he found several of interest. They were from an adult website. Again, using Angie's first name, he entered easily and found dozens of messages from one would-be suitor. It had a sexually tantalizing email address and after opening it, he wasn't disappointed.

The first email was fairly innocent asking Sandy if she wanted to meet. They continued to become more sexual as they progressed. She responded affectionately, leading him to have a clandestine meeting. The last one contained LMIRL (Let's Meet in Real Life). Further reading inclined Hastings to call Delton to check out the suggestive emails. The inspector scanned the first one and continued to read the others. It was evident a meeting had been arranged with Sandy Howard. Could this be the murderer? Delton had to identify the sender of the provocative emails. If nothing else, it showed that the victim was looking for more than a casual acquaintance.

Delton removed the night stand drawers on Sandy's side of the bed and proceeded to examine the contents. There were the usual face and hand creams along with nail files and a date book. Thumbing through the date book produced no red flags; just lunch dates and school activities.

Not satisfied, he reached into the back of the nightstand and felt an envelope. After removing it, several photos fell to the floor. Gathering them, they contained very tantalizing photos of the victim posing in alluring positions. The other detectives were quick to steal a glance at them and make crude comments. Inspector Delton realized it just became even more complicated. She was probably not an innocent victim but perhaps lured someone to her house for a sexual tryst. One of Delton's fellow officers emerged from the closet holding some sexual items. Delton asked, "Where were those?" The detective responded, "In the bottom of her shoe rack." There were snickers and guffaws from the other detectives as Inspector Delton separated them.

It was pretty clear they had a party girl as a victim, but something went horribly wrong at the party.

Chapter Two

After they had returned to the office, the detectives Delton and his young partner, Tom Smith, spread the evidence on a counter. Smith, who was a neophyte detective, was assigned to examine the datebook from one end to the other. Reading closer, it was apparent the victim kept every Friday afternoon open.

Smith thought, *was it possible she kept the Friday afternoons open for the obvious reason?*

Detective Smith motioned for his senior partner to join him scouring the datebook.

"Look here," Smith noted, "every Friday afternoon is open while the other days are full from morning 'til night. I'll have to go back and check her smartphone and laptop to see if she had any other rendezvouses scheduled for Friday afternoons.

"Let me know if you find anything," responded Inspector Delton.

Smith turned on Sandy's laptop and searched her emails more carefully. Not surprisingly, he found several that were even more provocative. One included pictures of the email contact in various stages of undress. The prospective lovebirds exchanged phone numbers and a rendezvous was scheduled for this Friday afternoon. Smith jotted down his email address hoping it could be traced. He now had two solid possible leads as to the murderer of Sandy Howard.

He summoned Officer Hastings to join him on the victim's laptop. As Hastings approached, Smith asked, "Do you think you can retrieve these two emails?"

Hastings smiled and said, "If I can find the header for your email provider, I can copy it and then paste it into my email analyzer. From there, it's a cinch to locate it. Within minutes, Hastings sat back and smiled. He stated, "The first email came from San Francisco. The second one came from an IP Address only thirty miles away, Saginaw."

The next morning, Hastings and Smith were discussing the emails Inspector Delton joined them. Smith said, "Hastings found two emails that are pretty suggestive. One of them is close and he's going to try to find the exact IP address. Inspector Delton glanced down the hallway and saw the victim's husband and daughter walking toward them.

Both detectives rose and approached them respectfully. "Thank you for coming," stated Inspector Delton. We'll have someone work with your daughter and see if she can give us a facial drawing of the man she saw."

Mike Howard nodded and asked Angie, "Are you sure you're up to this? We can do this another day."

Angie responded, "I want to do this while I can still remember what he looks like."

"Okay, honey, but we'll stop anytime you want and go back to Sarah's."

Inspector Delton made a phone call and soon a young female officer appeared. She was accompanied by a well-dressed woman.

At this point the inspector looked at Angie and said, "I would like to introduce a lady that is going to talk to you if you want. She's Doctor Noble. She specializes in cases like this."

Doctor Noble stepped forward and shook Angie's hand. The doctor said, "It's nice to meet you. I hope we can become good friends. I've talked to a lot of children who've lost a loved one. You go with this police officer and we'll talk later."

Angie nodded and Inspector Delton shook Angie's and Mike's hands.

Detective Delton looked at Angie and said, "This officer will take you to her computer and she'll ask you to describe the man that was leaving your house. Your dad can go with you. You are a brave young lady. We appreciate what you're doing."

Delton said, "After Angie gives us a facial sketch, we'll take it with us to the first IP Address."

As Angie was describing the intruder to the facial artist, Dr. Noble pulled Mike Howard aside.

She said, "I have worked with traumatized children over the years and I'm available if you want me to see her."

Mike Howard smiled and said, "Naturally. Whatever you can do will be great. When do you want to start?"

Dr. Noble replied, "Let's take things slow. Could I talk to you while your daughter is with the sketch artist?"

Mike Howard responded, "Certainly."

Dr Noble began, "Angie has witnessed a horrible tragedy. She's probably going to experience PTSD. She may have survivor guilt, that is feelings of guilt for having survived in this case, your wife's murder.

She may even blame herself.

Mike asked, "What are the signs of PTSD?"

Dr. Noble responded, "People, like Angie, with PTSD have symptoms of stress, anxiety, and depression. They usually include upsetting dreams or nightmares. Sometimes she may relive the event, these are called flashbacks. She may be jumpy or nervous when something triggers memories of the event

Under no circumstance should you try to relive it or ask Angie to talk about it. In addition to not talking about it, avoid activities, places, or people that are reminders of the event

It's common for people suffering from PTSD to have fears that the world is unsafe. She may even worry about your safety.

In addition, Angie may demonstrate a lack of interest in participating in regular activities. Sometimes, victims have feelings of detachment or may become estranged from people. Angie may not be able to have positive emotions such as happiness,

satisfaction, or feelings of love. She will probably have trouble falling or staying asleep and this could cause her to be cranky, grouchy, or angry. When you speak to her, Angie may have problems paying attention or focusing on what you say.

Signs of PTSD in teens are similar to those in adults. But PTSD in children can look a little different. Younger kids, like

Angie, can show more fearful and regressive behaviors. They may reenact the trauma through play. Symptoms usually begin within the first month after the trauma, but they may not show up until months or even years have passed. These symptoms often continue for years after the trauma. In some cases, they may ease and return later in life. For example, next year as your wife's death anniversary approaches, Angie may show a lot of emotions caused by bad memories.

She may have flashbacks that come on suddenly. It creates a short-term response, which we call acute stress disorder, to an event and can last many days or up to one month.

Sometimes, people with PTSD may not get professional help because they think it's alright to feel frightened after going through a traumatic event. Sometimes, people may not recognize the link between their symptoms and the trauma. Be sure to apprise Angie's teachers, doctors, school counselors, friends, and other family members so they can help her.

In special cases, medicine can help treat serious symptoms of depression and anxiety. This can help those with PTSD cope with school and other daily activities while being treated. Medicine is often used only until someone feels better, then individual or group therapy can help get the person back on track.

Finally, I'm a strong advocate of group therapy or support groups. They are helpful because they let kids like Angie know they're not alone. Groups also provide a safe place to share feelings."

Mike asked, "How can I help Angie now?"

Dr. Noble smiled and replied, "Right now, Angie needs your support and understanding. In the long run, help usually is needed from a trained therapist.

If you really want to help, here are some things you can do now. Give Angie time to adjust after this stressful event. During this time, it's important for you, Mike, to offer support, love, and understanding.

One big thing you have to do is try to keep Angie's schedule as similar as possible before your wife's murder. This means not allowing Angie to take off too much time from school, even if it's hard at the beginning.

When she is ready, let her talk about the traumatic event when and only when she feels ready. Praise her for being strong when you do talk about it, but don't force the issue if she doesn't feel like sharing her thoughts. Some kids may prefer to draw or write about their experiences. Either way, encouragement and praise can help Angie get her feelings out.

Reassure her that her feelings are typical and that she's not "going crazy." Support and understanding from you can help with handling difficult feelings.

As I mentioned earlier, some kids find it helpful to get involved in a support group for trauma survivors. Look online or check with your pediatrician or the school counselor to find a group nearby."

Dr. Noble continued, "This is important, get professional help immediately if you have any concern that Angie has thoughts of self-harm. If she shows any sign of suicide, it should be treated right away.

Help build self-confidence by encouraging her to make everyday decisions where appropriate. PTSD can make kids feel powerless, so you can help by showing Angie that she has control over some parts of her life. Mike, you might consider letting Angie choose a weekend activity or decide things like what's for dinner or what to wear.

Continually, tell her that the traumatic event is not her fault. Encourage her to talk about her feelings of guilt, but don't let her blame herself for what happened.

As I said, stay in touch with caregivers. It's important to talk to teachers, babysitters, and other people who are involved in your child's life.

If she regresses, don't criticize her behavior. If she wants to sleep with the light on or take a favorite stuffed animal to bed, it might help her get through this difficult time."

Mike answered, "I appreciate this information very much."

After shaking hands, Dr. Noble looked down the hall and said,

"It looks like they're finished making the sketch."

The two of them approached the two detectives and as they did, Inspector Delton said, "Dr. Noble has worked with our department for years and she's very good. She acts mainly as a sounding board for youngsters to be able to verbalize their feelings. It sounds easy, but when something traumatic happens people like to bottle it up inside. Children haven't learned that it's okay to feel sad and grieve." Mike shook his head approvingly.

By now, Angie and the sketch artist were returning to the detective's office. The artist smiled and said, "Angie did great. We have a very good drawing of the man she saw leave her house yesterday. Mr. Howard, you can be very proud of your daughter."

Mike Howard looked at the detectives and said, "I hope it helps catch the person who did this. They destroyed our family." Detective Smith relayed, "We'll do our best. This gives us a lead." As the father and daughter were departing, her dad looked at his daughter and said, "When we get to Sarah's house, I want you to rest, okay?" Angie smiled and thought, *if her Mother was here, they'd be doing something fun but that would never happen again.*

After the victim's family left the station, the sketch artist handed Inspector Delton the computer -generated drawing. The specialist said, "She did very well. It's amazing how she remembered so much detail of the man's face. It should help us a lot. They inserted the drawing into the photo copier and Inspector Delton's printer clattered and spit out duplicates.

The inspector handed the photos to the officers in the room. One patrolman examined it and said, "This guy looks familiar. Give me a minute. Yeah, now I remember. I rousted him about a month ago. His name is Bailey, Jeremy Bailey." The patrolman gave the two Midland detectives the address where they could find the suspect.

Armed with a name, the drawing and the IP address, the two detectives drove onto U.S. 10 East and hoped they might get lucky. Seeing the exit ramp 155, Detective Smith slowed down and tapped the suspect's address into his smartphone. Before long, they were parked in front of a dilapidated dwelling that passed for a house.

As they were stepping out of their vehicles, Smith said under his breath, "Even the rats abandoned this hole-in-the-wall."

They walked up the flight of stairs avoiding the broken rungs. Scanning the two mailboxes, they found their mark. Since it was a duplex, they had to use extreme caution. They didn't know if the people on the first floor could be accomplices.

They knocked on the first door and an older lady peeked through the window. Detective Delton showed his badge to the senior citizen and she slowly unlocked the door and opened it.

"Yes, can I help you, officer?" the old lady asked.

"I hope so," Detective Delton answered.

"Do you live alone?" asked Delton.

"Yes, but sometimes, my daughter comes downstairs and helps me with the house cleaning and the laundry," she answered.

"Does anyone live upstairs with her?" asked Detective Smith.

"Yes, my son-in-law, but he works during the day. I don't think either are home, but you can check," she replied.

"Thanks a lot. We'll just verify they're not there," reassured Delton.

She closed the door and the detectives continued up the flight of stairs stepping over loose boards.

Peering inside the door window, there were no lights on and after knocking several times, they returned to their vehicle.

Inspector Delton stated, "Let's drive over to Federal Avenue. We're going to need a warrant. I have a friend there that can cut through the red tape."

The Midland detectives arrived at their destination and Smith followed Delton into the Saginaw Police Station. As they passed the desk sergeant, Delton flashed his badge and the sarge just nodded. Maneuvering through a maze of offices, Delton suddenly stopped and took a right turn into the last office.

Smith could hear chortling and guffaws as he entered the room. Smith was a little surprised to see Delton in a bear hug with another burly man. By now, they were shaking hands and grinning from ear to ear.

The man seated at his desk, had risen and was shouting, "How the hell are you? You don't get this way very often."

Delton responded, "They keep me pretty busy in Midland. Whatever happened to that woman you were shacking up with?"

The man replied, "She left me when I ran out of money. I heard she hooked up with another cop in Grand Rapids. I hope he has better luck than I did."

Turning and facing his partner, Detective Delton said, "John, I want you to meet my new partner, Tom Smith. He's still wet behind the ears, but he's coming along. Tom, shake hands with the best detective in the state, John Bullock." Both Smith and the officer shook hands as the two Midland detectives sat down.

Bullock quipped, "Watch yourself with this guy. I don't trust him as far as I can throw him."

Getting down to business, John asked, "What brings you to our jurisdiction?"

Delton answered, "We're tracking an IP address that's located on the other side of town. After giving John the house address, John quipped, "You better be careful over there. There are some dangerous coyotes sneaking around."

Delton responded, "Yes, we know, we paid a visit there a few minutes ago and we're going to need a warrant with your help."

Detective Bullock responded, "I know a judge that'll give us one. He hates what's happened to our city the same way we do. You go over there and wait. I'll join you when I have the warrant."

Shaking hands, the two Midland detectives returned to scrutinize the premises. Upon arriving at their objective, both relaxed and prepared for a long stake-out. Settling down in the front seat, Delton stated, "We'll wait a few hours to see if either one shows."

Smith leaned back knowing it could be a long wait. Delton wound his window down and lit a cigarette.

As the sun was setting, a young woman approached the house,

and walked up the stairs and entered her apartment.

"That must be the daughter-in-law," muttered Delton as they exited their vehicle.

Smith followed his partner as they climbed the flight of stairs, again avoiding the broken rungs. Knocking on the door, they saw a silhouette peer through the door window. Delton flashed his badge and the woman opened the door and asked, "What's he done now?"

"Well, we're just here to ask some questions. We're from Midland. Can I ask your name?"

"My name is Lisa Bailey."

"What's your husband's name?"

The young wife responded, "Jeremy."

Inspector Delton asked, "Do you expect him home soon?"

"He works long shifts and sometimes I don't see him for days," she answered.

"It's important we talk to him as soon as possible," replied Detective Smith.

They returned to their vehicle just as Bullock and other officers arrived and parked behind them. Bullock, after sitting in their back seat, handed them each a cup of coffee. He stated, "I thought it would be awhile so I took the liberty of bringing you some nourishment. Careful it's real hot."

"Thanks," Inspector Delton responded. "I think we're going to be here indefinitely." They settled back and waited for their target to arrive. Smith asked, "Does he have a rap sheet?"

Bullock responded, "Yes, he has some priors including indecent exposure, public urination and lewd conduct. His wife is no prize either. She's been arrested for prostitution and child endangerment. The state took the child away last year. It probably saved the little one's life."

Just then, a straggly looking individual was seen making his way on the sidewalk. He turned into the yard and proceeded to walk up the stairs. Inspector Delton looked at Angie's generated photo and said, "Let's take him!" At once, they all jumped from their vehicle, including two uniformed officers.

"Mr. Bailey, can we have a word with you?" shouted Detective Bullock. Bailey turned and retraced his steps as the officers approached him, he stated, "What do you want? I've done nothing wrong."

Detective Bullock stated, "Your DNA was found at the scene of a murder in Midland last night. Where were you?"

"I was home with my wife. You can check with her," Bailey argued back.

"Believe me, we will. Let's take a ride to the station," retorted Detective Bullock.

Without arguing further, Bailey stepped into the police cruiser and was whisked to the station accompanied by two of Saginaw's finest.

The two Midland detectives along with Detective Bullock returned to the upstairs apartment and knocked on the door. Bailey's wife opened it and she quipped, "I see you took my old man. What'd he do now?"

Detective Delton answered, "We just have some questions for him regarding his whereabouts last night. Do you know where he was?"

After pausing for a long time, she responded, "Yes, we watched television until we went to bed. Is that a crime?"

Detective Bullock retorted, "Don't get smart. We want to check your computer. Where is it?"

"Wouldn't you like to know?" replied Bailey's wife.

Detective Bullock answered, "We have a warrant to search the premises. We can tear this dump apart or you can make it easy by showing us where it is!"

Lisa Bailey pointed to a pile of newspapers on the coffee table and said, "It's under the newspapers, but you'll never be able to open it."

Bullock picked up the laptop and said, "We have some pretty good computer techs downtown. Good day."

With the lap top in hand, the three detectives departed and returned to the station house.

As they entered his headquarters, Bullock said, "I'm pretty

sure our computer tech can open his files."

Delton and Smith took a seat in Bullock's office as the Saginaw detective tracked down his quarry. Finding the computer geek in the lab, he approached him and asked, "We have a laptop that we think was used in a set-up for a murder in Midland. Do you think you can decrypt it?"

The computer geek responded, "Sure, give me a minute to download the RAR file and then I can simply bypass the encryption. Within minutes, the computer geek smiled and said, "There it is. We're in. Do you need anything else?"

Detective Bullock responded, "Great, you may have just helped catch a murderer."

Returning to Bullock's office, the three detectives started to pour through Bailey's emails. After scrolling through dozens of weird sexual websites, they came across the emails from Sandy Howard. Opening one of them revealed Sandy and Bailey had a tantalizing conversation. "There you go, fellas," replied Bullock. "Case closed. You got your murderer."

"We'll get the paper work to transfer Bailey back to Midland. Can you hold him overnight?" asked Inspector Delton.

"No problem. We can hold him for 24 hours as you know. Try to be here by that time or else we have to kick him loose."

Inspector Delton responded "Got it. We'll be here before lunch tomorrow." They shook hands and departed positive they had their man. The two detectives enjoyed a relaxing ride back to Midland. They didn't know what was in store for them.

Chapter Three

Back in Mesabi County, things were pretty quiet. The boys and I had returned to our favorite restaurant, Millie's. Grumbling about the weather and our popular sports teams were a given. My comrades included lifelong friends, having solved many crimes together. They included my childhood soul-mate, John Baldwin, and our other two crime-fighting partners, Ben Meyers and Mark Kestila. They were now retired and enjoying their golden years.

A few years ago, John's son, Tyler, joined us in our mystery-solving pursuits. He was a local police sergeant whose contacts with the current law enforcement were invaluable. Tyler had recently married Carolyn Raft, the local medical examiner. She also proved priceless helping us.

Upon arriving home, I was greeted by my wife, Barb, with a concerned look on her face.

"What's up?" I asked.

She answered, "There's been a horrible homicide in Midland. One of our granddaughter's friend's mother has been murdered."

I tapped my cell phone and after connecting, my younger son, Roy, brought me up to speed on the circumstances of the murder. Naturally, there wasn't much known, but the little girl and her father had asked if they could stay for a few hours until they could find a place.

My son relayed, "I told them we wouldn't hear of them staying anywhere else. Angie and Sarah could sleep together and we had an extra bed in the basement."

I thought to myself *since the little girl saw the possible perp, her life might be in peril. If the girl and her father are staying with my granddaughter, my son's family could be in jeopardy.*

The more I conversed with my son, the more I wanted to investigate.

I asked, "Do you want me bring the guys to Midland and snoop around?"

"No," Roy responded, "I don't think that's a good idea. If we need you, I'll let you know."

I knew he was right as it would be too early to jump into the crime that wasn't even 24 hours old.

I answered, "Well, if you need me, you know where I am."

With that, we disconnected and I hoped that might be the last of it. I was wrong.

The next morning, I relayed the murder in Midland to my senior sleuth partners and that was the main topic for rest of the morning.

Mark suggested, "Maybe, it could be a serial rapist."

John brought up the point, "Maybe, she might have been seeing the perp right along and something went wrong."

Ben said, "I hear some suburban housewives have a sex ring while their families are away during the day."

Tyler added, "If she saw the perp, I hope they catch him before he tries to hurt the girl and everyone at your son's house."

Many possible scenarios were discussed and I concluded, "We'll have to wait to see what my son tells me as the case unravels."

Meanwhile, at the Midland Airport, Lisa Bailey was waiting for the next arrival. While she waited, she couldn't help but glance up at the 20th century bi-plane attached to the ceiling. As the time of the arrival neared, she gathered her belongings and walked toward the tarmac.

Soon, the luggage carousel began spewing various pieces as the passengers deplaned. It wasn't long before her anticipated arrival walked through the sliding doors. As they embraced Lisa asked her brother-in-law, "How did the drug deal go?"

He responded, "I brought two kilos back from Mexico."

The sister-in-law responded, "Where did you hide it this time?

He said, "I paid a couple of Mexican whores to swallow balloons filled with cocaine. We landed in Chicago and I waited for them to pass the balloons and then I dumped the women and sold the drugs to one of the gangs."

Lisa, impressed, responded, "Great, that'll make the boss happy."

The passenger asked, "How's my brother?"

Lisa replied, "We have a problem. They're accusing him of contacting a woman through the internet and then murdering her. He's being transported from Saginaw to Midland."

The brother responded, "They're going to have a hard time proving that. Being identical twins, Jeremy and I have the same DNA. Unless they have fingerprints, it'll be impossible."

Meanwhile, at the Midland Station House, two uniformed officers were transporting Jeremy Bailey to his cell.

Opening the cell door, Jeremy stepped in and introduced himself to his cellmate. "I'm Jeremy Bailey," as he extended his hand.

The cellmate reciprocated, "I'm Slick Bogan. What're you in for?"

Bailey replied, "They say I killed a woman."

Bogan retorted, "That beats me. I'm just in for a sex offense. How did I know she wasn't 16?"

Bailey continued, "It seems we're both in here on bum raps."

Bogan answered, "Lunch is in an hour. You might as well get some sleep."

Coincidentally, in the detectives' office, Delton and Smith were perusing the evidence to see if there was something they might have missed. Smith stated, "I think we have a good case against Bailey. His emails are pretty incriminating. His alibi isn't too good. If the DNA comes back positive, we got him."

Inspector Delton replied, "I know it looks like an open and shut case, but I've seen murderers and rapists walk."

Just then, the phone rang and Delton answered it. He listened for a long time and then disconnected. He looked at Smith and said, "Well, maybe, you're right. That was the M.E. and he said the victim was sodomized, stabbed 11 times and strangled with a curtain cord.

It appears she was still conscious when she was sodomized.

There's DNA on the body and the mattress. If the DNA comes back positive from Bailey's swab, we got our man. Case closed."

Later that day, Lisa Bailey and her brother-in-law, Wayne, paid a visit to the Midland Police Station. Upon entering, the desk sergeant did a double take. He asked, "How'd you get out? I thought we had you locked up!"

Wayne Bailey responded, "You have my twin brother back there, but he's innocent."

The desk sergeant phoned the detective's office and said, "I think you better see this."

Shortly, Inspector Delton and Detective Smith walked up front and likewise starred at Wayne Bailey.

Smith asked, "Are you telling me the one locked up has a twin brother?"

Wayne Bailey replied, "Yep, good luck prosecuting him if you don't have any fingerprints."

Both Bailey and his sister-in-law passed the speechless detectives and were taken to the visitor's room. Eventually, Jeremy Bailey emerged from the holding tank and smiled at his wife and brother. He started, "It's good to see both of you."

Wayne replied, "We'll get you out on bail and then they can try proving it wasn't you that murdered that bitch."

They exchanged general pleasantries, asking each other about nothing important. After a lengthy visit, Wayne retorted, "Hang in there, bro. We'll beat this rap."

Jeremy replied, "Hurry up and get a lawyer and some money. I want to get out of this hole."

Lisa pressed her hand against the Plexiglas and blew him a kiss.

After leaving the station house, Wayne asked Lisa, "Do you know any good mouthpieces?"

Lisa replied, "No, not really. They all suck. They just want their money."

As night was descending at the station house, the bailiff opened the holding tank door and ordered, "Lights out!"

Slick looked at Jeremy and said, "It's time for romance."

Jeremy replied, "No, I don't do that."

Slick responded, "Nobody's asking you."

Later that night, when the bailiff opened the holding tank door for the midnight rounds, he was taken aback at Bailey's face. It looked like he had been run over by a bulldozer.

The bailiff asked, "What happened?"

Bailey replied, "What'd you think? I fell out of bed."

In the morning, Bailey was led into the chief of police and he asked Bailey, "Do you want to report an attack?"

Bailey sneered and replied, "What good would it do? I just want to go back to my cell."

The sheriff answered, "Okay, you got your wish. Take him back and you can wait until we call you." Bailey returned to his cell and was pleased it was empty upon his return. He asked the bailiff, "Is that animal coming back?"

The bailiff replied, "Probably not. He's having his arraignment and most likely he'll make bail."

Bailey was scheduled for his later that morning. He wouldn't miss that pervert.

Hours later, the bailiff opened the holding cell door and shouted, "Bailey, it's time to see the judge." After staring into the cell, the bailiff gasped at the sight. Bailey had used his shirt to hang himself.

The bailiff rushed to the cell and felt Bailey's neck for a pulse. Nothing. He tapped his radio and summoned help. Immediately, several uniformed officers were assisting the bailiff but it was futile.

Coincidentally, Inspector Delton was typing Bailey's report for the prosecuting attorney when his phone chimed. Listening intensely, he replied, "I'll be right there!"

Entering the cell, emergency personnel were already checking for a faint heartbeat, but that was not to be.

As Delton was standing back to allow the medical personnel to do their job, Smith rushed in and shouted, "Oh, shit!"

Delton gazed at Smith and said, "See, you never know what's going to happen!"

Eventually, the body was removed to the morgue. Delton walked outside and lit a cigarette. As he was enjoying his smoke, Bailey's brother and wife approached him. Wayne Bailey stated, "We got a lawyer and we scraped some money together. We talked my mother-in-law into using her house as collateral."

Delton finished his cigarette and said, "That won't be necessary."

Lisa in a quivering voice asked, "What do you mean? I thought we could get him out on bail."

Delton hesitated and then said, "Your husband hung himself this morning."

Wayne shouted, "What do you mean? We just saw him yesterday and we told him we could beat the rap."

Delton replied, "I don't know why he did it, but he strung his shirt and tee shirt together and tied them to the cell bar and leaned forward."

By this time, Wayne was furious. He shouted, "I want to see him!"

The detective answered, "He's just been taken to the morgue. After the M.E.'s done, you can see him."

Both Wayne and Lisa sat down on the steps and grieved.

Wayne stated, "He was my brother. It was my job to watch out for him."

Lisa replied, "He idolized you. Don't blame yourself. I'll never see him again. We had some great times. We were hoping to get our kid back, but now that'll never happen."

Delton listened to them exchange stories and then thought there was nothing more he could do so he reentered the station house. As he was entering the building, he heard over his shoulder, "Wait a minute." He turned and spotted Dr. Noble jogging to catch up to him.

She said, "I've had my first session with Angie and she is pretty typical. She doesn't want to talk about the day. She mostly reminisced how much she's going to miss her mother."

The inspector replied, "I can't imagine a little girl having her mother taken from her. Is she having nightmares?"

Dr. Noble responded, "Naturally, she has a hard time sleeping. She often goes into her father's room and sleeps with him. It seems to calm her down."

"I can only imagine. On the other hand, the case seems to be solving itself. The accused murderer just hung himself in his cell. Those two individuals you passed on the front steps were his twin brother and wife. I have to say I'm glad the perp took his own life. It would have been a tough case to prove since he was a twin."

Dr. Noble stated, "I just wanted to bring you up to speed regarding Angie. I plan to see her every other day for a while."

Inspector Delton said, "Great. Keep me posted." They mutually separated as they went to their respective offices.

Chapter Four

That night, up north in Traverse City, the stars were twinkling overhead as the middle-aged woman waited for her city bus. It was as if the night sky was beckoning her, but she had no time for idle day-dreaming. She couldn't afford a taxi even though she was holding down two jobs. *Where was that bloody bus?* she thought.

Her mother, Gloria, was waiting. She reminisced that as a youngster, many times she and her mother sat on the front porch as they gazed skyward and the daughter dreamed of her future. While waiting, Sharon challenged herself to identify the constellations. No matter how hard she tried, her eyes were continually drawn upward. She remembered the brightest stars in the night sky belonged to the Big Dipper.

All of the stars in the eighty-eight constellations created a series of lights. Unable to control herself, she drifted into a metaphysical state of mind. Staring at each constellation, The North Star was always the first one she could identify followed by the Big and Little Dippers.

The screeching of the public bus's brakes brought Sharon back to reality. Entering the bus, she deposited the fare and checked her watch, 7:35. The nurses put her mother to bed promptly at 8:00, no exceptions. *She had to make it before 8:00. She hadn't seen her mother since she put her in the nursing home last week. With her work schedule, she couldn't squeeze in a trip across town.*

Even though she was a registered nurse for twenty-five years, she had to take a second job to keep her mother in the home. She was lucky to get another job, night shift at the 7-Eleven.

It was the last week in June and she knew only too well through her job, it was the week of the Cherry Festival in Traverse City.

During the festival, the city grew to ½ million people and she wished she could be enjoying the merriment. Many times, Sharon and her mother would make it an annual event to enjoy some of the celebrations. Now, that was all in the past.

Her mother had accumulated many illnesses in recent years, but now Sharon had been informed that morning, by the nursing home, her mother had contracted pneumonia. Sharon knew through her experience in nursing, that it could be deadly if a patient is not mobile. Chest pains, fever, chills, sweating, fatigue and other debilitating infections could cause death.

Because of the influx of people, the bus was making extra stops with great hordes entering and leaving. It seemed like an eternity but the bus finally arrived at the nursing home. Sharon had to worm her way through the throng of people and had to call to the driver to hold the bus so she could exit. Looking at her watch again, 7:57. *Could she scurry to her mother's room in time to see her?*

Racing through the front door, not even acknowledging the nurse at the desk, she arrived just as the nurse was closing her mother's door. "Couldn't you let me see her for just a minute?" begged Sharon.

"I don't make the rules. If we let one person stay late, then everyone will demand the same privilege. Residents need their rest. Visiting hours start tomorrow at 1:00. Good night," the nurse stated as she walked away.

Sharon turned and pretended to leave, but stopped short and waited for the nurse to disappear around the corner. Sharon tip-toed back to her mother's room and peeked inside.

The elderly lady in the bed didn't even resemble her mother. Now the patient looked like a ghost with tubes attached to both arms. Her mother looked so weak and helpless. Sharon quietly slipped into the room and over to her mother's bedside, leaned in and gently stroked her hair which resembled straw. Sharon remembered how beautiful her mother used to be and was the epitome of perfect health.

Now looking down at her, her mother was a pale skeleton that was sunk into the bedding. Sharon sat quietly at her mother's side and her mother's breathing now seemed to be labored. All the symptoms of pneumonia were apparent.

Noticing the chart on the counter, she began to read the codes and abbreviations left by the charge nurse. The usual, Prevar 13, was prescribed. Then she became alarmed when she saw that her mother was also being treated with Coumadin to reduce the chance of blood clots. She couldn't believe the next series of drugs. They were antipsychotic drugs, Risperdal and Haldol which were administered for bipolar disorder and schizophrenia. Sharon had never known her mother to be either of those. In fact, when she admitted her mother last week, her mother reassured her not to worry.

She had heard that some nursing homes over compensate just to keep the residents sublime. Clutching the medical chart, she raced to challenge the charge nurse. However, before she reached the door, her mother started to gasp for air. Returning to her bedside, she pressed the emergency button. Sharon was used to quick reactions by the nursing staff and couldn't believe there was no response. Watching her mother fight for breath, she ran to the door and upon opening it, saw nobody in sight. She screamed as loud as she could that finally brought the charge nurse who was preparing to castigate her for interrupting the silence.

Disregarding the charge nurse's ambivalence, she screamed, **"Get a doctor. My mother is dying!** Upon entering the room, the charge nurse was forced to agree. Sharon's mother's life was in jeopardy. Paging assistance, several nurses and a doctor answered the distress call.

Sharon stepped back hoping they could resuscitate her mother, but it didn't happen.

After the doctor stopped all lifesaving procedures, most of the night staff returned to their duties. Sharon stood thunderstruck. Shortly some LPN's entered and started to remove the tubes from Sharon's mother.

The doctor turned to Sharon and said, "I'm Doctor Collins.

I'm sorry for your loss."

Sharon mustered up the courage to ask, "Were you my mother's doctor?"

He replied, "Yes, I'm in charge of the senior residents."

Sharon asked, "Why were there so many drugs prescribed for her. She wasn't depressed or schizophrenic."

Doctor Collins responded, "In the past few days, she had become agitated and uncontrollable. She tried to hurt one of the nurses. I ordered those drugs to be administered to protect both her and the medical staff."

Sharon answered, "I don't believe it. I think you gave her that medication just to keep her asleep."

The doctor turned and left without answering.

One LPN said, "Could you wait outside while we clean her up?"

Overcome with grief, Sharon complied. She had nobody to call to inform them of the horrible news. Most of her relatives lived out of state and Sharon had not seen them in years. Eventually, one LPN stepped into the corridor and said, "You can come in now if you like."

Sharon entered the room and again stroked her mother's hair. *There was some consolation that her mother was no longer in pain.* While she was engulfed in grieving, a nurse entered and asked, "Is there any special funeral home you would like us to contact?"

Sharon had not given any thought to such details. She responded, "No, any mortuary would be fine."

The nurse answered, "There is one we usually use. I'll phone them and they'll come as soon as they can."

Sharon thought to herself, *they probably do this all the time.* Somehow, she had the perception to return to her mother's medical chart and using her smartphone photographed the contents. Even though it was very premature, she wanted to make sure that chart didn't disappear or become doctored. She just felt, somehow, the various medications had to contribute to her mother's demise.

Chapter Five

Back in Midland, the next morning, Inspector Delton had just seated himself in his office chair when his smartphone chimed. Answering, he said, "Yeah?" The voice on the other end responded, "This is John Bullock from Saginaw. You'll never guess what happened in our city. Last night, we had a woman that was sliced and diced just like your victim in Midland. Her name was Crystal Torres. She was a stay-at-home mom and led a quiet life."

Delton responded, "Are you kidding? What were the circumstances?"

Bullock responded, "Same scenario. Husband came home from midnight shift from his foundry this morning and found his wife strangled and murdered. Whoever did it, forced their way in through the side door. After they were through, they ate a bowl of cereal."

"Were there used wine glasses anywhere?" asked Inspector Delton. He continued, "If there is residue, could you have it tested. It'll probably be Courvoisier cognac.

"You must have ESP. Yeah, there were two. They're being dusted for prints. This is starting to appear to be a serial killer that is out of control."

"We have a big problem. The fellow we arrested yesterday hung himself this morning," added Delton.

"I don't like the direction this is going!" responded Detective Bullock.

"Has your computer geek checked the victim's emails?" asked Delton.

"He's going through them now as we speak," replied Bullock.

"There are a few incriminating emails to find." Delton gave the Saginaw detectives the emails addresses and they disconnected.

Detective Smith entered Delton's office and could see his senior partner had a strained look on his face.

Smith stated, "What are you worried about? Our case just closed itself. Bailey murdered Sandy Howard and he couldn't stand the thought of spending the rest of his life behind bars. I'll buy the first round."

Delton replied, "It's not that easy. I just got off the phone from Bullock. They have the same type of murder in Saginaw. The woman was killed in the same manner as our victim."

"You've got to be kidding," replied Smith.

They were still discussing the case when Delton's smartphone chimed. After identifying the phone number on Caller ID, he responded, "What'd you have John?"

Delton listened intently as Bullock updated him with more information. They disconnected and Delton stared at his junior partner and said, "It's deja vu all over again. The husband opened up their laptop for Bullock's tech, and sure enough, there were the same emails that were sent to our victim. There were no fingerprints on the bowl or spoon. It's almost as if the murderer's teasing us."

"If Bailey was locked up, he certainly couldn't have sent the emails," Smith said.

As they were discussing the case, Dr. Noble walked past their office. The inspector shouted, "Betty, I think you should hear this. As you probably heard, the case blew up in our face when another similar murder happened in Saginaw. We're back to square one."

Dr. Noble replied, "Yes, I heard by the water cooler your case fell apart. I'll keep talking to Angie and reassure her she's in no danger."

As Dr. Noble walked away, Detective Smith said, "It had to be somebody that knew his email address and used it to entice the second victim into a rendezvous."

Delton eyed his junior partner and said, "Let's play dirty. Get Hastings in here. I'm going to have him log in and pretend to be a lonely homemaker that's looking for action."

Computer specialist Paul Hastings was summoned to Delton's office and informed of the plan. Delton asked, "Can you enter that website and pretend to be a temptress?"

Hastings replied, "Sure, but where would we meet?"

Delton replied, "We have a safe house near the Arts Center just off St. Andrews Road. We can use that."

"Okay," responded Hastings, "but how should I describe myself?"

"We have an undercover female officer that will pose as the victim," answered Delton. The inspector gave Hastings a photo and description of the undercover female officer to use if he got a hit.

Hastings trolled the internet for the rest of the day without success. He returned to the inspector's office at the end of his shift with the bad news. He stated, "I cruised the website you gave me, plus several others, but no bites. I'm going home. Sell you later fellows."

"Catch ya later," responded Detective Smith.

The inspector exhaled and said, "Let's call it a night. Tomorrow's another day." Both exited the station house. Smith returned to his young bride and 15-month-old toddler, Delton to an empty house that had a photo of his deceased wife on the kitchen table. As Delton entered his small adobe, he glanced at his wife's picture. It had only been two months since cancer took her. He regretted not being by her side the last few weeks as she slowly slipped away. His job was more important. *Where did that logic get him? Now she was gone and he was sitting in the kitchen drinking a beer.* There would always be cases to solve, but he only had one wife and now she was in heaven.

He'll always remember holding her hand as she smiled at him for the last time. He couldn't imagine the pain she was enduring. The morphine was hardly working. He remembered her closing her eyes and falling into a deep sleep. Her breathing became labored as it continued into the night. The nurses assured him she wasn't feeling pain anymore. *Why was God punishing her? Why didn't God take him and not her? She led a pure life. She never said a bad word about anyone and was always the first to help someone. He remembered getting angry at her for adopting lost causes, but she just had to try to help.*

He had kept everything just as she left it. Maybe, he was fooling himself into thinking she might walk through the door carrying bags of groceries. He recalled how he would sit and listen as she went on about the latest charity and how they raised so much money. Now, he just looked at his beer and stared out the window. All he had now were memories.

Chapter Six

Back in Traverse City, over the next few days, Sharon was busy with her mother's passing. She was granted funeral leave from her employer that enabled her to tend to everything. When the funeral ended, she had some time. She turned to her smartphone and proceeded to inspect the photos she had taken during her mother's last moments.

Was it possible that her mother was over medicated just to keep her complacent? She decided to do some research. Perusing the internet, she discovered many nursing homes dispense unnecessary antipsychotic drugs. Sharon found that in one year, 88% of Medicare claims for antipsychotics were prescribed in nursing homes for treating symptoms of dementia, even though the drugs aren't approved for that. The federal government started a campaign to get nursing homes to reduce their use of antipsychotics by 15%. However, in reality, not all nursing homes comply.

Sharon continued to research other nursing homes that were affiliated with the one where her mother resided. If she was going to pursue this goal, she would need help.

Meanwhile, the pseudo-detectives and their wives decided to see what all the excitement was about at the Cherry Festival in Traverse City. The festivities began with a parade followed by a pie eating contest, and a cherry pit spitting contest. Where else can one eat one's fill of cherries and have fun doing it?

That night, we boarded the bus to return to our hotel and seated across from me was a distraught lady that looked troubled.

I stated, "Excuse me, ma'am, is everything okay?"

She didn't answer immediately, taking time to gather herself. Finally, she murmured, I'm all alone."

Trying to be sensitive, I continued, "Maybe, I can help."

She replied, "I doubt it. My mother died under unusual circumstances and I want to prove the nursing home was negligent."

I replied, "Well, guess what? You've come to the right place. See these old codgers behind me. We're retired police officers and we solved a lot of crimes. We're from the Superior Peninsula. If you give us a chance, maybe, we can help you."

She seemed to relax hearing this news. She answered, "I would be eternally grateful if you could."

I shouted, "Let's wait until we can hear ourselves talk without shouting over the uproar." She broke into a little smile and agreed.

We reached our hotel and everyone exited the bus complete with our new client. I said, "Allow me to introduce myself, I'm Bill Bennett." I introduced the rest of the gang as our wives continued walking into the hotel restaurant.

The lady introduced herself as Sharon Robinson. She never married and the last few years were consumed caretaking for her mother. She explained, "I feel so guilty. I'm a registered nurse. I never would have allowed my mother to be institutionalized in a place that was so cavalier with their drugs."

I began, "How can we help you?"

She answered, "I want to hold the nursing home responsible for my mother's death."

I asked, "Why don't you hire an attorney and let them do the legwork?"

She responded, "I don't have the money to hire an attorney. The nursing home where my mother was residing is affiliated with several others. Maybe, it's a policy for them to treat all residents the same. They keep them drugged and eventually they die."

I said, "We'll nose around and get back to you."

Sharon stated, "I don't have any money."

I replied, "Don't worry about it."

After she gave each of us a hug, we exchanged phone numbers. She gave me the list of doctors before she left.

I looked at the guys and I said, "Let's get to work. Each of us take a nursing home and see if we can uncover something."

The next day, after apologizing profusely, we were informed, "We'll spend the rest of the week enjoying the events and if you're still involved in the case, we'll simply return home."

Leaving our spouses in Traverse City, I selected the nursing home where Sharon's mother was residing when she died; possibly from a drug cocktail.

Entering the home, I told the desk receptionist that my uncle was in poor health and he was probably ready for a place such as this. The desk clerk paged the admissions officer and before long, I prepared myself to be inundated with glowing information and brochures from a professional salesperson.

The professionally dressed woman approached me, shook my hand and smiled. She started by introducing herself saying, "I'm Ann Hobbes. How are you? We're very proud of our facility. We treat all our residents like family." After I reciprocated the formalities, she continued on a cavalcade of positive reasons why my uncle would be lucky if he could spend his golden years at their nursing home.

As we were concluding our tour, I asked, "Do you mind if I look around on my own. I'd like to get a feel for the place."

Ms. Hobbes responded, "No problem, my office is down the hall. If you have any further questions please see me."

Wandering the corridors, it was pretty clear that this was the last stop for these folks. The only way they were leaving was feet first.

I finally found an older gent that seemed to be coherent. I introduced myself and he replied, "I'm Ned, Ned Ganders." I decided to pry into the make-up of the nursing home.

I asked him, "What's it really like living here?"

He answered, "I hate to say it, but it's hell. They keep us doped up so we just sleep all the time."

I asked, "Doesn't anybody check on the medications. I thought the government regulates how much a doctor can prescribe."

Ned was quick to reply saying, "They have ways around it.

They can just say the patient is uncontrollable. Nobody ever checks on the doctor's prognosis."

Now my curiosity was piqued. I continued, "Who is the doctor of record?"

The old timer looked both ways before he spoke, saying, "Dr. Collins."

I said, "Thanks. Let me know if I can help you."

Ned replied, "Just get the SOB before he kills somebody else."

The other four pseudo-detectives scattered throughout the Lower Peninsula, and found in each case, there was one primary doctor who controlled the prescriptions.

Meeting back at our hotel, all of the fellows had the same story. It seems there is a consortium of doctors that run the affiliated nursing homes.

I smelled a rat and we had to do something about it. I phoned Sharon Robinson with the good news. Listening to the information we had ascertained, she sounded happy. "Now, I can hire an attorney and all he has to do is draw up a civil case against the medical consortium."

Feeling our job was done, I disconnected, and along with my friends, we returned to the Superior Peninsula. A few days later, I was scanning the newspapers for updates on local events. A story caught my eye in the LP. In the story, a nursing home doctor was murdered in broad daylight during the Cherry Festival. Reading further, I found he was stabbed with a long-pointed object. Because of our recent trip to that city, I read further. It seems the doctor was murdered among the crowd during the celebration and because of the chaos; nobody paid any attention until he crumbled. Since, his relatives had not been contacted, the authorities did not release his name. My curiosity was aroused.

I dialed my inside man, Tyler Baldwin. He was a sergeant in the local Needleton Police Force and he would be able to relay the victim's name once he had time.

Tapping my smartphone, Tyler answered, "Yeah, what's up?"

I replied, "Remember a few days ago, when we advised that woman to hire an attorney. She claimed her mother's doctor was dispensing narcotics to keep the nursing home residents subdued?"

"Sure, but that's old news," relayed Tyler.

"I'm not so sure," I answered.

"What'd you mean?" he asked.

"A doctor was murdered during the Cherry Festival yesterday in broad daylight."

"Really!" he retorted.

"Do you remember the names of the doctors that prescribed meds in the nursing homes?" I asked.

"Sure, and you relayed the info to that woman," he quipped.

"That's right. But I wonder if she didn't take the law into her own hands!" I asked.

"I'll check on it and let you know," he retorted. We disconnected and I waited for the answer I didn't want to hear.

Several days later my cell phone chimed, and after checking Caller ID, I saw it was Tyler's.

Answering, I asked, "Yeah, anything on the murdered doctor's identity?"

"Believe it or not, you were right. It was the doctor from Robinson's nursing home. The preliminary M.E. report is that he was stabbed with something long and narrow like a wood carver's hand chisel," he relayed.

"I guess I'd better pay a return visit to the LP and find out what's going on," I answered.

"If you need help give us a call," stated Tyler. We disconnected and after touching base with my better half, I crossed the Mighty Mac.

I wanted to hear firsthand if Sharon Robinson was the murderer. Arriving at her house, she was pruning some roses as I entered her yard.

Seeing me, she stated, "I didn't think I'd be seeing you again. What brings you here?"

I relayed, "Didn't you hear? Someone murdered the doctor that had been treating your mother?"

She acted surprised and retorted, "No, I haven't watched the local news. How did it happen?"

After hearing my explanation, she went into further detail, "I contacted a couple of attorneys and explained my case to them. They just weren't interested. Apparently, it's almost impossible to prove culpability in medical cases. Most judges give doctors a lot of leeway in treating nursing home patients. Both of the law firms said the case would drag on for years and when it was over, I wouldn't get much money. I've been seething since."

I pushed by asking, "Seething enough to take the law into your own hands?"

She showed me an anguish look and retorted, "I'm a nurse and I'm sworn to save lives not take them. No matter how mad I was, I couldn't bring myself to harm that doctor."

I didn't think she was a good liar, so I apologized and decided the best thing to do was to visit the Traverse City Police Station.

Chapter Seven

The doctor's murderer was stalking the second victim. *All five of the doctors were going to pay. Collins was the first. Eventually, the remaining four would feel pain like she endured.*

After arriving at the second victim's residence, she saw Dr. Benjamin Gayle waxing his Bentley. The murderer approached him and asked, "Did you get the money to pay for that vehicle from murdering your patients?"

Dr. Gayle wasn't sure if he heard right. He mumbled, "What?" as he stood to confront his insulter.

With a quick thrust the attacker plunged her weapon into the doctor's torso penetrating the lung, thus prohibiting the victim to utter a sound. Dr. Gayle fell to the ground knocking over the pail of water. The attacker spit on the body and returned to her vehicle. *Two down and three to go,* she thought as she stepped into her vehicle and accelerated. There was a sense of justice that had been served as the assailant returned to her home.

Meanwhile, driving to the local police station and entering, it was apparent the place was in a state of flux. Officers were scrambling past me to exit the building. Something was happening so experience told me to step back and wait.

After sitting on a bench for a period of time, it seemed like the room was settling down. I approached the desk sergeant and asked the obvious, "What's happening?"

The officer replied, "Another homicide, but this one's in Grayling."

I asked, "How does that affect this city?"

The desk sergeant replied, "We're being asked to watch M-72 that connects us to Grayling."

"Do you have a description of the vehicle?" I asked.

"Yeah, someone described a late model gray mini-van leaving

the scene," the sergeant answered. "Can I help you?" he asked.

"Is the chief of detectives here?" I asked

"She's not here right now. You can wait in her office. Down the hall and to the right," the sergeant said.

"Thanks," I answered and made my way to her office and sat down.

After a lengthy wait, the female detective entered and acknowledged me. She asked, "Can I help you?"

I replied, "My friends and I are retired police officers from the Superior Peninsula. We're trying to help solve the murder of Dr. Collins."

"You don't say," replied Detective Melbourne. I could tell there was a hint of sarcasm in her voice.

I continued, "Really, we've solved a lot of crimes in the Superior Peninsula and even helped unravel the governors mess last year."

The detective softened her look and responded, "Oh, yeah. I heard about that. So, it was you and your buddies that solved that case. I suppose you're here to solve this one," she responded.

"We're just trying to find out who might have done this. Naturally, it had to be someone with a grudge."

She agreed saying, "That makes sense, but being a doctor at a nursing home, there's probably only two to three hundred people that might blame him for their loved one's death."

I had to admit she had a point. I replied, "I think I might know of one suspect that recently lost a loved one and was very bitter. The doctor had prescribed a lot of powerful medicine that kept her mother sedated 24/7. We've looked into it and my buddies discovered the same thing was happening in the other nursing homes that the doctors have a consortium and have complete control over dispensing the drugs."

Listening carefully, she replied, "Yes, but there's still hundreds who might have the same grievance against this consortium." She continued, "As you may have heard, we just got word a second doctor was murdered about an hour from here in Grayling. There might be a connection."

I said, "I have to agree. We're going to back track and see how many cases this consortium is accused of overdosing patients."

Since she was not able to provide any further beneficial information, I stood and shook her hand and departed. At least, she knew who I was in case our paths crossed again, and I was pretty sure they would.

With two doctor's dead, I made that phone call to my cohorts and within hours they arrived. After discussing our strategy, we decided to stake out the other three doctors believing an attack was imminent.

Meeting in a coffee shop on Eastman Avenue, Ben said, "Mark and I can find Dr. Garrett Willows and see if anybody comes after him."

John added, "Tyler and I can keep an eye on Bryn MacArthur. I think he's' in Grayling."

That left me with a Doctor Allen Windemeyer.

Suspecting an attack was looming, Ben and Mark made haste to find Doctor Willows. Using the GPS on their smartphone, they arrived at a mansion along West Grandview Parkway. They double checked the GPS to make sure the address was correct. The estate spanned many acres with a beautiful view of Lake Michigan.

"My God," Mark said, "I thought I'd seen everything. This place is bigger than most European palaces."

Ben agreed, "Keeping residents doped up all day must be lucrative."

Using a pair of binoculars, Ben could identify the massive garage with multiple doors.

Mark said, "My wife and I could stay in this place for weeks and we'd never see each other."

Ben asked, "What's the downside?"

Mark answered, "I didn't say there was."

"Let's introduce ourselves to Willows so he doesn't call the police thinking we're the stalkers. I'm sure he's heard about the first two deaths."

They exited their vehicle and were impressed at the perfectly groomed hedges as they neared the front door. Knocking on it resulted in footsteps that got louder as they reached the front door. The door opened and they were met by a dazzling beautiful woman that was probably being paid for many services.

She asked, "May I help you?"

Ben replied, "Yes, is Doctor Willows available. We'd like to speak to him."

"Who may I say is asking?" she answered.

"We're a couple of retired detectives investigating the deaths of two of the doctor's partners in the consortium."

"One minute please?" she asked.

Both seniors googled each other and smiled.

Mark said, "Sometimes this job isn't all bad."

Ben relayed, "I guess we have to enjoy the good perks when we have them."

They were still commiserating on the beautiful woman that opened the door for them when she returned and said, "Please follow me."

Ben and Mark were only too glad to accommodate her as she led them from one massive room to another. They finally arrived gaping at the doctor's personal planetarium. A large telescope was pointed skyward through a skylight.

Both seniors were marveling at the instrument when they heard. "Please come in and sit down. May I interest you in a drink? My name is Garrett Willows. I see you met my confidant, Ms. Burks"

Ben reciprocated saying, "My name is Ben Meyers and this is my partner, Mark Kestila. Yes, your employee is very beautiful. We're part of a group of retired detectives that are looking into the murders of two of your partners, Doctors Collins and Gales."

Dr. Willows responded, "Very interesting." Looking at his enhanced telescope he said, "This is my little escape venue. Whenever I'm stressed out, I flee to my constellations. Would you like to have a look?" Ben relayed, "Maybe, another time? Right now, as I said, we're investigating the death of your partners.

"By the way," Ben asked, "how is it you live here when your nursing home is located half an hour south of here?"

The doctor replied, "There's nothing like this in the community I work. When I saw this on the market, I just had to have it." Dr. Willows continued, "I pride myself on being perceptive and I believed there's someone out to get all of us from the time Collins was killed two days ago."

Mark asked, "Do you have an idea of who it might be?"

Dr. Willows answered, "Come now. You must be joking. The five of us have administered thousands of prescriptions. I couldn't possibly have a clue which family might be holding a grudge."

Ben said, "Yes, but some of them probably didn't need all the meds."

Dr. Willows now became defensive and replied, "It's a judgment call. Would you want to care for someone that was combative?"

Ben trying to hide his disgust responded, "These people are old and need TLC not narcotics to knock them unconscious just so the employees can have an easy day."

Noting the conversation was getting off track, Mark stated, "As we mentioned earlier, Ben and I are with a group of retired detectives that are trying to find out who's at the bottom of this. Do you mind if we watch your house?"

The doctor responded, "Not at all, in fact, I'll feel safer with you nearby."

Ben and Mark stood and shook the doctor's hand and departed. They enjoyed being led to the front door by the jack-of-all-trades Ms. Burks.

After they left the mansion, Mark said softly, "I'm going to have to get one of those employees."

Ben replied, "You're so old you wouldn't know what to do!"

Mark retaliated, "Yes, but I'd like to try."

Arriving at their vehicle, both men settled down for a long ordeal of babysitting a wealthy doctor. They resented that he made a fortune from prescribing drugs to keep nursing home residents comatose. They had to keep reminding themselves there was a murderer loose and the doctor might be the next victim.

After darkness arrived, Mark was fast asleep and Ben was fighting to stay awake. Just then, a vehicle arrived. It slowed down and the driver turned into Willow's driveway. Ben gave Mark a nudge, waking him, and together they kept a close eye on the vehicle.

The vehicle stopped and someone exited the driver's door.

Ben said, "I suppose we should check on it. Let's go."

Silently, Mark and Ben left their vehicle and using the hedges as cover, they stealthily approached the intruder. To their surprise, the intruder rang the doorbell and both seniors stopped in their tracks. They slid behind the building as the intruder was allowed entrance.

Mark asked, "What'd you think? Is this person legitimate or should we pursue it?"

Ben relayed, "We'd better look into it!"

As they approached the front door, Mark commiserated, "If nothing else, we get to see Ms. Burks again."

Ben smiled as he rang the doorbell.

There was a long wait before the door opened. This time Ms. Burks was dressed in a short nighty and a skimpy wrap.

Ben was able to compose himself first and asked, "Is everything all right?"

Ms. Burks responded, "Of course it is, why wouldn't it be?"

A scuffling noise echoed through the hallway. Ben and Mark shoved the gorgeous woman aside and dashed toward the commotion. It sounded like it was coming from upstairs. They arrived to find Dr. Willows bleeding profusely. The attacker had made their escape down the servant's stairway. Both Ben and Mark knelt over the doctor and realized blood was gushing out of the doctor's abdomen. Ms. Burks arrived and gasped at the sight.

Ben asked, "Okay, what happened?"

She replied, "Dr. Willows sometimes has evening guests. I

just let the women inside and I retire to my bedroom."

Mark shouted, "Are you telling us, you weren't involved in this?"

Burks answered, "Of course not, I was in my room from the time I let that woman inside until you rang the doorbell."

They heard a vehicle start and the motor grew fainter as the assassin disappeared into the night.

Ben shouted, "Who was the woman?"

Burks answered tearfully, "I don't know. I just let them into the house and go back to bed."

"Can you describe her?" asked Ben.

"After a while they all look the same. Young and beautiful. I think he has a contract with an escort service."

Mark pushed by asking, "Are you telling me, you and Willows aren't involved romantically?"

She responded, "Certainly not. I'm just his administrative assistant. He asked me to stay here because it would be more convenient."

Ben relayed, "I have a hard time believing that."

Burks relayed, "It's the truth. I just work for him. Nothing more."

Mark tapped 9-1-1 into his cell phone and relayed the terrible event to the dispatcher.

Shortly, emergency vehicles arrived and the place came alive with excitement.

Both senior detectives were detained and brow beaten as if they were suspects.

They were interrogated into the wee hours of the next day. By the time they arrived back at the hotel, they were exhausted. Knowing they would not win any popularity contest with us; they woke us anyway and explained the whole scenario.

After they finished, I asked, "Ben and Mark, why don't the two of you look into the escort business and try to discover the identity of the woman sent last night? I'll conduct surveillance on Dr. Windemeyer. John and Tyler, why don't you return and observe Dr. MacArthur?"

John stated, "Okay, now that we got that settled, let's get some rest. We have an early day tomorrow." I didn't even remember pulling the covers over me.

Chapter Eight

Bright and early the next morning, we departed for our targets. With only two doctors left, we had to be vigilant or they would both be massacred. As we were driving, I phoned Detective Melbourne and tried to learn an update on the latest murder.

She was cooperative to a point, but she wouldn't divulge too much. I did worm out of her that Dr. Willows was murdered with a long narrow sharp object. It was one of the few clues we had.

Ben and Mark drove to the seedy side of the community and looked for someone to interrogate. Seeing a group of young men occupying a run-down tenement building, they took a chance and decided they might be able to persuade one of them to give them some information.

Ben and Mark parked their vehicle and approached the group of teenagers. One youth shouted, "Cops." They started to run until Ben shouted, "I got fifty to whoever gives us the info we want."

The group stopped and approached them with apprehension. The biggest youth blurted, "We don't talk to the PO-lice or narc on anybody."

Mark relayed, "We're not the cops and we're not asking you to narc on anyone. We just want some information."

One of the youngsters replied, "If you're not the cops why are you packing?"

Ben replied, "We're private detectives trying to find someone."

That seemed to calm the crew down. One of them spoke, "What u say 'bout a "C" note?"

Mark answered, "We didn't say anything about a "C" note."

"What you want to know, whitey?" shouted one of the youths.

Ben barked, "We know there's an escort service operating in this city. Do any of you know where it is?"

The youths commiserated for minutes and one relayed, "We don't know who runs it, but there's a bar on Union Street that old white farts like yourselves seem to go. Try there. Now where's the money?"

Ben handed them the money and, along with Mark drove to the street. There were several bars and Ben and Mark decided to try all of them. One by one, the two senior sleuths entered and left without a snippet of information. Finally, coming to the last bar that looked like it had seen better days, Mark said, "I got a good feeling about this place."

Ben retorted, "I hope you're right."

Entering the bar, it looked like it was a home for losers. Bellying up to the rail, the barkeep wiped the area in front of them and asked, "What'll it be, gents?"

Ben said, "We'll take two drafts and some information. We're in town looking for some romance. I hear you help fellows find it." The bar tender replied, "The beers will be $10 dollars. In regards to the other item, you'll have to ask the man in the corner booth." Ben and Mark scanned the far wall and their eyes fell on a portly man sporting a goatee and a cheap suit. Ben and Mark grabbed their drinks and ambled to the corner booth. Sitting down, Ben struck up a conversation, "I hear you can hook up guys looking for action."

The man with the goatee responded, "Maybe, but I don't help undercover cops. It's been nice talking to you. Get lost!"

Mark relayed, "That's not very friendly." A behemoth walked toward them and said, "You heard the man. Get lost!"

Ben replied, "Okay, we can tell when we're not wanted."

As they stood, Ben karate chopped the giant in the neck and Mark slammed his head into the table.

Ben repeated himself, "As I said, we're looking for some action and you're going to tell us everything!"

The portly man appeared nervous with his bodyguard moaning on the floor. He said, "You're cops. You can't force me to talk!"

Ben whispered, "We never said we were cops. We're independents. Do you want to look like this loser in a few minutes?"

After mulling it over, the goateed man responded, "Okay, my name is Del Santos and I can hook you up, but it's ten thousand for each of you."

Mark answered, "We just want to know who was sent to Dr. Willows last night."

Del Santos answered, "I sent my best girl, Tiffaney, but haven't seen her today. I don't know where she is. Honest!"

Ben asked, "Where can we find Tiffaney when she's not hooking?"

"She lives in a trailer park on Meadow Lane."

Where can we find this trailer park and what's her trailer's number?" asked Mark.

Del Santos hesitated as the lump on the floor moaned. Mark kicked the lump in the head and shouted, "Shut up!" Mark smiled and said, "You were saying."

The pimp wrote down Tiffaney's address. Ben and Mark stood and looked at the barkeep and said, "Clean this mess up. How do you expect to run a respectable business?"

Entering their automobile, they drove to the address and found the trailer in disrepair. They exited their vehicle and stepped over beer cans as they approached Tiffaney's door. After knocking several times, they opened the door and shouted, "**Tiffaney, are you home**?" No response. Entering, they walked to the back of the trailer where they found their quarry. She was tied to a chair and had been tortured.

Mark stated, "I assume the assassin worked Tiffaney over until they got what they wanted."

"Yeah," Ben agreed. He tapped the 9-1-1 dispatcher and informed the police where they could find Tiffaney's body.

After the police arrived, it took hours of interrogation until Ben and Mark were released. As they returned to their vehicle, Mark said, "This police questioning is starting to become a habit." Ben nodded in agreement as they drove to their hotel.

Meanwhile, John and Tyler were being vigilant watching Dr. MacArthur's house. They took turns monitoring the house as the hours whiled away. The day turned into twilight, and both observers wished for a cup of coffee.

Both amateur detectives rubbed the sleep out of their eyes between yawns. John finally said, "Let's call it a night. I don't think anything is going to happen." The words were barely out of his mouth when a noise was heard from inside the house. In a flash, both men raced to the house and kicked the door in. With Glocks brandished, they went from room to room searching.

John heard Tyler shout, "In the master bedroom." John raced to his son only to find two bodies lying in their own blood. They felt for a pulse in each of the victims. John felt the man's pulse, but looked at his son and shook his head, indicating Dr. Bryn MacArthur was gone. Tyler kept feeling the lady's wrist and said, "I think I have one, but it's faint." Immediately, John dialed 9-1-1 to inform them of the carnage. John ran out the back door hoping to see something. Scouring the area proved futile. He returned to join his son to wait for the emergency personnel.

Upon their arrival, the EMTs checked the female's vital signs and began the usual procedure. One EMT looked at John and Tyler and said, "If she lives, she owes you her life. Nice job."

The police weren't as diplomatic as there were now multiple murders in the area. After informing the police, that they were partners with the other Superior Peninsula investigators, it failed to gain the boys any brownie points.

One of the officers relayed, "We've been hearing about you fellows. It seems wherever you guys are, death seems to follow."

John replied, "It does appear that way doesn't it?"

Like Ben and Mark, the two previous nights, John and Tyler were interrogated until they were exhausted. Finally, they were allowed to leave, but ordered to remain available if future interrogation was needed. The two pseudo-detectives collapsed into their beds once they arrived back at their hotel. Hearing their hotel door open and close, I looked in on them, but decided it was better to let them sleep.

Chapter Nine

The next morning in Bay City, Amy Lipton kissed her husband good-bye and handed her eight-year old son his Darth Vader lunch box and sealed it with a peck on her son's cheek as he and her husband exited the house. She couldn't wait until her husband's vehicle was out of sight hoping he wouldn't return until early evening.

She had a wonderful morning planned. A new love interest had sparked a flame in her that she had not felt for years. She still cared for her husband, Ted, and their son, Scotty, but it wasn't the same. Watching them disappear into the horizon, she couldn't wait to change into her new negligee.

She remembered her great teen years and an exciting college life, but now she was trapped in this suburban life that was squeezing the life out of her. She needed something exciting. This gigolo, she met online wouldn't mean anything to her, but it was something different.

She took out the Courvoisier cognac her gigolo had requested, and put it on ice. He was supposed to come soon and she wanted to be ready. Pulling the shades and lighting some candles help set the mood. She shouted, **"Alexa, play soft soothing music!"** Soon the voice of Taylor Swift could be heard. The table was set. All she needed now was Dimitri, who had promised to take her places she had never been.

There was a knock on the door. She walked to the curtains and peered through them. Her would-be lover was even more handsome than his photo. He was very buff with his shirt opened half way down. Sporting a tight black shirt and pants, he looked ever so dashing. His long black hair blew in the wind. *Was she ready for this?*

She slowly opened the door as to make a casual appearance.

"How do you do?" Dimitri asked.

"Great, it's nice to meet you," She reciprocated. She ushered her gigolo inside so as not to draw attention.

Dimitri continued, "I parked in the convenience store parking lot a few blocks away."

Amy replied, "How thoughtful of you. I hope this afternoon fulfills all my fantasies."

Dmitri responded, "I promise you this will be an afternoon you'll never forget."

"Let's start with some cognac, shall we?" asked Amy.

As he saw the bottle, Dimitri said, "My love, this is exactly what I would have ordered."

Dimitri poured the cognac and stared into her eyes. They slowly sipped the elixir as drink after drink was consumed until the bottle was empty. By now, Amy's inhibitions were subdued. As she stood, she had trouble walking to the bedroom. She looked over her shoulder and asked, "Shall we continue where we can be more comfortable?"

Dimitri smiled and replied, "But of course," as he followed her into her bedroom.

Once in bed, she was embraced like never before. He held her in her arms tight, and for an eternity their lips met. She could feel the room spinning as she feared she might faint. It might have been better if she had.

Suddenly a cord was wrapped tight around her neck. Her eyes bulged as she tried to scream for help, but Dimitri just stood and left the room. The attacker now stabbed her. Unable to breath, she was helpless against the onslaught. She felt the knife slice into her body many times and blood gushed out like geysers. The strangle-hold continued as she was at the complete mercy of the attacker. She could feel a large object being shoved inside of her and she wanted to scream but was unable. The slaughter continued for minutes.

Meanwhile, Dimitri had retreated to the kitchen to prepare a bowl of cereal. Rummaging through the cupboards, he found utensils and a cereal that he liked. Retrieving the milk and filling the bowl to the top, he began to enjoy himself.

After a while, the assassin entered the room and said, "It's' done. I left the knife in the bathroom sink. Let's get out of here."

Dimitri responded, "Not yet, did you forget we have one more job? He removed a knife from his pocket and walked to the side door. He pried the door jamb loose so it appeared to have been a forced entry. He turned to his accomplice and said, "Now, we can leave."

As they were returning to their vehicle, the assassin said, "You said that little Howard girl got a good look at you. We better take care of her next."

In the convenience store parking lot, reaching their vehicle, the assassin stated, "Wait here, I want to get a newspaper. Maybe, we're famous."

Entering the store, the assassin saw the newspaper stand and on the front page there was a computer sketch of Dimitri. Throwing some loose change on the counter, the assassin folded the paper and returned to his cohort.

The assassin entered the vehicle and started the engine. Dimitri asked, "Is there anything about us in the paper?" The assassin replied, "No, nothing much; just the basics regarding the murders. We have nothing to worry about."

Gambling that the police were not there, the assassin drove past the Howard's residence. Except for the yellow crime tape, it looked quiet. They knew the family could not be staying in the house, but where were they? The assassin stated, "We have to find that little rug rat before she fingers you." The assassin knew that was too late. Dimitri's picture was all over the media. He was now a liability.

Just as the assassin was considering driving away, they saw their possible target. A little girl was getting out of a car with a man that was probably her father. They slowed down to make sure. Dimitri said, "That's her." The assassin increased their speed and now a plan would have to be implemented.

Chapter Ten

Trying to catch some Z's, my smartphone chimed and I answered. My son, Roy, stated, "I think it's time for you and your buddies to come. There have been two more murders, one in Saginaw and the other in Bay City. Mike Howard wants to go somewhere else where they won't put us in jeopardy. Can you come?" He continued, "Whoever's responsible for these horrible murders, I feel is going to come after Angie. She helped generate a sketch of the perp and it's in the media."

"Certainly," I replied, "the guys are here and we'll leave as soon as we can get our gear together." We disconnected and I felt the apprehension in his voice.

I had to tell my wife what we were going to do without alarming her. I knew she would see right through me.

Trying to be subtle is not my strong suit. I phoned her as she was about to tee off on our golf course. I said, "Barb, Roy just called from Midland. As I told you earlier, he's taken in a family that had a loved one murdered a few days ago. There have been other murders probably committed by the same person. Roy asked for our help. The boys are packing and we'll leave in a few minutes."

My wife said, "By all means go and help. We don't want anything to happen."

We didn't spare the gas as we arrived by mid-afternoon and scoped out the area. It was a defensive nightmare. The cookie-cutter houses were close to one another and all of the yards were full of bushes and trees in full bloom. We had to establish a perimeter around the house.

I introduced myself to Angie's dad, Mike, and tried to reassure them, we would deploy and be inconspicuous. Mark climbed a tree and made himself invisible. Ben climbed over the back fence and scaled a tree. John and Tyler deployed down the street in either direction, and I lodged myself in my son's upstairs window. This gave us a 360-degree kill-zone, but at night or in bad weather anything could happen.

My son was instructed to pull the shades and close the drapes and stay away from the windows. Under no circumstances was anyone to venture outside.

We didn't know when or even if an attack was imminent but we wanted to be ready. We had done this many times before and we were all professional.

Evening arrived without fanfare, and I was thinking this would be the perfect time to try something. We noticed a woman approaching and we waited to see how the action revealed itself. She turned into my son's house and we watched as she rang the doorbell. In a few minutes, the door opened and she entered. Calling my son on his phone, I asked, "Who was the woman that just entered?"

He replied, "It's okay. It's just the psychiatrist that's been seeing Angie." I disconnected and waited to see if any more unplanned visits were going to occur. I was right. All of the house lights on the street were now dark as the locals turned in for the night. I didn't have to worry about the other guys. I knew they would remain vigilant. Later, we noticed the psychiatrist exit my son's house and disappear into the night.

In the early morning hours, a slow-moving vehicle could be seen maneuvering toward our kill zone. It continued driving past and it occurred to me there must have been a reason for the vehicle to drive so slowly. I assumed the worst and told the boys to be extra alert. I got three "Rogers," back and one "kiss my ass," from my old duck hunting partner Mark.

I heard "movement at 3:00" over the walkie-talkie and I removed my safety. From the voice, I knew it was John and if the perp continued, he'd be dead. I scoped the area where John had seen something, and sure enough, I saw a silhouette sneaking along the bushes. A second "movement at 6:00" was heard from another walkie-talkie. This time I recognized Ben's voice. I couldn't make out the second silhouette, but I knew if he kept crawling Ben would eliminate him. The one perp kept maneuvering along the hedges thinking he was invisible. With night vision goggles and a night scope on our rifles, it was no problem. These perps were crawling to their death.

One would-be assassin reached my son's house side-window and was about to pry it open when a crack was heard. The silhouette fell motionless. I assumed John had taken the shot. The other perp must have crawled away into oblivion. That villain would live to haunt another day. Nobody moved in case the fool that escaped made a return appearance. By sunrise, I felt the coast was clear and told everyone to rendezvous at the house.

Standing over the fallen perp, I removed the mask and he resembled the sketch Angie had described to the police. John phoned the shooting into the Midland Police and they arrived shortly. The place was alive with lights and sirens. My son and his family came outside and I told him, "We eliminated one would-be murderer but the second one escaped."

My son replied, "Thanks, Dad, I'm glad I called you."

I answered, "We'll keep an eye on the house for a while. Call your mother and reassure her everything's fine."

We were approached by a couple of suits that I assumed were the local detectives. I stated, "I'm Bill Bennett and together we're a group of retired police officers except the younger one over there. He's a sergeant in the Needleton Police Force. We're from the Superior Peninsula."

I continued, "This is my son's house and he asked us to protect his family and the Howards in case these idiots tried something. We got one, but the other one escaped."

Inspector Delton began by introducing himself and his partner Detective Smith. He continued, "This isn't the Wild West you know. You just can't set up shop and shoot people who you think are burglars."

I replied, "If you look at the dead body, you'll see he's probably the perp that murdered Sandy Howard and probably the other two as well."

Delton was rebuffed and became angry, "Listen, I just said, you can't take the law into your own hands."

I countered, "If we left it up to you guys, we'd be carrying body bags out of the house."

I could see we could argue all day. He finally relented and said, "I'm going to turn this over to the D.A. and let him make a decision. You guys stay in town and don't leave. You understand?"

Realizing that was probably the best offer I was going to get, I said, "Got it."

Concluding his remarks, he said, "I don't want you vigilantes posted outside here again. If you see something call 911!"

Always the instigator, Mark asked, "Should we call before or after we shoot?"

I thought the inspector was going to have a stroke. His partner pulled him toward their vehicle and I think we got off pretty easy. There would be an official investigation, but we had weathered them before and as far as I was concerned, I was satisfied.

Chapter Eleven

After Smith and the inspector re-entered their vehicle, Smith began, "You know those guys probably did the right thing. There's no way we could have prevented a mass slaughter."

The inspector answered, "I know, but I just don't want word getting around that this city is a free fire zone. I know those guys knew what they were doing, but we don't want every G.I. Joe trying that."

As they were driving away, they noticed a woman walking toward them. They pulled over and recognized the woman as Dr. Noble. The inspector wound his window down and shouted, "Betty, what are you doing here?"

The psychiatrist responded, "I had a session with Angie earlier and I was returning to follow up on a few things."

Inspector Delton replied, "We've just cone from there. Two assassins tried to break-in, but some hayseed detectives killed one and the other one escaped."

Dr. Noble responded, "Oh, my. I guess it can wait until tomorrow. Good-night inspector." She turned and walked away.

Inspector Delton said, "Tomorrow's another day. We'll have to check out Sandy Howard's funeral and see if anyone there might be a suspect. Murderers have been known to revisit their prey to gloat."

Meanwhile, after returning home and sweating profusely, the would-be assassin removed the black ensemble and fell into a chair. Breathing heavy, the murderer knew this killing spree would have to continue without Dimitri.

The assassin thought *those harlots who cheated on their husbands had to be punished. Men go to work thinking everything is fine and meanwhile back in the bedroom the slutty wife is screwing any man that answers the wife's emails. The plan could continue, just without Dimitri.*

Another problem that popped into the assassin's head was *who were those men that killed Dimitri? Were they police, private guards or neighbors?* The assassin wanted to find out but how?

The next day, most of Midland turned out to pay their respects for Sandy Howard and her family.

The police were observing from a distance and we also watched as hundreds filed into the church.

My son and his family sat behind Mike and Angie as everyone sobbed throughout the funeral. Dr. Noble sat close by in case she was needed by the youth.

The service was a tear jerker, and when it was over everyone exiting was wet-eyed.

In an attempt to patch things up with the Midland detectives, I approached them and said, "I'm sorry for the way I behaved yesterday. I was out of line. I know you fellows are the law, but we just wanted to protect my son's family and the Howards."

Inspector Delton responded, "I know you were only trying to help. My biggest fear is every amateur in the city will start to take the law into their own hands."

I asked, "Can I buy you a cup of coffee?"

Inspector Delton responded, "I guess. There's a nice quiet coffee shop on Eastman Ave. Follow us."

With that we reconvened over a hot cup of Joe. Delton said, "After we met yesterday, I did some research on you fellows. It seems you solved a lot of crimes in the Superior Peninsula. I read about the Maderis case and the meth business you shut down. That was some good police work."

I answered, "My son tells me Midland is one of the safest cities in the state." I appeared to be winning his trust. I continued, "How do you propose to catch the murderer that's still out there?"

Inspector Delton said, "First of all, I forgot to tell you, the perp you killed yesterday was none other than Wayne Bailey, the twin brother of Jeremy Bailey that was charged with the first murder."

I answered, "That doesn't make any sense. Why would the

twin brother try to murder the eyewitness after his brother was dead?"

Inspector Delton answered, "He probably wanted revenge for his brother's death."

I nodded and said, "I suppose that might be true."

The inspector paused for a moment, probably wondering if we could be trusted and then finally said, "We have a man checking the sex websites and if we see something suspicious, we're going to try to get the intended victim to help us. We have a safe house that we'll lure the murderer to and will take him/her down."

"Wow that sounds like a great plan. I wish we had money to have a safe house. In the Superior Peninsula, when we talk about a safe house we're usually talking about an outhouse."

"No," he said, "it's near the Arts Center," and he accidentally let the address slip.

We continued to discuss police matters and how the laws have changed.

In the interim, the assassin went online and once again trolled for a future victim. This time no photo was included. Within the hour, there were several possibilities. Most of them were too far to drive, but one in Midland sounded interesting.

Using abbreviations such as MorF (male or female), the assassin started to reel in the fish. As the exchange continued with the possible victim the assassin teased her with terms like FOL (fond of leather), ILF (I love female dominance), RUH (are you horny). The conversation lasted for over an hour when the assassin decided to play a little hard to get by texting WYRN (What's your real name?).

She replied Virginia Slim. The assassin replied LOL (laugh out loud) and H4Y (hot for you). This sealed the deal. The trusting victim relayed her personal information including her address and phone number. To tease the victim even more, the assassin disconnected and played a waiting game. Before long, the wood-be victim was online begging the assassin to correspond. The assassin waited and then replied. The vengeful murderer made it clear they could only meet certain times and days. That made the would-be victim even more impatient. Eventually, a time and day were established and the assassin closed out the chat and prepared the details of murdering victim number four.

The chat did not go unnoticed as we were monitoring the emails also. We had left John's son, Tyler, at the house to check the sex websites. Tyler was our computer tech and after many dead ends, he was finally able to talk to a woman that was planning to meet a man she didn't know. After engaging her in a sex conversation to make sure this woman was legitimate, he informed her she was being set up by a murderer.

Just in time, we returned, and told Tyler to use the Midland Police safe house as the rendezvous. Tyler continued to explain he was actually a police officer and would she be willing to give her gigolo the location of the police safe house, with a guarantee that she would remain anonymous. Tyler was able to gain her trust and asked that she inform him via an email when the sexual tryst was going to occur.

It wasn't long before the love-sick woman, Carrie Tonkin, came online and asked Tyler where the safe house was so she could dupe the would-be murderer. Tyler sent the address to her and in return she told him when it would happen.

Now we could tie up this mystery once and for all. The sexual rendezvous was going to take place tomorrow in mid-afternoon. The next day, we arrived early and easily picked the door lock and prepared ourselves. By the time of the anticipated rendezvous, we were ready for whatever came our way.

At mid-afternoon, we heard a knock on the door and Mark relayed in a high voice, "Come in."

The door opened and we jumped the assailant. Within seconds the intruder was bound with wrist ties and gagged. We had our man. Pulling him to his feet, we were surprised to discover it was a female. As we were busy searching her person for identification, a loud retort of an AK-15 was fired over our heads. We heard, "Drop your weapons or you're dead." Not being able to retaliate, we dropped our guns in unison. The bound woman ran to hide behind her rescuer. We heard, "Keep your faces turned to the wall!" We did as we were told and when we turned around, they were gone.

"Son-of-a-bitch," shouted Mark.

The rest of us, likewise, mumbled under our breath similar words of frustration. Ben shouted, "How could we be so stupid?"

We all showed our visible anger one way or another.

I said, "C'mon, we have to get out of here before Midland's finest arrive. I really don't want to

be here when they come through the door."

We exited the safe house and left as we heard sirens in the distance. I didn't want to have to explain how their safe house got destroyed by an AK-15.

As the two murderers were making their getaway, the assassin said. "Thanks, sis, they had me for a moment. If you hadn't come through a back window, I'd be in jail now."

Her sister replied, "Don't mention it. You'd have done the same for me."

Arriving back at our son's house, we commiserated about our failure to apprehend the other murderer. We made a wrong assumption that the murderer was acting alone. We couldn't make that mistake again.

We couldn't even go to the police and give them a description of the woman we caught. We'd have to explain the circumstances and that wasn't a possibility.

In the early evening we returned to our posts enveloping my son's house in a defensive perimeter. The only excitement we saw was the lady psychiatrist once again entering my son's house. I hoped Angie was able to confide in the professional. Later that evening, we viewed the same lady leave and disappear into the night.

Meanwhile, we had our own problem. There was a possibility the two perps might return. It was a long uneventful night and I was glad when the haymaker made its appearance.

We all retired to a bed in my son's house not even having the energy to undress.

Chapter Twelve

The next day my cell phone chimed, and I answered, "Yeah, who's calling at this time of the morning?"

The voice replied, "This is Detective Melbourne and for the record, it's afternoon."

I managed to ask, "What's up?"

She responded, "As I thought, the 4th victim was also murdered by a long narrow instrument. The good news, MacArthur's wife is going to survive. Once she comes out of surgery, hopefully, she'll be able to give us a description of the assailant."

"That's great. I assume you have a guard posted at the hospital."

"Of course, this isn't my first rodeo," replied Detective Melbourne.

I went into detail about a plan we used a few years ago. My buddies and I hid in a hospital room next door and waited for the fox to come to the henhouse."

Detective Melbourne wasn't as agreeable. She responded, "That bush league police work might work in your neck of the woods, but it doesn't hold water here."

I had to develop another plan to safeguard the MacArthur woman or else catch the villain before she struck again.

Rendezvousing at a coffee shop on West Grandview Parkway, we discussed our theories as to the best way to capture this murderess.

I began, "As I see it, we have one primary suspect, Sharon Robinson, and some others lying in the weeds. Since the police have a guard at the hospital, we can concentrate on protecting Windemeyer."

John suggested, "Let's take shifts guarding this last doctor."

Mark interjected, "This is our last chance. If this doctor is murdered, the murderess will disappear for good."

I suggested, "Let's all go to the doctor's home and see if we can establish a protective zone."

We enjoyed a hearty breakfast knowing it might be the only meal we got in a long time if we had to stake out the doctor's nursing home.

Windemeyer was in charge of dispensing his toxic narcotics to nursing home patients in Gaylord. We arrived at his house and to our surprise; his maid informed us he was at the nursing home.

As we were leaving, John stated, "I'm amazed he would have the fortitude to show his face there. He must be aware that he is the last member of the consortium."

We weighed in on the benefits and negative reasons for tending to his patients. It suddenly dawned on me, maybe, he wasn't being careless. I suggested, "What if he's only making it look like someone with a grudge is murdering the members of the consortium? What if he has a female partner that has been involved from the beginning?"

Again, everyone weighed in on that possibility. It would be very clever to use the vindictive angle to make it look like his life was in jeopardy.

Driving to the nursing home and entering, I said, "I can't wait to meet this individual." It wasn't long before a large jovial man exited his office and we began our introductions. After we identified ourselves and why we were there. He responded, "Yes, I heard you fellows were in the area. I would sure appreciate anything you could do to protect my family and me."

Playing it straight, I replied, "We thought we'd set up a perimeter around the nursing home and later, after hours, we'd do the same at your house."

He smiled and responded, "That would be great. The police don't have the manpower to guard my family and me 24/7."

We toured the facility, and like the others we had seen, most of the patients were heavily sedated or sleeping. I thought to myself, *I'm glad my parents didn't have to suffer through this degradation.* The few residents that were upright were near comatose or wandered like zombies. *Maybe, if there was a murderess, I should allow her to kill this bastard.*

Not certain if there was a villain trying to seek revenge, we decided to prepare for the worst. If there wasn't anybody, we could simply give Detective Melbourne our theory and return to the Superior Peninsula. On the other hand, if someone was trying to sneak in and murder the doctor, we'd be ready.

The day dragged as I contemplated my quandary. I kept mulling over in my mind; *maybe, Sharon Robinson was innocent all along.* That evening as twilight was starting, a vehicle entered the parking lot. Using our walkie-talkies, we bantered back and forth what our options were. I said, "Let's see how this plays out." We left our posts and entered the nursing home. Quietly, we crept through the hallway to Dr. MacArthur's Office.

We could see through the glass window that he was having a heated discussion with a woman. We readied our firearms as we entered the office. I couldn't identify her since we couldn't see her face. It was apparent; Dr. MacArthur was trying to placate her.

Entering the office, I spun the woman around and was disappointed to see it was Sharon Robinson. We trained our weapons on her and I shouted, "Hands, I want to see your hands!"

She had a very confused look on her face as she complied. John searched her body and Tyler sifted through her purse, but there was no weapon.

I exclaimed, "What are you doing here?"

She replied, "I wanted to stop this drug abuse. He is the last doctor alive from the consortium. He could halt the heavy medications if he wanted."

I asked, "You mean you didn't come here to kill him?"

She answered, "Heavens no. I took an oath as a nurse to save people no matter what they've done."

I escorted her outside, hoping to calm her down.

Once in the open air, I said, "Sharon, you can't stop this by threatening one doctor. The AMA has to get involved. Probably even the state. You could become a patient's advocate and lobby our legislators. That would be more productive than trying to persuade one doctor to stop the madness."

Sharon listened and she appeared to compose herself. I kept discussing possible positive alternatives as I escorted her to her vehicle. She seemed to be getting control of herself and when we finally parted, she gave me a hug.

Once I returned to the nursing home, the pseudo-detectives and I commiserated and decided we had to maintain a vigil on our last potential victim.

The doctor emerged from his office carrying his coat and hat. We agreed to follow him to his house and duplicate another protective zone around his chateau.

Chapter Thirteen

The next day, leaving the doctor under the protection of my comrades, I made it a point to drive to the Midland Police Station. Upon entering, I saw my new friend, Inspector Delton. As I approached him, he said, "Good morning. I hope the night was quiet."

I said, "Fortunately, yes."

He responded, "It seems excitement follows you characters wherever you go. A few days ago, someone shot up our safe house. You wouldn't know anything about that would you?"

I shook my head negatively and tried to look innocent.

The inspector was pretty insightful as he asked, "I suppose you want something?"

I replied, "As a matter of fact, yes. Could I review the police reports? Something isn't right."

Delton said, "I suppose I better allow you to see them, I don't want them to turn up missing."

I think he was getting to know me.

The inspector tapped his laptop and printed the reports. He said, "You can use Dr. Noble's office down the hall. As you can imagine, she's busy counseling the other children."

I gathered the three reports and found the empty office. Spreading them over the table, it appeared the only thing they had in common was that the wives were looking for a sexual rendezvous.

Flipping the scenario around, I looked at the families closer. *Did the children have anything in common besides being counseled by Dr. Noble. Did they belong to the same church or social group?* Nothing. Frustrated, I stood and stretched. Gazing out the window, a Midland Chemical truck rumbled by the station.

Wait a minute. Where did the fathers work? Looking closer, they were all employed by the same foundry, Midland Chemicals. Could there be a connection among the fathers?

Mike Howard was a vice president, Crystal Torres' husband was a truck driver, and Amy Lipton's husband was a chemist.

I thought to myself, *could that just be a coincidence?* I called Inspector Delton to check my theory. He entered the room and asked, "Do you have something?"

I related, "Maybe, we've been looking at this serial murder all wrong. Look at the jobs the three husbands have."

Inspector Delton perused the three reports carefully. He looked up and said, "I think you have something." Having another thought, I asked the inspector, "I know Jeremy Bailey worked at a foundry. Is it possible he worked at the same one?"

The inspector replied, "Let's see." He walked over to his computer and logged into his files. Scanning through until he found Bailey's, he leaned into the computer and said, "Yeah, he worked at the same chemical plant."

That put a whole new perspective on the murders. *Maybe somebody was murdering the women to make it look like a sexual tryst had gone wrong. It might not be a serial murderer after all, but some kind of retribution against the people involved in some kind of illegal plot involving some of the employees at the plant.*

It wasn't a stretch to imagine what illicit drugs could be made at a chemical plant if there were enough people involved.

Delton continued, "We'll have to put the plant under surveillance."

Thinking out loud, I said, "I'm going to research and see what drug(s) they could be selling on the black market." I asked, "Do you mind if I use a computer?"

Delton said, "Sure, I'll type in the password and you can take all the time you need."

Sitting down at the laptop, once Delton bypassed the encryption, I searched the internet on manufacturing illegal drugs. One drug that seemed to be capable the Midland Chemistry Corporation could manufacture was LSD.

Intrigued, I wanted to know more about this hallucinative drug. It's produced in crystalline form and later mixed with other chemicals to prepare it for ingestible forms. The liquid solution is either distributed in small vials or, more commonly, soaked in sugar cubes. Recently, tablet form is the most popular method.

Reading closer, I found it takes at least two days to produce a supply of pure LSD. Potency is at least 20 micrograms per dose. This is actually less than forty years ago when the dosage was much higher.

I was surprised how inexpensive it cost; usually about $5 a piece to produce. Most of the large illegal manufacturing centers were found in northern California.

One concern I had was these chemists must be extremely careful in working with ergot because of its toxicity. I remember from my college history days; people were poisoned by rye bread during the Middle Ages? I thought to myself, once Tonkin and Lipton obtain the fungus, they have to carefully extract the ergot alkaloids. They probably have a darkroom to avoid the fungus decomposing under bright lights. I read where LSD might even break down when exposed to them.

On the down side, I read that the solvents and the compounds used to bring about chemical reactions are also incredibly dangerous. The solvent anhydrous hydrazine, for example, may explode when heated. It's extremely poisonous and carcinogenic. Another chemical often used in the process, chloroform, can cause long-term effects, cancer, not to mention damaging the kidneys and liver. Both substances are easily absorbed through the skin or inhaled.

I learned that the ergot alkaloid is synthesized into a lysergic acid compound through the addition of chemicals and heating processes. Then the iso-lysergic acid hydrazide has molecules rearranged through a chemical process. It's cooled, mixed with an acid and a base, and evaporated. What remains is iso-lysergic diethylamide which is isomerized again to produce active LSD. It's then purified and crystallized.

Finally, LSD used to be made into tablets, but now it is

usually dissolved in water or other liquids or made into gelatin windowpanes. Today, it's usually dissolved in ethanol. Sheets of blotting paper are then dipped into the LSD solution and dried. These sheets of blotter acid are usually printed with funny characters or other colorful graphics. The sheets are perforated into small squares, about a quarter of an inch wide. Each square is one dose, and a sheet can contain 900 doses.

Apparently, users chew and then swallow the little bits of blotter paper. You can inject LSD, but it's not really necessary because it's so readily absorbed through oral means. Then, the drug's powerful effects quickly take hold.

I returned to Inspector Delton and said, "If these clowns are manufacturing and selling LSD on the black market, we have to stop them."

Inspector Delton stated, "We're going to keep surveillance on the chemical plant. If we get some kind of idea of their routine, we could stop that truck and get a warrant to search it."

I knew he had to abide by the law, whereas the pseudo-detectives and I didn't have such constraints.

Returning to my son's house, my partners and I considered our options. After being updated about the possible LSD ring at the three men's plant, we decided to split up and each interview one of them. We eliminated Moran since he was deceased.

John said, "Tyler and I will take Mike Torres, the truck driver."

Ben spoke saying, "Mark and I can take the chemist, Henry Lipton. One of us can check out the 4th woman who unknowingly doesn't realize her husband was probably involved in the LSD trade."

John replied, "Don forget about Bailey. I'm sure he was involved."

Tyler interjected, "I wonder if the two Bailey wives are involved. Wouldn't that be something?" I paused and said, "They certainly could be. It's probably a big ring smuggling LSD from the plant."

Mark evinced a dark thought saying, "I wonder if they're bribing the DEA to look the other way?"

I replied, "I don't want to think about that, but anything's possible when millions of dollars are involved."

We went our separate ways agreeing to meet at my son's house later that evening.

John and Tyler found the Torres residence near Plymouth Park. It was a clean looking modest house with toys in the front yard. Walking to the front door they didn't have to ring the doorbell since the homeowner saw them through the front window and acknowledged them.

After opening the door, a burly man asked, "Can I help you?"

John replied, "Are you Miguel Torres?"

He replied, "Yes, that's me. Is it about my wife's murder?"

John realized Torres probably assumed they were Midland Police Officers and they decided to take advantage of it.

"Indirectly, it is. We're following up on all three of the murders. We noticed one thing in common. The three victims' husbands worked for Midland Chemical. How do you account for that?"

Torres suddenly became nervous and replied, "I don't think I should be talking to you without my lawyer."

Tyler quipped, "It's better to talk to us then have some criminals come after you. Was your wife murdered to keep you and the other husbands quiet?"

Torres became wet eyed and slammed the door.

John looked at Tyler and said, "I think we touched a nerve."

Tyler said, "Let's text Bill that we're going to wait and see where this fellow goes tonight."

They drove to a secluded corner where they could monitor Torres' house from afar. As they were leaving, a professionally dressed woman exited the Torres' house.

Ben looked at Mark and said, "That must be that psychiatrist we saw entering Bill's son's house the other day."

Mark shook his head as they continued their surveillance.

Across town, Ben and Mark arrived at the Tonkin residence that was located along the Sanford River. As they stepped out of their vehicle, they were impressed by all the boats on the water enjoying the beautiful day.

As they approached the house, they noticed several big ones on lifts in the Tonkin backyard. The house was a two-story colonial. Mark said, "It must take a lot of shekels to pay for this place."

Ringing the doorbell, there was a long delay before someone opened the door. A middle-aged woman, who I assumed was the nanny, said, "Mr. Lipton isn't seeing anyone today. He's not feeling well. Could you come back another time?"

John didn't feel like complying so he replied, "We'd like to talk to Mr. Lipton. It relates to his wife's demise."

"Just a minute, I'll see if he's able to talk to you." She closed the door and there was a delay before a handsome man, tall in stature and well- dressed, opened the door. He stated, "I don't feel

good. Could you make it quick?"

Tyler said, "We're investigating the death of all three women and we've discovered all of their husbands worked at the same chemical plant. We don't think it's a coincidence."

Mr. Lipton replied, "I just lost my wife. I don't care what you think. I have to protect my family now."

John retorted quickly. "If you and the other husbands are involved in drug manufacturing and selling, do you think the murderers are going to leave you alone?"

Mr. Lipton winced and closed his eyes. "Are you with the media?" He continued, "I can't comment on that right now."

Tyler answered, "Actually, no. We're private detectives and we're helping find who murdered Mrs. Howard."

Mr. Lipton replied, "Why don't you guys leave it alone. I don't want anything to happen to my children." With that he shut the door.

As John and his son were leaving, a well-dressed lady passed them on the sidewalk and smiled as she walked up to the Lipton's front door. Upon ringing the doorbell, she was admitted after some small talk. John and Tyler looked at each other and shrugged their shoulders.

John said, "We're getting close. I think we should continue to follow this lead. Let's park down the street and see if this bird takes us anyplace."

Tyler acknowledged Doctor Noble as she walked by them on the sidewalk. Both smiled at one another as they passed. The doctor rang the doorbell and after the door opened, she entered.

John replied, "She seems to know the Upton family."

Continuing my investigation, I drove back to my son's house and prepared to discuss Mike Howard's wife's murder, and persuade him to come forward with information to save his daughter.

I realized now the attempt on the Howards was probably just as much to scare/kill Mike Howard as it was to eliminate Angie as an eye witness.

While driving there, I realized that I had to pick the right time to interrogate the father. He wouldn't be forthcoming if his daughter was near.

Entering the house, my son's family, along with Mike and his daughter were watching *Frozen* for the umpteenth time. I was pretty sure I could pry Mike away from Amy. "Mike, do you have a minute?" I asked.

"Sure," he replied.

I led him outside so we'd be free of any prying ears. Once we were far enough away from the house, I asked, "Mike, my buddies and I have been going over the evidence again and it seems of all the women murdered, the only thing they have in common is that their husbands were employed, along with Jeremy Bailey, at the chemical plant. We're guessing the fact that all of you worked at that plant is a red flag."

Mike began, "It's just a terrible coincidence. A lot of people work at that plant."

I now got testy, "Mike, cut the crap. You and those other guys were involved in manufacturing LSD and distributing it. Weren't you?"

Mike replied, "As God is my witness, I'm not involved in any drug trafficking!"

I now pushed even harder, "Mike, if those people come after you, they're not just going to kill you and your daughter, but my son' entire family as well. I can't allow that."

There was a long moment of silence. Mike now walked over to a lawn chair and sat down. He looked like he had the weight of the world on his shoulders.

Feeling I was making progress, I joined him and sat in a chair next to him.

Mike finally muttered, "How did I get myself into this mess. I don't care about myself but I'm so worried about Angie."

I replied, "Don't worry about her. I promise you the five of us will give our lives to protect her. The only way out is to spill the beans. If this is big enough, they can put you in the federal witness protection plan."

Mike argued, "Even that's not fool proof." He pulled out a photograph and handed it to me. It was a photograph of his daughter walking to school. Mike said, "I found it on my desk at work. They can infiltrate any place."

I asked him to explain the make-up of the crime family he was dealing with. He started, "They're from Detroit and it's been around for years. There are probably over 70 made men that belong[update]. At the same time the organization has proven itself to be a very resilient crime family. Most of their members are related by blood or marriage making it hard for the FBI to penetrate their gang. This has led to very few people becoming informants against the family and has made building a criminal investigation against them almost impossible."

Mike proceeded to lay out the whole scheme. He continued, "There was an outdated research lab that was closed at our plant. Lacking internet connection and with antiquated storage facilities, it would have cost a fortune to renovate. The new way of doing things is simply to build a new building and leave the old one alone. That's exactly what happened."

He continued, "Somehow, the gang in Detroit found out about the abandoned lab and they told us they were going to use it to run an operation. We were approached by a gangster from Detroit who threatened our families if we didn't cooperate. Lipton and Tonkin, being chemists, would manufacture the LSD, Bailey was to do the bull-work. Torres was to transport it to Detroit for distribution. I was to make sure there were no interruptions."

He continued by saying, "The money was great, but after a few months, Tonkin, Lipton, and I had reservations. We didn't like spreading that poison throughout the country. When we voiced our objections, we were visited by some unsavory characters and they told us that on no uncertain terms, we were going to continue the process. When we finally refused, Jeremy Bailey reassured the gangsters, he would take care of it. He cooked up a scheme to terrorize us by meeting and murdering our wives on the internet.

The Bailey wives, Lisa and Helen, met our wives at a sex addiction therapy session. The Bailey women got to know my wife, Amy Lipton, and Carrie Tonkin over drinks. Later, Jeremy, his wife Lisa, his twin brother Wayne, and his wife Helen, arranged to meet the unsuspecting wives on a sex chat line and then proceed to murder them."

He continued, "They told me the two sisters, Lisa and Helen, took the philandering wives to the extreme and felt they should be punished for cheating on their husbands.

After Jeremy strangled himself in jail, his brother, Wayne, went nuts. That's when he and Jeremy's wife came after Angie and me. Wayne's wife, Helen, was also an accomplice. It was she that rescued her sister, Lisa, at the safe house. They called and told me all this to make it clear they could get Angie and me if I didn't continue to cooperate. I was supposed to hire Wayne Bailey to replace his brother, until he was gunned down. Murdering his wife had the desired effect on Torres."

After he finished, I said, "Let's play it cool. You continue as if nothing happened. I'm going to get my crew together and devise a scheme." He seemed a little relieved as he returned to the house and I drove away to improvise something.

I decided to investigate this so-called abandoned laboratory to see if it indeed was producing LSD. The others had contacted me informing me they were keeping tabs on the two chemists, Tonkin and Lipton.

As luck would have it, both Tonkin and Lipton were driving to the Midland Chemical Plant. The pseudo-detectives and I texted one another and we agreed to meet outside the plant.

Upon arriving, we wanted to develop a plan. Mark asked, "Should we sneak inside and see if we can catch Tonkin and Lipton red-handed?"

Tyler said, "Maybe, we should call the Midland Police before we get in too deep?"

Ben added, "I think it's a chance we have to take. We can always call if we find the chemists with the drugs."

John said, "I reconnoitered the plant yesterday, and there's a fence on the north side my wire cutters will make quick work of if we want to do that."

I asked, "Is everybody agreed, we go in and see if we can catch those chemists with the goods?"

Everybody nodded and John led us to the north side and after John cut the wires we were sneaking toward the building. Fortunately, the security was pretty lax at night with only a few employees. I assumed the chemists thought it was a good time to prepare their drugs for market.

As we approached the lab, a large delivery truck backed up to the loading dock. I muttered to the others, "That's probably Torres picking up another shipment."

John said, "Tyler and I can take him, after he's loaded."

I said, "That works for me. Ben, Mark and I will infiltrate the plant and catch them with the goods."

We didn't realize the plant had motion detector lights near each building. As we were about to enter the so-called abandoned lab, the compound lit up. John and Tyler charged Torres but he accelerated at warp speed. Ben, Mark and I charged through the door with Glocks drawn.

Tonkin and Lipton were busy preparing the shipment for Detroit. Hearing the commotion, the two chemists dropped their boxes and ran for the front exit. I shouted, "Stop, or we'll shoot!" Fortunately, the two chemists turned and raised their hands. John shouted, "Lay face down on the floor." They did as they were ordered. After we had them under control, Mark applied wrist ties to them and we felt relieved. What could have been a disaster seemed to be ending peacefully.

Meanwhile, Torres was high-balling to the front gate. John and Tyler were unable to catch the speeding truck before it made its exit. The truck crashed through the gate and disappeared into the night.

Mark relayed, "At least we caught two of them. Let's work them over and find out more about this operation!"

I said, "I don't think we're going to have to lean too hard on these two white-collar criminals."

Ben and Mark picked Lipton and Tonkin up from the floor and threw them into a load of pallets. Lipton screamed and said, "I want my attorney."

Ben smiled and retorted, "I think it's time for you guys to take your own medicine. Ben opened a roll of the blotter paper and prepared to shove a handful down Lipton's throat. Ben pinched Lipton's nose closed, and punched him in the stomach, making Lipton gasp for air. "Now," Ben said, "open for the birdie. You're going to ingest as much of this LSD as I can shove down your throat." Mark prepared to do the same with Tonkin. Both Lipton and Tonkin screamed. Lipton blurted, "Okay, what do you want to know?"

I said, "Now, we're getting somewhere." Both Lipton and Tonkin were very cooperative telling the story of their role in the LSD manufacturing. I did have to ask one important question. "I know the Drug Enforcement Agency keeps a close eye on the amount of lysergic acid you're given. How do you get away with that?"

Both Tonkin and Lipton looked at each other and went mute. Ben said, "Okay, you two idiots had your chance. Open up and swallow."

Lipton and Tonkin fidgeted and murmured, "One of the DEA agents is in on it too."

Mark and Ben shook them and said, "Quit stalling, out with it." They were about to give us the DEA accomplice when shots rang out in the lab. The room went dark and immediately, gun fire was sprayed everywhere. All of us hit the deck and looked for the shooter. We turned on our flashlights and both Lipton and Tonkin were lying in their own blood.

Ben shouted, "Damn it. Just when we were about to crack this case. Now what do we do?"

"For starters, I said, "Let's get the lights back on." We searched the large tomb-like behemoth before I felt the circuit breaker box. Flicking the lights turned the lab into a brilliant beacon.

Mark stated, "Well, that should destroy any remaining LSD." By the time we reached the outskirts of the plant, Midland security guards were swarming the site. We placed our weapons on the ground and followed their instructions. I had to admit we did look pretty guilty with two dead chemists with their hands bound.

We waited for the Midland Police to arrive and I hoped Inspector Delton would be among them. Fortunately, Midland has a limited police force and Delton appeared along with his partner, Detective Smith.

I could see the disgruntled look on the inspector's face as he approached us. Inspector Delton asked, "Why did you shoot these two fellows?" I replied, "If you check, you'll see they were shot by an automatic and we're only carrying hand guns."

Detective Smith answered, "How do we know you didn't have time to ditch the gun somewhere on the property?"

It didn't look good as we stepped into the patrol cars and were driven to the station house. We would have to explain everything.

Chapter Fourteen

As the two assassins drove away from the plant, both Lisa and Helen Bailey removed their masks and Lisa said, "It's a good thing Torres texted us after he escaped and told us that those old guys were breaking into the lab. If Torres can make it to Detroit, we can at least pocket that money from the shipment and lay low."

Helen replied, "The boss said, we should disappear after we took care of Lipton and Tonkin."Lisa replied, "We earned a rest after cleaning up all the messes the Midland chemists left behind."

They were returning to their hideout, when Lisa's cell phone chimed. "Yeah, we just took care of the two chemists, Tonkin and Lipton. Torres is on his way to Detroit. We're planning on leaving town soon."

The voice on the other end said, "I have one more job for the two you. Since the whole LSD plan has fallen apart, I want you to track down the DEA agent, Jack McCallahan, and put a bullet in his head." The voice gave Lisa the location where the agent could be found. They disconnected and Lisa

looked at Helen and said, "Guess what? We're not done yet. The boss wants us to take out the DEA agent, McCallahan, as well!"

Helen said, "That's going to be tricky."

Lisa answered, "The boss gave me his home address. He's outlived his usefulness."

The two female murderers drove to the home of the agent and put the agent's house under surveillance.

Hearing that the LSD plan had unraveled over his radio, Agent McCallahan returned to his house to plan a quick exit. He was filling his suitcases as fast as possible and had booked the first flight out of Midland. He could always take a junket to an international airport and from there to South America. He had just finished closing his last suitcase when he heard a voice. "Going somewhere McCallahan?" The agent glanced up but before he could respond, Helen put two 9mm shots into his forehead. The two assassins backed out of the room and disappeared into the night.

As they were returning home again, Lisa said, "I better call the boss and tell her mission accomplished." Upon phoning the boss's cell number, the voice on the other end responded, "Good job. Everything is nice and tidy. You girls take some time off and I'll do the same."

The women returned home and were relaxing watching old episodes of *Breaking Bad* when there was a knock on the door. Lisa opened the door and was met by a revolver in her face. "I thought you two would be here," Miguel Torres retorted. You thought you could take out the chemists and I'd disappear. I want my cut. I asked the Detroit guys and they said the boss has already been paid and everyone knows you take care of the money. Give me my share and I'll be on my way. If not, there will be a couple of dead women here."

Lisa said, "We don't have any money. The boss has it downstairs." Torres started to back out of the apartment. He opened the door being careful to keep his gun pointed at the women. Stepping back into the doorway, he suddenly stopped and raised his arms.

A voice from behind him said, "We had a hunch this would be the rendezvous for you bums." Torres stepped back into the Bailey apartment as we relieved him of his hand gun. Ben and Mark approached the two Bailey women and attached wrist ties. "I overheard you say the boss was downstairs." I nodded for John and Tyler to take care of the old lady.

Quickly, John and Tyler fast-tracked to the lower apartment and kicked in the door. The old woman didn't have time to react as she was manhandled by Tyler and thrown onto the couch with her wrists bound.

I contacted Inspector Delton with the good news that we had apprehended the leader and her two daughters.

Delton arrived and we had the three women and Torres sitting on the curb trussed up and ready for delivery.

The four drug felons were placed in police cruisers and whisked to the Midland Station House. Delton looked at me and said, "I have a million questions for you."

I responded I'm sure you do." I recalled the events that Mike Howard had informed me of and along with Inspector Delton, pieced together the rest. I stated, "It appears the Detroit mob heard there was a lab available at the Midland Plant and they pressured, Howard, Lipton, Tonkin, Torres and Jeremy Bailey to have a role in distributing LSD." Delton interjected, "They just found a DEA agent, Jack McCallahan, dead in his home. He had his bags packed and had booked a flight at the Midland Airport. McCallahan must have been the dirty agent that allowed the chemists to obtain extra lysergic acid."

I resumed, "You might be able to get some information out of the two sisters, Lisa and Helen, their mother, who ran the operation, or even Torres."

Delton answered, "It seems the old lady was married to one of the crime bosses from Detroit before he was gunned down in a territorial dispute. She moved here to lay low, but heard about the available lab from her son-in-law, Jeremy. She saw a chance to make a lot of money and used some Detroit enforcers to intimidate the Midland chemistry employees."

I continued, "They used the online dating ruse to throw us off and it almost worked."

Inspector Delton said, "The only thing left to do is pick up Mike Howard."

I replied, "I hope the DA goes easy on him. If it wasn't for him, we wouldn't have solved this crime spree."

"I'll tell the DA what you told me and maybe, they will," he continued, "I sure feel sorry for the kids involved. Thank God they have a good friend in Doctor Noble." I agreed, but I was just happy to have solved the *twin killing*.

Chapter Fifteen

Returning our attention to the nursing home murders, and realizing Sharon Robinson was not a suspect, we now had to resume our interest in another direction. We knew a woman was involved since one entered Willow's house and stabbed him. Whoever committed the murder had to have a working knowledge of the escort service.

The fellows and I discussed our options over coffee the next morning. We had to uncover who the mystery woman was that gained entry into Dr. Willow's house under the guise of being a hooker. I looked at Ben and Mark and asked, "Do you think it would be worthwhile for all of us to pay a visit to the bar that runs the escort service?"

Ben replied, "It probably couldn't hurt."

I spoke, saying, "I think that's the key to the whole murder case. Someone's pulling strings from above and we're looking down below."

Mark stated, "We're probably going to have to take that fat cat pimp outside with no witnesses and interrogate him. I doubt if he's going to divulge any incriminating information without being persuaded."

Tyler interjected, "I'm afraid I can't be a party to anything like that. I don't want to lose my job or pension."

I reassured him by saying, "No problem. The four of us will interrogate him and hopefully, he'll give us his police contact."

After driving to the bar, Tyler reluctantly exited the vehicle and took a seat on a park bench.

The rest of us marched into the bar, not even stopping to make small talk with the pimp. John put a gun to the pimp's bodyguard and said, **"Don't move! Understand!"**

The bodyguard, still nursing his bruises from his last beating, nodded in agreement.

Del Santos was carried outside and the four of us threw him into our vehicle. We whisked Del Santos away with a common goal.

The pimp stated, "You can't do this. Who do you think you are? I demand you let me out at the next intersection."

I opened the door and John increased his speed and I asked, "Do you really want that?"

The pimp swallowed hard and related, "No, not now. What do you want?"

Ben said, "Remember when we asked who you sent to Dr. Willows? We found her tied and cut to pieces in her trailer. Any idea who might have done that?"

Del Santos shook his head and said, "No, I have no idea."

Mark added, "Well, you'd better remember because the next time we ask, it's going to cost you a finger every time you don't."

By now, we were well out of town on M-131 with ample dirt roads intersecting it. Sarcastically, John said, "Okay, fat boy, pick a road and we're going to show you how we do things in the Superior Peninsula."

Del Santos said, "Honest, I don't have any idea of who might have killed Tiffaney."

Mark held up the pimp's little finger and said, "Say good-bye to your little pinkie."

Turning onto a road that looked like it would serve our needs, we found a grove of trees that offered privacy. The pimp was kicked out of the vehicle and we followed suit. John motioned to a tree stump and said, "This will do nicely."

Del Santos resisted, but we carried him over and knelt him against the stump.

Mark asked, "Do you want to watch or wait for the pain?"

By now the pimp was hysterical and begged for mercy.

Mark removed a large hunting knife and struck the stump for effect. Apparently, it worked.

John held Del Santos' hand against the stump and Ben as I restrained the pimp.

Del Santos was screaming profusely to let him go as Mark separated the pimp's little finger from the others. Mark raised the knife and was preparing to deliver a horrific blow when the pimp screamed, "Okay, I'll tell you!"

John shouted, "There's no second chance. If you're stalling, my partner's going to cut off two fingers!"

We relaxed our hold on the fat pimp and he collapsed into a blubbering heap. I shouted, "Out with it, little man. Now!"

Del Santos screamed, "I'm supposed to meet her tonight!"

John asked, "Why should we believe you? You're probably just giving us a name to save your fingers. You have to prove that she is involved or your hand is back on the chopping block."

"Where's the meeting?" I asked.

"It's at an old opera house that's been converted into a coffee shop. There's a fire pit where we usually meet and I pay her."

"What time are you scheduled to meet?"

"7:00," he answered.

I said, "Well, fella you're going to keep that date. We're going to mic you and we'll be listening."

Del Santos responded, "Are you nuts. I'm not wearing any wire. Forget it!"

John said, "Okay, boys put his hand back on the stump."

I interjected, "The wire isn't what you think it is. They've come a long way. It's a simple belt that you wear. We'll hear your conversations wearing the high-grade leather belt with a body wire transmitter. It sends your voice to a radio receiver. It'll tape record everything. Once she admits her guilt, we've got her. That's all that's to it. Del Santos seemed relieved to hear it wasn't going to be an elaborate wire that's seen on television or in the movies.

We inspected the café later that day and we each designated a place we would be close but out of sight. We were ready. The question was, could we outsmart an experienced criminal?

That night the murderer was punctual. I'm sure greed was a great motivator. She entered and sat down next to the fire pit. Because I'd been in the police station a lot, and since it was a dirty cop, she'd recognize me so I decided to stay out of sight. We were scattered throughout the perimeter.

Del Santos, strolled into the back area and it was obvious he was very nervous. Sitting next to the suspect, he removed the money envelope and placed it on the arm of the chair. We heard some bantering between Del Santos and the executioner. Del Santos protested, "Why did you have to kill my best working girl?"

The perp responded, "All she had to do was tell me where she was going?"

"Do you know how much money you cost me? She was my best girl. Every guy wanted Tiffaney. Now I got nothing in the stable."

"You'll find a new girl," retorted the murderer.

I was getting worried that the suspect wasn't going to talk about the money. She still hadn't admitted her involvement. Del Santos did a good job of trying to lead her on and admit she murdered Tiffaney, but the murderer didn't bite.

Del Santos next tried to coax his accomplice into a conversation regarding Willow. Somehow the pimp had to get the sly murderer to admit she committed the murder.

Del Santos asked, "How did you get past Willow's administrative assistant?"

Finally, the murderer's vanity got the best of her. The perp said, "It was easy. I just acted like a bimbo and pretended to be a whore. I'm not bad looking you know when I get cleaned up. I can still hold my own."

Del Santos pursued his line of questioning. He asked, "Why did you kill Willows? I thought you were partners with the consortium?"

The accomplice let her guard down saying, "Eight years ago, my mother was a resident at one of their nursing homes. After she died, I brought it to their attention that they kept her over medicated. They paid me $100,000 a year if I didn't bring legal action against them. But then four of the doctors got greedy. They said they weren't going to pay anymore because the authorities would be unable to prove the consortium acted in a reckless manner. In addition, these cases are usually handled in a civil court and not criminal. Worst case scenario the consortium might face disciplinary proceedings but no legal action. You know the rest."

Del Santos asked one more question. "What was the weapon you used?"

Looking skyward, she replied, "I thought it would be ironic if I used one of my mother's darning needles."

I shouted, "That's it! Take her!"

In a flash, the five pseudo detectives flocked to our quarry. The suspect didn't have time to reach for her weapon.

She protested shouting, "What are you doing?"

I turned her around and I gasped. It was Detective Melbourne. I relayed, "It's over, we have you on tape," as I slipped the belt from Del Santos' waist.

"It'll never stand up in court. You'll see. It's my word against the pimp's! This is entrapment. I was setting up my own sting to find the murderer."

I contacted 9-1-1 and informed them of the dire arrest. Several cruisers arrived and after a scuffle with Melbourne, she was led away to the station house.

The next day, the pseudo detectives along with our wives returned to the sanctuary we call the Superior Peninsula.

A few days later, I received a thank you note from Sharon Robinson. In her note, she expressed deep appreciation for the pseudo detectives and me for helping her in her hour of need. Further, she took my advice and became a patient's advocate. She has even been asked to deliver a plea on the state legislative floor requesting they look into over medicating seniors in nursing home.

Dr. Windemeyer avoided prison time but he did have his medical license revoked.

I was satisfied my friends and I ended the *Diabolical Consortium.*

Part II

CRACKING the FRACKINIG

Chapter One

"Great job," senior engineer, Lance Skylar, shouted to his foreman, Mitch Avery.

The water pressure was flowing and the chemicals were added. "What's the depth?" shouted Skylar.

"5,000 feet and still going," relayed Mitch Avery. He added, "It's looking good."

The two had worked together for over twenty years fracturing for oil and natural gas all over the world. Their company was one of the first to convince investors to take a chance on their procedure. Now they had sunk hundreds of wells and Skylar's drilling crew made their investors millionaires many times over.

Even though Lance Skylar was only the project engineer he was given carte blanche to oversee the entire operation.

Skylar knew fracking as well as anyone. Hydraulic fracturing is a process of oil and natural gas extraction. It involves injecting fluid into subterranean rock formations at high pressure. The high-pressure fluid produces a fracture system that allows crude oil and natural gas trapped inside dense rocks to flow into what is called a wellbore and drawn to the surface.

Under Lance Skylar's guidance, the investors didn't even ask questions. They had impeccable confidence in their boy.

Under Skylar, the company usually used 5.5 million gallons of water to drill a typical fracking well. This produced an average of 2.5 million cubic feet of natural gas a day for a month until it dried up and had to be capped.

One problem he was running into was the shale formation crossed into one of the Great Lakes watersheds. Environmental groups were starting to make waves. It was true there were no proven statistics to show that fracking caused any ecological problems. However, various environmental organizations raised the question what happens when there is an ecological disaster.

To appease the bureaucrats, he knew how to play the game and whose palms had to be greased in Lansing.

Companies like Skylar's are primarily responsible for regulating their own activities, as fracking is exempt from most federal laws targeted toward environmental protection, such as the Clean Water Act, National Environmental Policy Act, and the Safe Drinking Water Act.

Michigan laws also largely exempt fracking from key water protection statutes. In fact, Michigan's Great Lakes Compact under the Natural Resources and Environmental Protection Agency exempts the oil and gas industry from complying with the requirements of large quantity of water usage, including procuring a water withdrawal permit.

Fracking, done as part of an oil and gas activity, is exempt unless it results in the diversion of a river. Considering that fracking has been occurring in Michigan over the past four decades, and deep horizontal well drilling has been in abundance since 2010, Michigan's laws and regulations are minimum at best. Gas and oil companies use the fine print to evade the state and federal laws.

This was one job in which experience was worth a great deal and nobody was going to stop Skylar and his crew.

"How far are we down now?" asked the project engineer.

Mitch Avery responded, "About 5,300 feet!"

"It looks good. Keep it up," responded Skylar.

The project engineer was trying to forget the recent phone call he had with his wife. She had given him an ultimatum; it was either his work or his marriage. He knew he hadn't been a good husband or father with his job taking him away for months at a time. He loved both but just couldn't part with his job. He got such an adrenaline rush when they drew oil or gas out of the ground. Maybe, he could patch things up with his wife, Judy, when he got home.

Just then, Dutch Stanton arrived in his truck and motioned for Skylar to join him. Frustrated, the project engineer exited his platform and joined his public relations director. "What's up?" asked Skylar as he approached Dutch.

"I hate to tell you this, but we got trouble. There are over a hundred protestors at the gate. They won't get out of the way when our trucks try to enter."

"Did you phone the police?" asked Skylar.

"Of course, I did, but they don't have the manpower to send a dozen deputies here. They can only spare a few," relayed Stanton.

"Okay, I'll take care of it. Give me a ride to the main gate," barked Skylar.

There was no way he was going to allow a handful of demonstrators to interrupt his drilling schedule. Arriving there, Skylar bolted from the truck and strode into the crowd of protestors. Ignoring their chants of "**No Fracking**" he searched for their organizers, who he knew only too well, Lucy Edington and Kim Holland.

Skylar shouted, "Lucy, Kim, can I have a word with you?"

Emboldened by the crowd chants both Kim and Lucy stepped forward.

"Com'n let's talk," shouted Skylar over the crowd.

The young women followed Skylar through the gate into a tool shed and Skylar turned and barked, "You know you're going to get arrested if you continue preventing my trucks from crossing your picket line."

Kim was the first to reply, "That's too bad! You're destroying the environment. The watershed in this area is being devastated. You're affecting the Great Lakes. What are you going to do if the chemicals that you use drilling, surface along the shoreline? Explain that!"

Lucy Edington added, "I don't care if you are my father. This is wrong!"

Being a father for a minute, Lance Skylar responded, "I've drilled using fracking all my life and I've never had an incident yet. I've provided a good home and an education for you and this is how you repay me? Now you turn on me? Girls, why don't you take your protestors and find another cause to champion? Surely, there's a lot out there!"

Lucy was incensed that he asked them to leave so easily. She bantered, "We're here until you quit destroying our drinking water."

Kim chimed in, "You can bring in the police and chase us away, but we'll be right back tomorrow. We're not going to quit. We're here to stay!"

Skylar was frustrated he couldn't persuade the young women to leave.

He returned to the front gate and stepped into the waiting supply truck. Skylar put the truck in gear and slowly inched his way forward. Some of the protestors laid down on the ground preventing him from going any further. Totally exasperated, he jumped out of the truck and pushed his way through the chanting protestors and returned to his drill site.

As the two men returned to the drill location, Dutch asked, "What are we going to do? If we can't get supplies in and the gas out, we're screwed."

Skylar replied, "I know!" He knew he had to solve this problem one way or another.

Chapter Two

We were preparing to return to the Superior Peninsula when we felt slight vibrations. My wife and I immediately were under the impression they were tremors that were preceding an earthquake.

Looking around, nobody else was reacting. I stopped a lady passing by and I asked her, "Are my wife and I the only ones that felt those sensations?"

The woman smiled and said, "Those are tremors from fracking being conducted in the next county."

I had heard of this new type of drilling, but I didn't realize it was so prevalent.

My wife and I gleefully finished loading our vehicle and returned to our beloved peninsula. We have a cottage on a beautiful river that is home to many wild animals and birds. In the morning, we are usually awakened by various sounds of Mother Nature. As we enjoy our morning coffee on the deck, it is not unusual for ducks or geese to come ashore and feed.

If we're lucky enough, some of our grandchildren visit us and bring joy to our hearts.

Swimming, boating and fishing are a must. The floating dock is perfect for the older grandchildren to dive from. Sometimes a pontoon boat ride is in order. When we do, we maneuver to the middle of the majestic river and enjoy a cool refreshing dip. In the evening, there is nothing like roasted hot dogs or s'mores over an open fire.

Occasionally, the neighbor's dog, Bowser, will pay us a visit looking for a hand-out. I'd like to think the dog is just being friendly, but I know better. The hardest part is getting the grandchildren to fall asleep.

Our golden years couldn't be any better. This was truly nirvana but that was about to change. In the morning, my cell phone chimed and as I answered it, a voice I recognized from the past said, "Hey, Bill, how are you? This is Inspector Delton from the Midland Police."

I responded, "Inspector Delton, I'm good. How's everything in Midland?"

The inspector replied, "Okay, but I have a problem."

"What's up? I'll be glad to help if I can."

He said, "Normally, I would handle this myself, but I'm retiring at the end of the month and I want to go out with a clean slate. We had a murder here a few days ago and I'd like to have it solved before I clean out my desk."

My interest was piqued as I said, "Tell me about the case. I'm all ears."

He began, "As you know, they're doing a lot of fracking north of here. One of the engineers was murdered the other night. His body was scattered all over the tri-city area!"

"My God!" I exclaimed. "Any leads?"

"His wife was leaving him. His own daughter was one of the protestors outside the gate. In addition, he ran a pretty rough crew. Many of them have been arrested for bar fights, drunk and disorderly, public urination, lewd conduct; you name it. They're not choir boys. We've started interrogating them, but most of the rough necks don't remember anything the night of the murder, they were so drunk. In addition, we don't know if he was in tight with any state bureaucrats."

I responded, "Let me talk to the boys and see if they're available." I texted the guys I wanted to meet the next morning at our favorite restaurant, Millie's.

As I entered, I thought I heard some grumbling among them. As I sat down, John began, "This better be important. I gave up a date with a trout stream."

Ben added, "My motorcycle is gassed and I'm looking for a ride."

Tyler chirped in, "Unfortunately, my lawn needs to be cut."

Mark climaxed the conversation saying, "My wife wants me

to paint the house. Anybody want to switch?"

Taking all of this in stride, I said, "Do you remember Inspector Delton from Midland? It appears they had a murder in the tri-city area. Somebody dismembered an engineer from one of the fracking sites. The inspector hated to call, but he's retiring at the end of the month. He'd like to walk out the door with a clean slate. What do you think?"

There was a hush and I could see all of the guys were thinking. Trying to bait them, I added, "John, you could bring your fishing equipment. Ben, you could ride your bike there and Tyler, the grass will keep. As for you, Mark, you have the rest of the summer to paint."

Finally, they agreed with me and nodded their heads. I said, "How about if we retrieve our gear and meet here after lunch?" With that, we dispersed to gather our supplies.

After loading everything, we drove across the Mighty Mac to another adventure.

After entering the village, I took it upon myself to visit the local police department. Upon arriving, I found Inspector Delton at his desk. I could tell he was at the end of his rope. The inspector began, "I've never had a case like this. Usually, after questioning the people involved, I get a picture of what happened. Not this time. All of them had a reason to dislike Skylar. He was a bad husband, his daughter despised him over fracking, dozens of demonstrators disliked him, and on top of all that he had a crew that would scare the French Foreign Legion."

I answered, "Inspector, we'll start tomorrow fresh and early. We'll check everybody out and see if we can't get some leads. You go home and get some rest. After all, you have retirement waiting."

He replied, "That's what bothers me. I don't want to leave this case to somebody else."

I didn't have an answer for him so I just said, "We're here to help."

We found a motel just on the outskirts of town. That way, we would be less conspicuous.

The pseudo-detectives were unloading our weapons and equipment when it became apparent that the other guests were gaping wide-eyed.

Mark looked at the onlookers and said, "We have mice." At least, I was pretty sure, we wouldn't have anybody snooping around while we were gone. It wasn't long before we were fast asleep with CPAPs working in unison.

Chapter Three

It was finally here! College graduation had only been a dream for all five young men, ever since they had become inseparable in junior high school. The five geeks had weathered everything together.

If one of them was being bullied, the others would cook up a scheme to gain retribution. There was one time a group of upper classmen had super glued one of their lockers shut. The geeks snuck into the locker room and applied invisible mortar glue inside their football helmets. The maintenance man was able to remove the face masks, but the bullies had to wear the helmets until the glue became porous. Needless to say, it was the last time anybody messed with the Fab Five, as they called themselves.

The Fab Five consisted of Paul Baker, Drew Payne, Cal Graham, Nate Shaw and Travis Knight. They conducted many pranks during their high school days, especially Halloween when they attached a video camera to a drone and had it hover outside the principal's bedroom window. The video went viral and the principal suddenly became ill for several weeks.

They knew their IQs were off the charts and college would probably be a bore, but they knew they had to jump through the hoops. They had numerous academic offers from every major university in the country. They selected the engineering and computer school in the Superior Peninsula for one main reason. After extensive research, they chose that college because it had a 98% hiring rate after graduation. It was a can't-miss guarantee. Knowing this, they continued the same shenanigans during their undergraduate years. They knew they were guaranteed a cushy job in a research lab after graduation where they could play all day. What a life they were going to have.

Right now, they could enjoy commencement. They did

the normal things. Photo ops with families, hugs with other graduating classmates, and then off to the bars. The Fab Five didn't remember much that night. The next morning, they woke up in their underwear on Lake Gitchigoomie beach.

The first thing they did was check to see if there was any evidence on YouTube. Sure enough, their friends filmed the Fab Five doing all sorts of immoral things. Not satisfied with raising hell in the bar, they retreated to a farm in the outskirts of the city and opened every pen they saw. It was only when the farmers' house lights came on, did they beat a hasty retreat.

Now it was time to wait for the job offers to pour in. None of them even gave a thought to look for a summer job. That was for losers. A few days passed and nothing. A week elapsed and they heard some of their classmates were picked up by big ones like Apple and Samsung.

They were going to hold out in order that they could be hired together. Certainly, Foxconn and Amazon would be hiring. They'd even consider Intel, Dell, LG, Sony or Panasonic if they could all stay together. The second week passed and still nothing. Now they started to make calls. Why weren't they getting contacted by the large Intel corporations?

Their calls went unanswered and their resumes were ignored online. What was the problem?

Chapter Four

The Fab Five decided to have a meeting. Paul Baker stated, "Listen, guys we know we're the best computer geniuses coming out of college this year. Does anyone have an idea why we've been ignored?"

Drew Payne said, "Is its possible companies got wind of our antics and didn't want us even though we're the best of the best."

Cal Graham relayed, "I thought I'd be making $100,000 by now, driving a Lamborghini."

Nate Shaw said, "If I don't get a job soon, I'll have to go back home and work in my old man's lumber yard."

Travis Knight chimed in saying, "Let me make some calls and see if we're being black balled from the technology industry."

Drew Payne asked, "How are you going to do that? Nobody's going to admit anything."

Days passed, and young Payne made some contacts in the computer tech world. Nobody came out and said as much that the Fab Five was being ignored by the human resource managers. Days turned into weeks that in turn evolved into months. Each computer genius had to resort to a minimum wage job. Baker and Payne were hired as general laborers, while Shaw and Knight got to wear cute little paper hats working at a fast food restaurant. Graham probably had the most degrading position, back at his father's lumber yard working in the warehouse.

At their next meeting, Knight began, "I've been on YouTube and some of our practical jokes and antics have been seen by thousands. Is it possible that they were noticed by the big companies and they decided to overlook us?"

Graham sighed and said, "I guess I have to agree with you. Maybe, we went overboard in college. We know we're geniuses but tech companies want reliable employees, not clowns."

Paul Baker jumped in and said, "I think we should teach everyone a lesson."

Drew Payne responded, "What exactly are you talking about?"

Nate Shaw said, "Maybe, we can use our brilliance to make some money on our own."

Cal Graham said, "Anything's better than working in my old man's warehouse forty hours a week."

Knight said, "I'm sick of refilling the condiment dispenser at work. What can we do?"

Paul Baker said, "Remember in junior high we made homemade drones and flew them in town. We terrorized people."

Drew Payne retorted, "Yeah, I got grounded for a week."

Baker asked, "Why not make some sophisticated drones and use them to rob banks?"

Travis Knight said, "I like the idea, but how do we control the drones and what's to keep the police or bank guards from simply shooting them out of the air?"

Paul Baker answered, "We make five of them and we develop a plan. It's very easy. When someone opens the bank door, we fly our drones inside. We attach a note demanding money or we'll explode the drones. We include a demand that one of the bank tellers open the doors for the drones to leave. There's no way banks or police can stop them."

The other four were enthusiastic and discussed plans to build powerful drones loaded with IED's. Paul Baker and Drew Payne assigned themselves the task of building drones that could fly with a powerful electrical system that included a formidable Power Distribution Board. The flight controller didn't have just the normal four or six gears, but they engineered the drones to have ten.

Cal Graham and Nate Shaw went on the internet to learn to construct lightweight IED's that could be released by the Flight Controller if needed. Travis Knight's job was to inspect the local banks and credit unions and see which were the most vulnerable.

Finally, the drones were ready. The Fab Five took the drones into the country to give them a test run. With the drones' batteries fully charged and all of them carrying disconnected IEDs, the boys flew them for over a ¼ mile radius. The geeks even released the IEDs in a field and everything worked splendidly. Would they work in the city was the question?

The boys were eager to give them a try under real conditions. There were five banks in Bay City, one for each. Travis Knight had done his job. Each bank was inspected over several weeks and it looked like Monday morning would be the best time to strike.

The night before, the Fab Five had a celebration of sorts including wine and lobster. They toasted their good fortune and felt their plan was foolproof. The worst-case scenario was if someone shot a drone down, the gang member operating the flight controller would detonate the IED thus destroying all evidence.

The plan was simple and efficient. The next morning saw the boys eager to commence their mission. They carefully placed each drone in a backpack that the thieves would wear. After driving to midtown, at precisely 10:00, the robbers turned the drones on and allowed them to hover outside the five banks' front doors.

An unsuspecting customer opened the door either to enter or exit and the flight controller, from a safe distance, they maneuvered the drone inside. The mini flying fortress flew to the nearest teller and lowered itself in front. Once the teller read the note the employee had a confused look. The floor manager was summoned and thinking it was a hoax thought it could be ignored. A flight around the bank's interior by the drone was used to convince the employees it was not a joke. The drone dropped a large bag with a list of instructions. The tellers were ordered to place all their loose cash in the bag and pass it to the next one. Once, the bag was filled, the last teller accompanied the drone through the doors, if the double doors were sealed, the IED would be detonated, killing the teller. Once the teller opened the outside door, it would make its escape and the drones flew to a designated field outside of town.

Each robbery was timed to take under three minutes, and by the time the police arrived they could only see the aerial thieves flying into the distance. Naturally, they gave chase but once the drones were out of sight, it was anybody's guess where they landed.

Hours later, when the Fab Five felt it was safe, they went to the field and retrieved their drones and the spoils.

Knowing a bank teller would drop a GPS tracking device into the bag, the robbers were quick to remove it and throw it in the back of a passing truck. They also suspected the money was either marked or consecutively numbered. They agreed beforehand to store the stolen money indefinitely.

Meanwhile, the police were in a quandary. They had never heard of thieves using drones to rob a bank, let alone five banks simultaneously. They would be ready next time. The FBI was contacted and hopefully, their expertise could be utilized.

The Fab Five knew they had to return to their routine jobs the next day. This time they didn't resent them as much. Even Cal Graham didn't mind sweltering in his father's warehouse.

Months passed; the winter set in with its cruel repercussions. The Fab Five thought it might be safe to conduct another aerial robbery. Since Saginaw was a larger city, they thought they could rob the next five banks.

The morning of the robbery, the thieves were positioned out of sight, but still able to maneuver the drones inside the banks and let them do the work. Each teller passed the bag among themselves and just as before, a GPS tracker was slid into the bag. Again, using the final teller as a hostage, the terrified teller had to open the outside door to allow the drone to escape. The police arrived late again. The boys in blue gave chase but lost the drones in the trees. To tantalize the authorities again, the tracker was discarded in the back of a county truck.

They were getting their revenge on society. Meeting again clandestinely, the five thieves thought one more job was in the offing. They sized up the banks again in Saginaw and decided to rob the next five. Paul Baker said, "Let's do it the week of

Thanksgiving. All of the banks will have extra cash on hand for Black Friday."

The plan was set and after proper scouting, it was hatched the morning after Thanksgiving. Everything went fine until a teller became hysterical and refused to accompany the drone as a hostage. To instill fear, the flight controller, Nate Shaw, maneuvered the drone around the inside of the bank to terrorize the employees and the customers. Everyone dropped to the floor as the drone continued to travel at warp speed.

One brave customer was able to open both doors allowing the drone to escape. By this time, the Saginaw police arrived, and they made quick work of the aerial thief. The drone dropped from the sky and exploded. Fortunately, nobody was injured, but Shaw had to beat a hasty retreat empty handed.

The state police bomb squad was asked to help and they inspected the burnt wreckage. The other four thieves were able to conduct their robberies successfully. The GPS tracker was found on a helium balloon, the Fab Five attached the tracker to, just to torment the police.

Paul Baker replied, "Don't worry about it. We can build another drone and we'll be ready to do it again just before Christmas."

Chapter Five

Meanwhile, months earlier, at the Simmons residence, Lucy Edington and her husband stepped out of their vehicle and raced across the lawn to embrace her mother. Lucy started, "I'm so sorry this happened!"

Her mother responded, "I know. We had an argument over the phone the night he was killed. I told him to make a choice, the job or me. I feel just horrible. That was the last time I talked to him."

Lucy's husband, Frank, tried to console his mother-in-law saying. "It's not your fault. He was a rough guy and that's how he lived his life. His job meant a lot to him and he couldn't leave it."

Lucy also trying to console her mother said, "Let's go inside and sit down. The sun is getting hot and you need to cool down. We'll help with the funeral arrangements."

Judy answered, "Lance wouldn't want a fancy funeral. He was a very private man."

Frank said, "Lucy and I can go to the funeral home and take care of everything if you want."

Judy shook her head and replied, "I want to go with you. It's the least I can do."

They entered the house and sat on the patio while Lucy made some lemonade.

In the afternoon, the trio arrived at the funeral home and searched for the director. A distinguished-looking man approached them and expressed his sorrow for their loss. He introduced himself as Dan Blackwell. Without missing a beat, he guided them into a room where they discussed the plans for the wake.

With every step in the funeral process, the two women, Judy

and her daughter, Lucy, teared up, and they simply nodded as the funeral director guided them through it.

Meanwhile, the roughnecks had gathered at the work site and were wondering when or if they would ever start fracking again. One of the men, Clem Haskins said, "Skylar was tough but fair. We had some run-ins, but he didn't carry a grudge."

Another roughneck, Wes Bentley said, "He gave me my first job. I'll always appreciate it." The others chimed in adding similar epitaphs.

Mitch Avery and Dutch Stanton stepped out of the office and Avery said, "Let's see if we can get some drilling done today. Everybody knows what to do. Let's start with I-13. I'd like to get a few hundred more feet down by sundown."

The men climbed into their trucks and followed Avery to the site.

Dutch Stanton watched the trucks drive away and he looked skyward and said, "Skylar, I know you'd want Mitch to get the boys back to work."

Across town, at the local university, some of the youths that had participated in the protest were commiserating among themselves. One youth stated, "Maybe, they'll stop now that the project engineer is dead."

Kim Holland retorted, "Don't count on it. They're a pretty rough crew. I have a feeling they'll continue drilling."

Others offered their own insight into the future of the fracking site.

After a hearty breakfast the next day, the pseudo-detectives and I discussed assignments.

I asked, "We have a host of people to follow up on including, Skylar's widow, his daughter, the demonstrators, the roughnecks, and even a Lansing bureaucrat or two. All of this is going to take time. "Who wants to take the widow?" I asked.

John signaled he would take her.

"What about the daughter?" I asked.

Tyler motioned he could do that.

"Who wants to question the roughnecks?" Mark said, "They

sound like my kind of people!"

I looked at Ben and asked, "Do you want the protestors or the Lansing bureaucrats. Ben said, "I'd rather stay here so I'll take the protestors at the university."

"That leaves me with the Lansing bureaucrat," I said.

Before departing, we agreed to meet back in a few days at the hotel.

John drove to the widow's residence, exited his vehicle, and hesitantly rang her doorbell.

After a period of waiting, the door opened and John was taken aback by a beautiful middle-aged woman that could have passed for half her age. "Yes, may I help you?" Judy Skylar asked.

John composed himself and then said, "Hi, Mrs. Skylar. My name is John Baldwin and along with some of my friends, we're looking into the death of your husband. Do you have time?"

Mrs. Skylar paused and said, "I guess we could talk. I haven't seen him in over a month. We had a very unusual marriage."

John said, "That's what I understand. It must have been hard with him gone for extended periods."

Judy Skylar responded, "Yes, I pretty much raised my daughter on my own. I was unhappy and the last conversation I had with him, I told him I planned to leave him. That will haunt me until the day I die. I feel so guilty."

John said, "I'm going to ask you some questions, but please, don't be upset." Trying to reassure her, he said, "You can't blame yourself. Did he gamble or have a drinking problem?"

Judy answered, "He didn't gamble, but he wasn't opposed to having a drink at the end of the day. He had a lot on his mind and he drank to relax."

"I see," said John. "What about other women. Were there any signs he might have had relationships? When a man is away from home, he gets lonely."

Mrs. Skylar bristled at the thought her husband was a philanderer. She retorted sharply, "Definitely not!"

"Were there any signs he might have used heavy drugs?" John asked sheepishly.

Mrs. Skylar now grew angry at the question and said, "I think we're through here."

John, trying to coax information from her, continued, "How's your daughter coping with her dad's murder?"

Judy Skylar answered, "Pretty good. They weren't close. In college, she became very active in environmental causes."

John now wanted to feel her out on how she was dealing with everything. He continued, "Mrs. Skylar, after the funeral do you have any plans?"

The widow reacted, "What do you mean?"

John persisted, "I mean do you have any plans to visit relatives or take a trip. Sometimes, after people lose a loved one, they just want to get away for a while."

Judy Skylar said, "I haven't thought that far ahead. But maybe, I'll visit my sister in Vermont."

John wanting to get a full picture asked, "Did you ever work or graduate from college?"

Judy shook her head negatively and said, "I was always a stay-at-home mom. Raising Lucy was my pride and joy." John shook Mrs. Skylar's hand and said, "I'm sorry for your loss. I can see myself out. Thank you." John closed the door behind him as he left.

Tyler had a harder time tracking down the daughter. After contacting the inspector, Delton had told him that he could probably find her at the environmental protest office. After getting directions, he found the young woman busy drawing posters for a future rally. Tapping the young activist on the shoulder, he asked, "Are you Mrs. Edington?"

She said, "Yes, who are you?"

Tyler replied, "I'm working with a group of retired detectives who are trying to solve your father's murder."

Lucy Edington replied, "I never had a father."

Not knowing how to reply, Tyler simply said, "I'm sorry to hear that."

He had to get some information from her and it just got harder. He persevered, "Can you be specific as to why you hated him?"

She said, "It'd take all day. Pass me the green marker, will you?"

Not giving in, after handing her the marker, Tyler asked, "What made him the kind of man he was?"

She let her guard down replying, "He never cared about my mother or me. His only love was his work, fracking."

Tyler asked, "Do you think he ever showed his love?"

She now gave Tyler an icy stare and said, "He missed all my birthday parties, holidays, my high school graduation and now, through no fault of his own, my college graduation. The irony is, he wouldn't have come to that, either, if he was alive. No, I have no feelings for him. He wanted to drill underground for oil or natural gas whatever the consequences. He didn't appreciate this earth. If it's destroyed, we don't get a second chance. He couldn't see that. He just went from one drill site to the next."

John had a pretty good idea of how Lucy felt about her father. Whether she could be involved in his death was another matter. He thanked her for her time and left.

Mark probably had the toughest job and he knew it. He was hoping his rough nature would appeal to the roughnecks. He drove to the mine site and approached the main office. A man opened the door and after introductions were exchanged, Dutch Stanton told Mark he could find the men at I-13. Before he left, Mark asked, "Mr. Stanton, how did you feel about your boss?" Stanton gave the company answer, "We had a working relationship. My job was to keep the public informed what we were doing and play down any bad news. When I made mistakes, Lance let me have it. I have to say it was a strained relationship, but that's the way Lance was. He was a man's man. No fooling around. If you were on company time, you better be working or you were fired."

Dutch continued, "I remember once, one young man came to work with his cell phone and thought he could take incoming calls when he wanted. You can imagine what happened. Lance saw him standing next to the drill talking like he was at Grand Central Station. That boy was gone in an hour. However, if he found that you worked extra hard, he complimented you like you were his best friend."

Mark said, "Thanks, you said I could find the crew at I-13?" Stanton gave him directions to get there and within minutes, Mark was parked in front of a pretty gruesome bunch. He stepped out of the truck and hoped they didn't throw him down the hole. He advanced toward the group and most of them ignored him. He shouted, "Can I ask who's in charge?"

A burly broad-shouldered man stepped forward and said, "What'd you want? We're busy!"

Mark spoke as loud as he could over the noise, saying, "I'm Mark Kestila. My friends and I are looking into the murder of your boss, Lance Skylar. Do you have some time to talk?"

Avery led Mark away from the group and said, "Make it quick!"

Mark said, "Did Lance have any men he had trouble with?"

Avery replied, "Look around, at one time or another he had an argument with all of us including me. Anything else?"

Mark knew he couldn't waste time. "Listen, you can either talk to me or to Inspector Delton at the Midland Police Station. What's it going to be?"

Hearing this, Avery relented and said, "Okay, you can talk to the guys one at a time if you want. I know you're going to get the same answer I gave you." Avery returned to work and sent one of the roughnecks in Mark's direction. The man approached Mark and said, "I'm Ron Emerson. The boss said you wanted to talk to us about Skylar's murder. What'd you want to know?"

Mark proceeded to ask the standard questions: did he ever have an argument with Skylar and did he know who might have wanted him dead?

After interviewing most of the men, he came to the same conclusion Avery had told him. Skylar was a tough boss but if you pulled your weight, he left you alone.

Mark waved to the guys as he drove away, but they ignored him.

Ben probably had another challenging job; interviewing young idealist people who believed they could make a difference.

He drove to the eco-warrior's headquarters and pushed his way into the main office. There was an aroma of marijuana permeating the room. Ben thought if he stayed too long, he'd get high himself.

Speaking in a loud voice, Ben asked, "Can I talk to someone about the murder of the project engineer at the fracking mine that you people were picketing the other day?"

I young woman stepped forward and asked, "What do you want? Don't look for us to shed any tears for that bastard."

Ben said, "I'm Ben Meyers and my friends and I are helping the Midland Police look into this murder."

The woman replied, "I'm Kim Holland and my best friend is Lucy Edington. Even she hated her father's guts."

Ben asked, "Could we talk somewhere more private?"

Kim walked outside and Ben followed her. Once they were far enough away from the protestors' headquarters, Ben asked, "Are you sure, his daughter really hated him or did she just say that to make it sound like she opposed fracking?"

Kim, said, "Her father was a cold fish. He didn't care about her. He missed every important event in her life. Lucy even got married last year just to have someone to love."

Ben asked, "Could you tell me his name?"

Kim retorted, "So you can hound him also? No way!"

Ben replied, "We're just trying to solve a murder. A man's life was taken. You of all people should appreciate that. You say you care about the world, then prove it. Tell me his name."

Kim said, "All right. Lucy's husbands name is Frank. Frank Edington. There, are you happy now? Go turn his life upside down." Ben tried to shake Kim's hand, but she refused. Ben could see the resentment in her eyes that exists when the youth become disenchanted with the older generation. Ben gave her a friendly wave that was not returned.

Meanwhile, I had the most time-consuming job. I had to drive to the capitol and find the Department of Oil, Gas, and Mineral Division. Once inside the capital, I scanned the directory to point me to the right office, MDEQ. I climbed the stairs and walked down the hall to the cold stares of the employees. I saw the lettering and opened the door. An administrative assistant looked at me and she asked, "May I help you?"

I replied, "I hope you can. I'd like to talk to the person that distributes the drilling permits."

She asked, "Do you have an appointment?"

I'm sure she knew the answer but she had to go through the formality.

I answered, "No, but it relates to the murder at one of the drilling sites a few days ago."

I think I caught her off guard. She was ready to give me the canned answer that I needed an appointment. She said, "One moment please?"

She entered the office and I could hear a dialogue between her and her superior. After a lengthy discussion inside the office, she exited and said, "Mr. Arden can give you a few minutes."

I thanked her as I entered the bureaucratic lair. I could feel the coldness in the air as I sat down. The small bespectacled man with thinning hair said, "I'm Jim Arden. How may I be of service?"

Even his introduction sounded fake. I answered, "I'm Bill Bennett, as your administrative assistant may have told you, my friends and I have been asked to investigate the murder of Lance Skylar. Could you check and see how many permits he's been given since you've been in office?" The little bureaucrat tapped his computer and leaned closer. Scanning the data, he replied, "About a thousand."

I replied, "Don't you think that's a little excessive for one company?"

The head of MDEQ took offense to my question and replied, "If you must know, I don't give out the permits. The Supervisor of Wells is in charge of permits."

Now, we're getting somewhere, I thought. "Can you tell me his name and where I'll find that person's office? After giving me directions to the next bureaucrat's office, I could tell he was glad to be rid of me.

Finding the Supervisor of Wells office was simple; getting to see the person was a different story.

As before, I entered and introduced myself to the administrative assistant and explained my mission. As before, the state employee excused herself and entered her boss' office. This time, she returned and said, "I'm sorry, he's on a telephone conference call. You can leave your name and he'll get back to you."

Not to be outsmarted, I replied, "That's okay. I'll wait."

She wasn't ready for that reply and she returned to her laptop and started crunching data.

Hours passed and it was obvious he was giving me the cold shoulder. Two can play at that game. I left the Supervisor's Office and returned to the main foyer. Examing the Directory again, I made note of who was the Supervisor of Wells. I knew all of the department heads would be identified by position in the Michigan Government Directory. Logging into my smartphone, I soon had the MDEQ on my screen. Scrolling down until I came to the Supervisor of Wells position, I tapped and a smiling middle-aged man appeared on my screen. Now, I could wait for him to exit the building and continue our conversation.

Relaxing on a park bench in front of the state executive's parking lot, eventually scores of government employees appeared at the end of work day. I scanned the crowd and sure enough, there was my pigeon. I made haste toward him to cut him off and we reached his vehicle simultaneously.

Naturally, he was nervous as I started my conversation. I commenced, "Mr. Riley, it's nice to finally meet you."

Confused, he asked, "Have we met before?"

I replied, "I was in your office and waited, but your administrative assistant said you were on a conference call. It must have been a long phone call."

He said tersely, "What is it that you want?"

I said, "My name is Bill Bennett, and along with some friends who are retired police officers, we are trying to discover who killed Lance Skylar."

He replied, "How would I know anything about that?"

I answered, "Well, it seems you have given him over a thousand drilling permits since your political party's been in office."

He answered, "Most of those permits are completed online. I have nothing to do with it."

"Are you telling me anybody can get a drilling permit if they fill out the form and send it into the MDEQ?"

He backed off and said, "It's not quite that easy. Once you develop a pattern of filing the request for a permit, an aid sends it through and it'll be investigated. The hardest thing is getting the first few approved and after that it becomes simple. Have I answered your questions Mr. Bennett?" I had to acknowledge, "Yes, thanks." With that, he entered his vehicle and drove away. I felt I had wasted an entire day chasing my tail.

Frustrated, I returned to exchange stories with my cohorts at the motel.

Chapter Six

There's nothing like a good cup of coffee to jumpstart the day. We were enjoying our second cup as each of us relayed our experience with the Skylar family and even those who did not wish Lance Skylar well.

Mark began by saying, "I have to say the roughnecks overall liked Skylar, but anyone of them could take a life if they were pushed."

Ben said, "My experience with the demonstrators went as expected. The one I spoke with, Kim Holland, knew Lucy pretty well, and said the daughter got nothing from her father. That's why Lucy got married last year."

John said, "Skylar's widow wasn't much help. There was no love lost between the two. She was planning to leave him. I guess he was never home so after all these years she had enough."

Tyler chirped in saying, "That brings us to young Lucy. As Ben said, the daughter was angry at him for never being there. They were on opposite sides of everything especially fracking. She is idealistic and wants to make the world a better place."

I said, "I spent a day in bureaucracy land. It wasn't fun. How those guys can push paper and double talk is beyond me. Anyway, I finally spoke with the Supervisor of Wells, Riley, and he said the reason Skylar got so many permits was that they're just sent to a computer and if they're legitimate, they're approved."

I asked, "Can we narrow our search?"

Mark said, "Right now, I have to rule out the roughnecks. If we come up empty, we can always circle back. From what I saw at the site, they're barely keeping their jobs. They had too much to lose in my opinion."

"Anybody else?" I asked.

Ben said, "I don't think the young college kids would have it in them to murder someone and then scatter the body in three cities."

"Okay. that's two down for now." I said. "John, or Tyler, do you think the mother or daughter could be involved?"

John replied, "I don't think the mother cared enough to kill him. She already had one foot out the door."

Tyler thought for a while and then responded, "I think it's quite possible that the daughter could have been involved. If we're just going by who hated him, I'd say she despised him the most."

I joined in saying, "The bureaucrat gave Skylar a lot of drilling permits."

"If we're narrowing it down, the daughter is the number one person on our list. Does everyone agree?"

The fellows nodded their head affirmatively.

Since we streamlined our suspect down to one, I felt it was appropriate to see Inspector Delton. After all, he was crossing off the days until he could grab that golden parachute and leap out the front door.

Entering the Midland Police Station, I found the inspector in his office. The soon-to-be-retiree smiled and said, "Good timing, I'm just about to review the M.E. report on Lance Skylar. Have a seat."

I entered and sat down and the inspector started reading the report out loud. Inspector Delton said, "I'll spare you the gruesome parts. I'm sure you've heard them all too often. I'm going to skip to the coroner's conclusions. The coroner writes: The murderer may have had skills in dissection because the body was so cleanly cut and mutilated.

He looked at me and now we had a whole new angle to examine. *Could the murderer be a medical person?*

I replied, "I think that changes the game plan. I'll contact my friends and we'll start digging into everybody's past and see who would know how to dissect a body."

I couldn't wait to get back to the hotel and tell them about our new lead. Driving into the parking lot, I knew where to find the boys. Sure enough, as I walked into the bar, I could hear the boys blowing off steam. As I approached the table with a drink, it was apparent they were in the middle of a good poker game. I began, "If I could interrupt for a minute, I have some critical news. The M.E. report concludes the murderer had special training the way the body was severed into three parts."

You could have heard a pin drop as the formerly rambunctious jovial fellows became instantly sullen and I could see their minds working. I asked, "Who do we know that has medical training?" All of the pseudo-detectives shook their heads. I said, "Well, we're going to have to return and find out who fits that description."

We finished our drinks and retreated to our rooms to get an early start in the morning.

Chapter Seven

We agreed to revisit our first targets and try to find out who had medical training.

As we were enjoying our morning Joe, John said, "Skylar's widow was a homemaker. She never even went to college. I doubt if she could be a suspect."

Mark added, "I have to say, I doubt if any of the roughnecks had any medical training."

That left the Supervisor of Wells, Lucy and Frank Edington and a host of students.

"Ben could you and Mark research the demonstrators and see if any of them are in a pre-medical program?"

Ben said, "Sure, if we find one, maybe, they'll want to do a lobotomy on Mark?"

Mark responded, "Very funny!"

"Since you're pretty sure Skylar's wife couldn't have cut him up surgically, why don't you help your son, Tyler? Don't forget to see if her husband had any medical training," I said.

John replied, "I can do that. Let's go Tyler."

I added, "I'll return to Lansing and see if the Supervisor of Wells could be a suspect. Let's meet back here in a couple of days." With a plan laid out, we dispersed.

Ben and Mark decided it would be easier if they went to the College of Medicine Building and nosed around. Arriving, they entered, and approached the bulletin board. They saw the poster that called for students to protest at the fracking site. The organization that was responsible had an eco-friendly theme. The contact person was Steve Haskins. Mark wrote down the cell number and together, they found the dorm room of the organizer. They knocked on his door and soon a sleepy-eyed youth opened the door and rubbing his eyes asked, "What's up, Dude?"

Ben stated, "Are you Steve Haskins?"

The youth nodded his head and still appeared to be groggy.

Ben continued, "We're helping find the murderer of Lance Skylar. My name is Ben Meyer and this is Mark Kestila. Do you know if any of the pre-med students were involved in the protests the other day at the drilling site?"

Haskins responded, "That's pretty heavy stuff man. Are you serious?"

Mark relayed, "Very serious!"

The youth replied, "Kim Holland is very involved. I'm just the contact person. Check with her." He closed the door unceremoniously.

Mark said under his breath, "That's our future generation!"

Checking his smartphone, Mark identified the young protestor's home address. They arrived off-campus and found a house that looked like it saw its share of parties. As the two men walked up the steps, the porch was littered with booze bottles and empty pizza cartons. They rang the doorbell and after opening the door, a young female attired in pajamas asked, "What's up?"

Ben introduced himself and Mark asked,

"Is Kim Holland available? We would like to speak with her."

The young girl nodded, turned, and shouted, "Kim, it's for you!"

In a few minutes Kim appeared dressed and holding her laptop. She said, "I'm late for class, is this important?"

Mark said, "Yes, we're helping to find the murderer of Lance Skylar. I have to ask, what degree program are you involved with?"

Kim replied, "Why is that important? If you must know, I'm majoring in micro-biology."

Ben and Mark said, "Well, thanks, you better get to class."

After the two men returned to their vehicle, Mark said, "I doubt if she has any training in cutting cadavers."

The next stop was the Edingtons and after locating their address on one of their smartphones, they arrived in the downtown section of Midland. John and Tyler prepared to knock on the

Edingtons' door. The apartment had seen better days, but it passed for married housing. Before they knocked, Tyler peeked through the window and saw something that startled him. There on the floor was Lucy Edington. Tyler smashed the window and unhooked the latch. The father and son bolted through the doorway and raced to the young woman lying on the floor. Tyler felt for a pulse and started CPR. John tapped the emergency number and gave the dispatcher the address.

They continued chest compressions until the EMTs arrived. John and Tyler stepped back. Knowing her husband would want to be contacted, they scoured the room for Lucy's cell phone. Finally, locating it between the couch cushions, Tyler dialed her husband's number.

The voice on the other end said, "Yeah, what's up honey?"

Tyler wasn't sure how to tell her husband so he just said it as plain as he could. "Mr. Edington, I'm a private detective and we're checking relatives of Lance Skylar. We're at your apartment and I looked through the window and I saw your wife unconscious. The EMTs are working on her now. I think you better come home."

Frank Edington answered, "I'll be right there!"

While Tyler was speaking to the husband on the phone, John surveyed the room. He saw narcotic bottles on the coffee table. Being careful not to touch them, he knelt down and read the labels. They included Zaleplon, Emazepam, Belsomra, Trazodone and Zolpidem.

John took Tyler aside and said, "Look at the narcotic bottles on the table; they're empty."

John relayed the same information to the EMTs and he stepped outside so as not to impede their work. Within a few minutes, Frank Edington's vehicle roared down the street, he jumped out and raced past the two sleuths to his wife.

Both John and Tyler had seen enough overdose cases in their careers to know the prognosis was grim. The EMTs removed Lucy on the gurney followed closely by her husband.

Soon, the ambulance sped away accompanied by her husband

hoping they could save her.

John looked at Tyler and said, "Let's nose around inside. Maybe, we'll find something. After watching the police leave, the two pseudo-detectives started searching the apartment. They checked the toilet tank, under the sheets, the night stand, behind the mirror and other usual places people hide things.

Sorting through the floor of the closet, Tyler tapped the floorboards. It was common for the boards to be loose and people kept their important items hidden there. As he softly tapped the boards, he heard a hollow sound. Sure enough, using his pocket knife, he pried up one of the boards. John stopped what he was doing and looked to see what Tyler retrieved. Unwrapping a cloth, was a large butcher knife covered in dried blood. Both John and Tyler stared at each other. They knew they had discovered the knife illegally, and it would be inadmissible in court.

John said, "I think we have our murderer. I doubt if Lucy would have the strength to do it, but

Frank certainly would."

Tyler said, "Let's find out what hidden skills Frank has. I'm betting he knows how to handle that knife."

After being informed of the events, I said, "As usual, we'll have to set a trap for the husband. I'll turn around and be there in a few hours."

Rendezvousing at the motel coffee shop, we had to wait for the family to deal with Lucy's overdose. We were sure of the outcome. I said, "Let's wait until after the funeral and we'll take him down." I wondered, *could Lucy's overdose be a result of her role in murdering her father?*

John said, "I doubt if the son-in-law would do this heinous crime on his own. I wonder if his wife, Lucy, helped him. He must have hated his father-in-law to cut the body up and distribute it in three cities."

Now we were pretty sure who the murderer was, but who else was involved?

As expected, Lucy didn't survive the heavy overdose of

barbiturates. Inspector Delton informed us of the somber news later that afternoon. Knowing it would take several days for the arrangements, I felt sorry for Lucy's mother losing a husband, even though estranged, as well as a daughter.

Chapter Eight

Hoping for a reprieve from investigation for a while, we returned to enjoy the fall in the Superior Peninsula. The weather is usually perfect for any type of hunting or fishing that you desire. I recalled deer hunting last fall; my compatriots and I had hunted together since time immemorial. We each had our hunting area claimed and knew not to intrude on each other.

Remembering back to last deer season on opening morning, it was still pitch black when Tyler served up breakfast. Traditions differ, but in our camp, the youngest is always the designated camp cook. We finished skillet-fried eggs with toast, and just before sunrise, we went our separate ways, each of us heading to our preferred designated hunting site. After being together for years, we all knew the location of each member of our group. If there was a shot, we would know who had fired it and from which direction. With their military training, some of the guys swore that they could even tell the caliber of the rifle.

There was always light-hearted bantering among us; it wouldn't be hunting season if there wasn't.

Mark began, saying, "You guys wait for my shot and then you can come help me field dress it and drag it back to camp."

Ben retorted, "You couldn't hit the broadside of a barn, you old coot."

"The only thing you'll be dragging back to camp is your sorry ass," John said.

Once, we separated, I walked slowly on the trail toward my favorite location, being sure not to step on the leaves. I needed to get to my blind without being detected. If I wasn't careful getting there, I would hear a deer snort, followed by the pawing of a hoof; in a flash, the deer would be gone.

I always sat on the side of a hill facing the wind, usually about half way up under cover of some prearranged dead branches. I wanted to be comfortable as possible because I was going to be there for a good many hours. If it was foggy, rainy or snowing, my chances of seeing deer were pretty good. The enemy was wind because it took away one of their natural defenses and if it was breezy, the deer became very skittish. We old deer hunters know how to use the elements to our advantage.

Once settled, I knew the deer would be on the move, moseying toward a sunny glade where they'd spend the afternoon in their day beds.

Hours passed, and I was getting ready to quit, when I heard something over the rise. I raised my .308, slowly pulling the hammer back. There it was, a beautiful ten-point buck. I'd seen it a few times on my trail cam and now I could hardly believe it.

I raised my rifle slowly taking aim, and then squeezing the trigger. The buck leaped, then fell. It was a clean kill.

It wasn't long before the guys arrived to give me a hand field dressing it. Always a fierce competitor, John repeatedly said, "That isn't much of a deer." I knew better.

After dragging it back to camp, hoisting it on the buck pole, we celebrated with a shot of Jack Daniels. It didn't get any better than that. John kept mumbling, "It isn't much of a deer."

Truth be told, my real preference is waterfowl hunting. The reason is in the Superior Peninsula, the weather is warmer because the season is earlier, and there's a lot more action.

I had a good friend, former classmate, Ben Bonetelli that owned a duck camp near Lake Michigan. It was situated right in the middle of the Canadian and duck migratory routes. Just before the birds chose to cross Lake Michigan, they'd land on Ben's lake. Enhancing our good fortune, one of our hunting buddies, Scott, had a beautiful retriever, Abby. It was not uncommon for Abby to retrieve two ducks at a time. You couldn't teach that skill. She was just a natural and it made hunting that much more enjoyable.

Years ago, when I first started duck hunting, I could identify the easy ones, like mallards and buffleheads. In time, Ben helped me recognize the others such as wigeons, teals, ring-necked, scaups, and the real trophy everyone wanted, goldeneye. The two that were despised were wood ducks and hooded mergansers because of their horrible taste.

Everyone had a twelve-gauge semi-automatic shotgun. Some invested a lot of money in them and I certainly respected that, but I was satisfied with my old Mossberg.

It was critical that hunters arrive early before the waterfowl started looking for a landing sight. That meant we had to arrive before sun-up. If you haven't navigated in a small Jon boat across open water wearing chest waders, heavy hunting jacket, gloves, face mask, and hat you've haven't truly experienced life to its fullest.

This past duck season one dark morning the fog was so thick you could cut it with a knife. After we were underway, Ben gave me the flood light to shine ahead through the murky waters. He was very skilled and I had a lot of confidence in him. There were a few times we got stuck in the mud and had to push out, but eventually we found our blind. It took additional time for us to spread our decoys and we tried to line them up so they mimicked a flock that had just landed. It was only after we were safely settled in the blind did my hunting companion say, "That was interesting."

Trying to make conversation, I said, "You got that right. You did a great job."

Ben answered, "Yeah, that's the first time I did that."

I tried to act unemotional, but it was difficult. Not sure how long it was before I took my next breath. Such is water fowl hunting.

In the evening, we would reminisce about the day's hunt. It was natural to embellish our shooting prowess, and we enjoyed ribbing one another about the ones that got away. We knew the cardinal rule, anything that happens at camp stays at camp.

Because we were serious about duck hunting, after our shotguns were taken apart nightly and cleaned, it was usually an early night. Nothing is worse than sitting in a duck blind and having trouble staying awake. That was the exciting part of waterfowl hunting. The birds flew in so fast, cupped their wings and landed, you had to be ready.

The smaller ones like buffleheads and teals were lightning fast, both landing and getting airborne. Ring-necks and goldeneyes were a little bigger, but you still had to be ready. It goes without saying, if someone accidentally shot a decoy, they faced the wrath of the rest of the partners that night.

Another nemesis to duck hunters was walking through the marsh. You had to pick clumps of grass to step on and hopefully they held your weight. It seemed that whenever you were in a hurry, that's when you found a pocket of mud and sunk up to your knees.

I came to the conclusion that the worse the terrain and conditions were, the better the hunting was. If it was sunny and bright, the ducks and geese would put down for the day and be content. If it was windy accompanied by dark clouds, the hunting seemed to improve. The overall controlling factor for all hunting was the wind direction. If the wind was in our face, we could count on some flocks finding the decoys. If the wind was at our back, the game usually found someplace else to put down.

Sharing a blind with a hunting partner is a treasure. You get to know your partner pretty well. Families, old classmates, and of course, the girl that got away comes up. When it's all said and done, it's a great time to relax and be young again. You have no responsibilities, problems or obligations. Your only concern is being ready when the birds land.

At the end of one hunting excursion, my cell phone chimed and as I answered I heard, "Hey, Bill, how are you doing? I know you're duck hunting but something's come up."

I recognized the voice as John Baldwin's. I had heard that voice since junior high and was proud to call him my friend. However, there are exceptions and I was going to make it clear that this better be important.

He began, "You'll never guess. They're having trouble in the Tri-Cities again.

Your wife called me and brought me up to speed; it seems that your daughter-in-law works in the Midland bank. The drone thieves have hit the Bay City banks as well as the Saginaw ones. It seems like a good chance they're going to rob the Midland ones next. I phoned the Midland police, but they said neither they nor the FBI has the manpower to stake out all the banks indefinitely."

After hearing this, I realized I had to cut my duck hunting short, and along with the boys, travel to the Tri-City area again.

I collected my gear and thanked my old classmate, Ben, for a great time. I explained the situation and he said, "Of course you have to go. Family comes first." I returned home, packed and the next day the pseudo-detectives and I were traveling to the Tri-City area. I knew the police and FBI were great, but I wanted to make sure my daughter-in-law was protected.

Arriving mid-day, we were content to relax at my son Roy's house.

Ben looked around and said, "It feels like we didn't even leave."

Mark chimed in saying, "I'm getting to know the mail lady. She's single and likes distinguished, older-looking men."

Ben relayed, "That's probably true, but why does she talk to you?"

Mark just snarled at Ben.

I checked the city map and noticed there were five major banks. I asked the guys, "Should we stake out all five or should we concentrate on the one where my daughter-in-law works?"

We discussed the pros and cons of both and we decided, since the thieves were probably going to hit all of the banks, we should establish surveillance on all of them. If any of us saw a drone, waiting to enter one of the banks, shoot it.

John and Tyler would each take one of the banks located on Saginaw Road, Ben and Mark would take the ones on Ashman Road, and I would be concerned with the one my daughter-in-law managed on Eastman Ave.

We discussed how we were going to deploy without being

conspicuous. Also, with Christmas shopping now in full swing, every bank was going to be very busy. How could we protect the banks without calling attention to ourselves? Mark suggested an ingenious idea. What if we approached each bank and asked if it would be acceptable if we pretended to be Santa Clause? After all, we didn't think the customers would mind and it would be good PR for the bank.

The next day, we made it a point to visit each bank individually. After we explained the drone thieves had already robbed banks in both Bay City and Saginaw, it was a pretty good chance they were going to rob the banks in Midland. Did the branch managers want to take a chance of an armed drone entering their bank and terrorizing everyone? There was also the possibility that one of the IEDs attached to the drone could be detonated. Would they want to be responsible for the death of some of their customers or employees? I didn't say it, but I thought each manager probably didn't want to get blown to hell either.

Fortunately, all of the managers agreed to allow us pretend to be Santa Clause. The plan called for us to wait outside and simply shoot the drone out of the sky providing no innocent pedestrians were near.

We scouted each bank and all of them were pretty standard. They all had a closed-circuit camera behind each teller and other devices that will not be discussed. My daughter-in-law was amused that I was going to play St. Nick from 9-5 every day until Christmas.

We overnighted the Santa Clause suits from Amazon. The next day, putting the suits on was like walking into a sauna. The heavy suit didn't breathe and it didn't take long for my body temperature to climb. I felt I was either going to pass out or lose weight wearing this monkey suit. The others felt the same way, doing their usual grumbling as they squeezed into the suits. It could be said, only Tyler needed a pillow to fill out his stomach.

We were ready bright and early the next morning dropping each of the Santa Clauses in front of their respective bank. The Salvation Army graciously loaned each of us a red kettle. If nothing else, we would be able to raise some funds for a great cause with Christmas approaching.

Little ones were glad to see their favorite elf especially since they had all been good little boys and girls during the past year. At least that's what they told us. A few older urchins thought they could give Santa a hard time. The misguided youths usually left with an attitude adjustment knowing first-hand what an atomic wedgie felt like.

Everything was going fine. Day after day, we rang the Salvation Army bell and collected donations. Unfortunately, all good things must come to an end. I was ringing the bell wishing every customer a Merry Christmas as they entered or left the bank when I saw trouble. Two of my grandchildren were making their way to see their mother. They were accompanied by my son who apparently didn't get the memo of me pretending to be Santa at his wife's bank.

I kept ringing the bell and smiling as people passed. I opened the door for my grandchildren as they passed through the doorway. Great. Then they both stopped in their tracks and turned to face me. They stepped closer and peered into my eyes. I tried to turn away but both of the tots screamed in unison, **"You're not Santa Clause. You're Bumpa!"** Now I had big trouble. How do I explain this without ruining their belief in the jolly elf? There was only one thing to do. **Lie.**

I began, "Hi girls. You're right. I am Bumpa Bill, but I have to let you in on a big secret. Santa Clause is way behind in his toy-making and he asked me to help him. You can't tell a single soul. You have to promise me you'll keep this secret or Santa won't bring you anything Christmas Eve."

Both little ones nodded their heads and gave me a big hug. My son rolled his eyes as he opened the door and ushered his two little ones into the bank.

Whew! I dodged a bullet there. I hoped they bought it. Just then a whirling noise was heard approaching me. It stopped and it hovered overhead. I reached into my pocket and felt my Glock. I released the safety and prepared to take this floating tin can out of the sky. As I was drawing my weapon, a customer opened the bank's entrance door and the drone shot through following the customer into the bank.

Normally, I remain calm, but my grandchildren were in jeopardy. I knew I could not run into the bank and begin shooting. If the IED exploded, my son and grandchildren, along with all the other customers and employees, would be hurt.

I assumed the other four pseudo-detectives were experiencing the same crisis. Thinking quickly, I opened the door and prepared to deal with the carnage. Once inside, I could see the drone was following the same MO, appearing before the first teller on the left and allowing her to remove the note. The tellers had been notified such an event could happen, so the teller calmly removed the money from her drawer and placed it in the bag along with a GPS tracker. One by one, each teller replicated the steps.

Finally, the drone turned to fly toward the door. Knowing I was being watched by the flight controller, I pushed the interior door open and allowed the drone to hover between the two doors. I had to make a choice: if I let the drone outside, it might shift into warp speed and disappear, or I could jeopardize my life and blast the flying scrap metal. My pride prevented me from doing the first, so I reached into my pocket, withdrew my revolver and fired at the drone. After being hit, it reacted by spiraling out of control. Another thought entered my mind. *Why not let this wounded duck outside, and maybe, I could shoot it again before it escaped?*

My son, grandchildren and everyone else were safe. It was between this flying pile of nuts and bolts and me. I opened the outside door and allowed the metal bandit through the doorway. Again, taking aim before it could hit warp speed, I fired a second time. The metal thief fell like an anvil. I shouted for people to keep their distance. The last thing I needed was for a curiosity seeker to approach it and be blown to bits.

The flight controller realized his part of the plan was foiled. He started to run into an alley to his vehicle. Seeing him out of the corner of my eye, it didn't seem natural for a young man to be racing away from so much excitement. I gave chase as best I could. It must have been unusual to watch a youth being chased by Santa Clause. The thief entered his automobile, but had trouble locating his keys.

Finding them, he prepared to start his engine, but not before I dived though the passenger window. I had to say the Santa Clause suit served a nice purpose. We struggled for the keys and I prevented him from turning on the engine. I squirmed across the front seat and removed my Glock. I shouted, "Do you want to be the first person killed by Santa Clause?"

He relaxed and knew it was over. I flipped the door handle and ordered him outside. Painfully, we both landed on the pavement. He rolled over and tried to run. I shouted, "You're being a bad boy. Do you want to feel what a Glock castration feels like?"

He took a few steps and halted. I shouted, "Get on the ground!" He obeyed and I pushed him face first into the sidewalk. I shouted, "Put your hands behind your head and cross your ankles!" Again, complying I could see he was not a battle- tested thief.

As I waited, I caught my breath. I couldn't believe I chased this idiot for over a block wearing a heavy suit. I was fortunate that schools were in session and no little ones were nearby. That would have required extensive explaining. In time, a police cruiser arrived and I was glad to turn the robber over to them. Now I had another problem. *How do I avoid being seen by youngsters who believed Santa Clause was a kind old soul?*

Looking around, I found the perfect hiding place. A bar. I sauntered inside and sat on a stool. The barflies all seemed to enjoy the entertainment. One of them even staggered over and said, "Nice job, Santa! Can I buy you a beer?" What a stupid question. I replied, "Sure, but don't forget my eight reindeer on the roof!" By the time I left the bar, I had a pretty good shine going. Eventually, my cohorts found me staggering toward the bank. They had changed back into their street clothes and had many stories to relay.

Ben said, "I saw that contraption and I opened fire. The drone fell into the back of a pick-up truck. I didn't see the flight controller. He must have lit out for the hills."

Mark spoke, saying, "I started shooting as soon as I saw it and it disappeared over the rooftops."

John and Tyler had similar experiences as they chased the flying robots away with gunfire.

I answered, "I was lucky. I shot the drone down and the youth that was controlling it made a run for it. He couldn't get his vehicle started in time and I bailed through the passenger side window. This Santa suit came in handy. I think I'm going to lose the deposit on it as it has a lot of tears. They got the thief at the local station house. After I get out of this monkey suit, we can have a shot at him if the locals will allow us."

After consuming many cups of black coffee, I joined my partners as we entered the Midland Police Station. I approached the desk sergeant and I said, "I'm the one that tackled the would-be bank robber today. Is there any chance we can talk to him?"

The sergeant said, "That's not for me to say. See the chief in the back room."

With that, we made our way toward his office.

We entered the chief's office and I read **Chief Brooks** on his name plate.

I introduced myself, "Hello, Chief. You don't know me but my name is Bill Bennett and these are my buddies. We've worked with Inspector Delton. We know he's retiring soon."

The chief looked at us and smiled, "Yes, Delton told me about you guys. Didn't one of you make a citizen's arrest earlier today?"

I answered, "That'd be me. I was wondering if we could talk to the young fellow."

The chief shook his head negatively and said, "You know I can't let you do that. His attorney would have a field day. We'd be sued every which way to Sunday. No, I appreciate what you fellows have done for our community, but I can't let you see the guy."

I asked, "Are you allowed to tell me his name?"

The chief smiled, and said, "I think I can do that. His name is

Drew Payne."

I continued trying to learn as much as possible.

"Was he a local boy?" I asked.

The chief replied, "No, he's from Bloomfield Hills."

I asked, "Where is that?"

He said, "I can tell you're not from Lower Michigan."

I asked, "What'd you mean?"

The chief responded, "Everybody knows that's one of the upscale places. I'm guessing he comes from big money. Probably graduated from a major university and is just plain spoiled. We have to wait for his attorney to arrive. He's coming from Ann Arbor." He continued, "I recognized the law firm. It's a very prestigious one. He's high class. The mouthpiece will probably get the kid time served since it's his first offense, maybe, even probation. The lawyer will argue the kid was just flying his drone when it got away from him. Don't be surprised to see the kid get a get-out-of-jail card."

I understood what the chief was saying. As we left the station house and returned to our vehicle, John said, "Let's see where the kid's old haunts are. If we can find his buddies or an old girlfriend, we might get an insight into who the other four idiots are."

Chapter Nine

We had time before the four surviving robbers tried something again. Knowing we were on a time schedule, the next morning the five pseudo-detectives drove to Bloomfield Hills.

The area was only five miles in diameter, but driving through we saw what Chief Brooks meant. Each home was more luxurious then the previous one. We knew one of the robbers, Drew Payne, lived in this area. We had to discover if he had any friends or even girlfriends.

I asked, "John, why don't you and Tyler visit the county courthouse and see what you can find?"

"Ben, could you and Mark find the parents, if they're available, and interview them. Go easy. I'm sure they're distraught that their son is accused of robbing banks."

"I'll take the academies. I doubt if he attended public school." Having only one vehicle put a damper on our investigation. We dropped John and Tyler at the county courthouse on Telegraph Road and I could see one academy so I thought I would start there.

Ben and Mark had a challenge. Luckily, they could find the youth's last name in one of their smartphones and several names appeared. Maybe, they'd get lucky and the first one they interviewed would at least be related to the family.

Ben and Mark entered the Oakland County Courthouse and examined the directory. Making a mental note of it, the men proceeded to the records office. Upon entering the room, they couldn't help but notice the beautiful panoramic view.

As Ben approached the front desk, a young assistant asked, "May I help you?"

Mark responded, "Yes, we're looking for the birth records of a Drew Payne. We believe he was born in this county. Can you help us?"

The young smartly dressed assistant said, "Let me check." She crunched some data into her computer and she said, "Yes, he was born in Oakland County."

Ben asked, "Could we have whatever information you have? He's accused of a robbery in Midland."

Making a serious face, she tapped the keyboard a few times and before long her printer was spitting out pages. She returned and handed the papers to the senior detectives and said, "That's all we have!" Both Ben and Mark nodded and left the office.

On the way down the front steps, Ben said, "Our boy is definitely local. His parents' names are here. I'll call John and Tyler and save them some time. Tapping his cell phone, Ben waited for John to answer. "Yeah," John asked, "what'd you have?"

Ben proceeded to give John the relevant information relating to the robber.

After listening intently, John relayed, "Thanks, Ben, I owe you one." Checking the map on their smartphones, John said, "It's only a couple of blocks from here. Let's go."

I wasn't having much luck after stopping at the first two academies. I had never seen a community that prepared their students for the future so well. The only private school I could discount was the one for the performing arts. Feeling frustrated and ready to call in reinforcements, namely the other senior sleuths, I thought I'd try once more.

Arriving at the third academy, and impressed with its splendor, I was buzzed through the main door. I approached the matronly looking administrative assistant who could have beaten Attila the Hun to a pulp.

She forced a smile that would intimidate a water buffalo. She replied, "Can I help you?"

I said, "I'm in town with a group of private detectives. We're trying to ascertain some information. Do you remember a former student, Drew Payne?"

By the look on her face, I knew I was in the right place. She stared at me and asked, "What did that fool do?"

I replied, "He's in jail, accused of robbing banks."

She said, "That doesn't sound like him."

I answered, "With a drone."

She quipped, "Now, that sounds like him. What do you want to know?"

I said, "There were five robbers, each was using a drone."

She thought for a minute and answered, "He hung with a gang of geeks. They thought they were smarter than everyone else. Let me see, who were the others? Wait a minute. Now I remember." She gave me four names and I wrote them down as fast as she said them.

I answered, "Thanks a lot. You have been a big help." I shook her hand and left the academy. I couldn't wait to share my information with the others.

In Bloomfield Hills, Ben and Mark found the Payne address. They stepped up to the door and pressed the button. A voice from a speaker asked, "May I help you?" Ben and Mark looked at the closed-circuit camera in the upper corner. Ben replied, "We would like to speak with Mr. and Mrs. Payne."

The voice responded, "What does it pertain to?"

Mark said, "We know Drew is in jail for robbing banks. We're private detectives that are looking for his partners. If your son doesn't give the others up, he's probably going to prison for his adult life."

The door unlocked and the voice said, "Come in and take a seat in the room on the left."

Ben and Mark entered and could hear the echo of their footsteps as they walked into the receiving room. Mark said, "I've never seen such exquisite paintings and statues."

Ben agreed saying, "This place is bigger than the White House."

Eventually a handsome couple entered the room.

Mr. Payne began, "We are aware our son has some legal issues, but our attorney has informed us, since he has no criminal record, he will pay a fine and receive probation."

Ben said, "He used an IED attached to a drone to rob banks. If you use a weapon in the commission of a crime, that's five years minimum."

Mrs. Payne answered, "We have complete confidence in our attorney. In fact, we just sent money for our son to get out on bail. Our attorney is going to petition the court to allow him to return home so he can receive counseling."

Mark bellowed, "Counseling? That kid needs a kick in the ass. If that IED exploded, it would have killed dozens of people."

Mr. Payne said, "We can argue all day about this, but our son is coming home and we'll put him under a doctor's care. Now, if there's nothing else, good day. My wife will show you to the door." Mark snorted, "Don't bother, we'll find our own way out."

After leaving the mansion, Mark said, "I can't believe the arrogance of those people."

Ben said, "I agree, they just throw money at problems to make them disappear. Obviously, the kid was allowed to do what he wanted his whole life. No wonder he's the way he is."

As Ben and Mark approached their vehicle, a young woman walked up to them and asked, "Did you just come from the Payne residence?"

Ben answered, "Yes."

The young woman explained that her boyfriend is their son. "He and I were in love in high school, but he went to college and I stayed here and attended a local university. I heard he's in trouble. Do you know anything about that?"

Mark answered, "As a matter of fact, we do. We're private detectives and we helped arrest him. He's accused of bank robbery."

The young lady said, "My name is Sherry LaPoint. If you see him would you tell him I still love him?"

Ben retorted, "We can do that. But he has to give up the other thieves or he might be going to prison for the rest of his adult life."

Sherry answered, "I imagine he's still hanging with those four idiots. They think they're too good for everyone. They goofed off in high school and probably college and now they're in big trouble."

Mark replied, "If we see him, we'll pass along that you still care for him. Those four friends of his have done nothing but get him in trouble."

Sherry walked away holding back tears.

We reconnected and the five of us exchanged stories as we returned to the Tri-City area. We decided to stop at the Midland Police Station and I wanted to touch base with the sheriff again. As I entered the station, I asked the desk sergeant "Is the sheriff in?" The sergeant nodded as we proceeded to his office.

I smiled as we entered his office. I looked at the sheriff and said, "You hit the nail on the head regarding life in Bloomfield Hills. I got to see some of the academies. We toured some of the streets and saw how the other half lives."

The chief smiled and said, "I won't say, I told you but they march to a different drummer."

Mark interjected, "I'm surprised they don't have moats around their houses."

Ben said, "We talked to Payne's parents and they said their son was going to make bail. Is that true? Even though he used a dangerous weapon to rob banks he's going to be released!"

The chief said, "The attorney is arranging everything right now as we speak. He'll be out by 5:00."

An idea popped into my head and I could see the others were thinking the same way. "Well, chief, we'll keep you posted if we hear anything." We left the station house and parked in an inconspicuous place. We were going to wait until young Payne left with his attorney and I was hoping he couldn't wait to hook up with his fellow thieves. I doubted if he was in any hurry to return to Bloomfield Hills to commence psychiatric counseling.

Sure enough, at precisely 5:00 the two exited the station house. It was clear they were not on the same page. Young Payne became very agitated as well as demonstrative. I could tell the attorney was not looking forward to telling the Paynes their little boy didn't want to come home.

After an argument barely short of fisticuffs, the attorney threw up his hands and stepped into his vehicle and left.

The young man tapped his cell phone and after concluding the conversation, he sat down on the curb.

We waited patiently for what we hoped would be a break in the case. Our prayers were answered as an old wreck soon arrived and young Payne stepped inside the vehicle. As usual, our best driver, John, was at the wheel. He had negotiated some tremendous driving hazards and we put our faith in him completely. Almost!

John allowed the older sedan to put some distance between themselves and us before he started to follow. As we followed the young thieves, John kept a half mile behind them to allow them a false sense of security. The only problem was that we didn't know the area. If they turned onto a dirt road, it would be hard finding their trail. The surveillance continued for miles as they traveled on 10 East then turning onto I-75. The heavier traffic made it easier for us to stay far enough behind until they suddenly took the exit that led to the Wildlife Sanctuary.

John slowed to a crawl allowing the thieves to gain ground and prevent us from being seen. We finally came to a straight stretch and the criminals were nowhere to be seen.

"Damn it," shouted Mark.

I thought for a moment and asked, "Did we bring all of our supplies?"

John said, "Naturally."

I said, "Remember how we caught that sex trafficker in Venice, Florida a few years ago?"

Everyone smiled as we stepped out of our vehicle and opened our trunk.

Mark was our go-to man in this department so we stepped back and allowed him to prepare our intelligence gathering device: our own drone.

Within minutes, Mark had it buzzing and it lifted upward. The weather conditions were perfect as he reached several hundred feet. Knowing we had driven too far; Mark simply had to back track and look for dirt roads. When he found one, he adjusted the joystick to follow the road. If it became undriveable, he simply reversed directions and maneuvered elsewhere.

"There they are," Mark said as he pointed to the monitor. We leaned in and now we knew we had them. We recalled the drone and stowed it back in the truck. I could tell the boys were itching to get into it with the arrogant bandits.

The thought of terrorizing innocent people by using a drone and an IED was disgusting to all of us.

Backtracking, we made an educated guess that we were turning onto the right trail. We drove a few hundred feet more and then decided it was best if we went the rest of the way on foot. Everyone took their favorite automatic rifle along with several pistols.

Walking through the thick brush we were careful to avoid any broken branches. Being winter, there were a few inches of snow that made maneuvering easy. As we got closer, we dispersed. We wanted to provide a 360-degree killing zone in case they wanted to shoot it out with us. Some of the fellows carried several fragmentation grenades. They had a 3.5 second fuse and released 110 grams of explosive on contact.

We now dropped to our stomachs and crept ever so slowly. We didn't have our white camo so to avoid detection, we had to be sure we set up near a deadfall or patch of high grass. The thieves had taken refuge in an old abandoned cabin. I thought, *it must be quite a comedown for these spoiled brats raised with a silver spoon.* We had to wait for Ben and Mark who had to crawl the longest distance behind the cabin. John was on my left and Tyler took my right flank. Patience was critical. When Ben and Mark texted that they were ready, I thought I owed it to the punks to give them a chance to surrender.

I called, "**To you in the cabin, we have you surrounded! If you throw out your weapons and come out with your hands up, you won't be harmed!**"

As I expected, from the cabin, they started firing wildly in every direction. Knowing they had a limited amount of ammunition, we allowed them to fire until they stopped. Again, I repeated my warning and the result was the same. When they were finished shooting, I shouted, **"Let 'em have it!"** We blazed away for a few minutes until the cabin was nearly cut in half. I shouted one last time, **"If you don't come out now, we're going to lob fragmentation grenades inside that will disintegrate the place!"**

We heard some shouts of capitulation inside the former cabin that we had reduced to toothpicks. One by one they stepped outside, bleeding profusely, and threw their weapons down. Only four exited and I shouted, **"Where's the fifth one?"**

One of them winced, "I think he's dead. He's not moving."

My comrades slowly stepped forward with their automatics trained on the robbers. As I approached them, I said, "If you try anything, we'll unload on you and there won't be enough left to fill a Petri dish."

It was clear they had enough. No longer were they tough bank robbers willing to scare innocent women and children. Standing over them, they looked so young. I said, "Do you idiots realize how many lives you risked to be showoffs? I've a mind to beat the tar out of all of you."

Thank goodness the boys held me back. All I could think of was two of my grandchildren and one of my sons being disintegrated inside that bank.

Luckily, calmer heads prevailed and we trussed them up and tossed them in the trunk of their vehicle. I didn't care how uncomfortable they were. When we were finished with the four bums, we poked our heads inside the shredded cabin. We shoved some of the shredded timber aside and there was the fifth thief, Drew Payne, dead.

Mark sarcastically said, "I think he's going to be late for his counseling session."

Ben said, "What a waste!"

We returned to Midland knowing we had *out smarted the drones*.

Chapter Ten

With the closure of the drone robberies in the Tri-City area, we could now turn our full attention to the death of Lance and his daughter, Lucy. Making it a point to attend Lucy's wake, we were careful to keep our distance. Lucy's funeral, since she was young and well-connected to the university, was enormous. The church was filled and the overflow remained outside in a respectful manner.

With the conclusion of the service, people left the church and proceeded to the cemetery. Likewise, we did the same. Led by the hearse, there was ample grief for the family. I always hate graveside services since they aggravate the pain. Finally, the last prayers were said, and Lucy was lowered into the ground next to her father.

I couldn't help noticing the mother was being consoled by none other than the State Well Supervisor, Riley. *Something wasn't right!*

I said to the guys, "Don't look now, but the man escorting Judy Skylar is the State Well Supervisor."

Was he involved with the family or was he just being a Good Samaritan? We had to find the answer. We all had theories about how he was that close to the widow.

After the graveyard service concluded, some people congregated back at the Skylar residence. We decided to continue our surveillance although I think Mark just went for the free food. We entered and milled among the mourners. I tried to eavesdrop to see if I could hear anything helpful. I heard nothing but compliments of the deceased. The widow was consoled by the Well Supervisor and I suddenly had a thought. *If the Supervisor could keep Lance Skylar busy year-round with drill permits, wouldn't it be easier for him to have a romantic engagement with the distraught wife? It would be pretty simple to plant seeds of discontent towards the husband while comforting the upset wife. Now with Lance out of the way, he could swoop in and grab the prize, Judy.*

I shared my thoughts with the others and they listened intently. Right now, our main problem was to get the son-in-law to catch himself in the mousetrap or admit his guilt. I doubt if the latter was going to happen.

Riley finally left the grieving widow/mother to refill their drinks. This was my opportunity. Immediately, I made haste to the punch bowl and approached Riley from behind. I said, "You sure are a wonderful state employee to come here and care for the brokenhearted mother." Riley turned and said, "Oh, it's you again. What do you want?"

I replied sarcastically saying, "Do you go to everybody's funeral that does business with your office?"

He said under his breath, "Go to Hell!"

I must have touched a nerve. I couldn't quit now. I followed him to the mournful mother. As he was about to sit down, I continued, "She must really appreciate your concern. It's mighty nice of you to drive all this way, just to provide solace." Riley's face turned red and he stood and said, "Let's continue this outside."

I followed him outside and when he turned to throw a haymaker, I nailed him in the nose and added several more to the stomach. He dropped to his knees and I shouted, "Did you give those permits to the husband just to keep him away from Judy?"

"I don't have to answer that!" he replied.

I asked, "Do you want some more? You're a sneaky scumbag. I can do this all day!"

By now my comrades had formed a circle around my mark and I had made up my mind I was going to pummel this bum until I got some answers.

Seeing my friends, he broke down, and said, "What if I did give Skylar drilling contracts. It's not against the law!"

"It is in my book. I started to swing again when he shouted,

"Okay, I'll tell her I did it on purpose. I'm not going to tell her now, because she's too fragile."

I replied, "I can live with that." The boys and I re-entered the house and I felt good about gaining some redemption. It just wasn't right for one man to make arrangements so he could take advantage of it.

Sitting in the dining room, I asked, "Does anybody have a suggestion how we can snare Frank Edington?"

Watching him now, my heart almost went out to him. It was obvious he was grief-stricken, losing his wife. I overheard two elderly women chatting that Lucy was ten weeks pregnant. That had to make Lucy's suicide even more stinging.

John leaned over and said, "I did some reconnoitering regarding the husband. He's working his way through college in a computer repair shop. He couldn't sew a button on a shirt let alone surgically dissect a man into three sections."

I said, "I guess that crosses him off the list. Who else do we have?"

We bantered several names among us, but none of them seemed culpable. I said, "I guess we're back to the drawing board, and Delton retires tomorrow."

Ben relayed, "Since, we're desperate, we might as well go back to Lucy's friend, Kim Holland." I looked around the room and I didn't see her. I asked, "Where is she?" If Kim was Lucy's best friend, she certainly would have come to the funeral. I didn't see her at all. Does anybody see her?"

All of the pseudo-detectives shook their heads. I continued, "Let's find out why her best friend didn't come."

Helped by Ben and Mark's directions, we found our way to Kim's house that she shared with a host of young women. We approached the door and knocked. A petite young lady with a towel wrapped around her torso answered and said, "Yeah." I asked, "Could we speak with Kim?"

The young co-ed responded, "She went with her boyfriend to the park."

Since we weren't familiar with the city, I asked, "Which

park?"

She gave good directions and as we left, Ben said, "It sounds weird she would go to the park when her best friend is being buried."

On the university campus, we found the park that was centrally located and we scanned the area. Not being able to see them, we spread out and scoured the grounds. We found our quarry under a large tree. They had spread a blanket on the ground and Kim was nestled in her boyfriend's lap. We approached cautiously and I shouted, "Kim, do you have a minute?" It was apparent she was very annoyed being disturbed, which I completely understood. As I approached her, I stated, "I'm surprised you weren't at your best friend's funeral. Can you tell me why you weren't there?"

She shrugged her shoulders and said, "We had a falling out the last few days."

"Was it so important that you couldn't pay your respects to her mother?" I asked.

Her boyfriend ordered, "Why don't you leave her alone?"

Ben said, "You look awful familiar."

Mark added, "Yeah, now I remember. You're Steve Haskins, aren't you?"

Ben said, "If I remember, you're in medical school, aren't you?"

Haskins replied, "What if I am?"

I answered, "Well, Stevie boy, it seems whoever sliced and diced Lance Skylar had medical training. All the cuts were done as if by a surgeon. Do you see why we're interested?"

Kim stood and shouted, "It was you who killed Lucy's dad!"

Steve Haskins screamed, "You're crazy!"

Kim looked at us and said, "Lucy's baby was also Steve's. I know Lucy told her parents she was pregnant. Naturally, her father was happy assuming the baby was her husbands. When Lucy told me, Steve was the father and not Frank, I went nuts. I confronted this jerk and he admitted he got Lucy drunk one night and had sex with her. It took a long time for me to forgive him. I never dreamed Steve would kill Lucy's dad."

I asked Haskins, "What about it? Did you kill Lucy's dad?"

Haskins answered, "I had no choice. The old man came to my apartment. He was a crazy man. He had a terrible temper. He slugged me several times. That's when I saw the kitchen knife. He kept coming and I stabbed him in self-defense. After he was dead, I rolled him into a carpet and dragged him down the stairs. I thought if I could divide the body into sections, it would be impossible to prove who did it."

I asked, "How did the knife get in Lucy's and Frank's apartment."

He replied, "I didn't know where else to hide it. Frank showed me the loose floorboard once."

While I was interrogating Haskins, John called 9-1-1.He passed the relevant information to the dispatcher and we waited for the cruisers.

It wasn't long before they were in sight. We explained the circumstances of the murder and they led young Haskins away.

We returned to the Midland Station House in time to see Inspector Delton cut his retirement cake. I relayed the good news to him, that we had solved the fracking case. To say he was overjoyed would be an understatement. He said, "Now I can walk out of here with a clean slate. Thanks guys." He gave each of us a big hug and a hearty handshake.

As I watched him leave, I thought to myself, *it was a tragedy that caused so much sadness. Nevertheless, we were satisfied to have solved the fracking* case.

Part III

Double Trouble

Chapter One

My wife and I had just returned home to enjoy the early spring days at our cottage. The melting snow had provided a beautiful backdrop for our stay. Once the fire was roaring in the hearth, we usually enjoyed a walk in the woods looking for moose sheds.

In the ensuing months there would be dozens of boats on the water at any given time, but now it was quiet. The only sound was our boots crunching along on our homemade trail. Occasionally, one of us would stop to point to something Mother Nature had provided. The sun was shimmering as the tree boughs were swaying in the gentle breeze.

At one point we walked to the top of a hill overlooking the river. We could see for miles as the river wound its way to the dam. We stopped to rest on a stump and gazed at God's beauty. It was probably as close to heaven on Earth as you could get. You couldn't put a price on this moment. Eventually, we had to start our return to our cottage, but not before my cell phone chimed.

Barb said half-heatedly, "Don't answer that." We both knew it would probably put an end to the idyllic day. I answered, "Hello!"

The other end said, "Dad, do you have a minute?"

I wanted to say no, but I never wanted to discourage one of my sons from phoning me. I replied, "Sure, what's up, Roy?"

My son replied, "We have a problem in the Tri-City area."

I answered, "What sort of problem?"

He continued, "As you know, I manage an adult-care facility. I think we have a scam in progress."

I asked, "What kind of scam are we talking about, Roy?"

He replied, "It's hard to explain. An attorney has gotten himself appointed as a legal guardian of several wealthy adults. He has continually petitioned the probate court and the judge has ruled in his favor to name him legal guardian. I just reviewed the financial report of one of his wards and before he took control of one individual, that person had several million dollars. By the time this person passed, the account was drained."

Thinking out loud, I said, "It's probably going to be hard to prove. The attorney probably went through all of the legal hoops and with the probate judge appointing him guardianship, it will be hard to prove any dishonesty."

My son added, "In addition to that, I went to the police and they told me to check with the DA.

I did, but the district attorney said that if the judge signed off on the guardianship, they don't think they can pursue it."

I answered, "Let me talk to the boys and see if they think we can help." We disconnected and I mulled the whole idea over in my head. *How could the pseudo-detectives and I prove collusion? We were not attorneys.* As we returned to our cottage, I broached the topic with my wife.

She responded, "You could always look into it and if it's impossible to prove anything illegal, at least you can say you tried." Good advice, and with that I convened a meeting the next day at Millie's.

Before the meeting, I wanted to know what was involved in becoming a guardian. Checking the internet, I discovered that the probate court may appoint a guardian if it finds by clear and convincing evidence that the individual for whom a guardian is sought is an incapacitated individual and that the appointment is necessary as a means of providing continuing care and supervision of the incapacitated individual.

Next, I wanted to discover what qualifies an incapacitated individual. The legal definition is someone that is impaired by reason of mental illness, mental deficiency, physical illness or disability, chronic use of drugs, chronic intoxication, or other cause, not including minority, to the extent of lacking sufficient understanding or capacity to make or communicate informed decisions.

I was surprised to learn that there is no specific illness,

infirmary, or mental deficiency that automatically qualifies an individual for a guardianship and each case is evaluated on its own merits. In other words, the probate judge makes that decision.

In Michigan, guardianship is usually determined in the probate court in the county in which the person resides or is present.

After filing the paperwork, the court will provide a hearing date. If there is an emergency, the court may grant a temporary guardianship. However, even if temporary guardianship is granted or denied, within a few weeks, a full hearing will take place.

Prior to the hearing, a person will need to serve a petition relating to the ward outlining what is happening. It will also have to be served to all other interested parties. After this is done, a proof of service will need to be filed prior to or on the hearing date.

In between the filing of the petition and the hearing, the court will appoint guardian ad litem. This person is an attorney who prepares an independent third-party report for the court regarding their recommendations for the proposed guardianship and advises the proposed ward of their various rights in the process. The report is filed with the probate court prior to the hearing.

At the hearing, the judge evaluates the information presented by both the third party and the person(s) applying for guardianship. In other words, it wasn't too difficult for a person to be appointed guardian of a ward if the probate judge was receptive.

I was not impressed with the difficulty needed for someone to become a guardian in our state. It certainly opened the door for characters with unsavory morals to become guardians of friends or relatives that may or may not be incapacitated.

Chapter Two

The next day at Millie's, the others were already enjoying a cup of Joe. As I entered, John stated, "I got out of a nice lawn chair for this. This better be important, Bill."

Ben added, "My truck engine barely turned over this morning. I think you should pick up the bill for getting us here in this weather."

Mark and Tyler added equally insulting remarks. I started to explain the circumstances of why I called the meeting, knowing they were just toying with me.

I began, "My son phoned me yesterday and informed me there may be something illegal happening in the Tri-City area.

"It appears two attorneys are running a scam. It happens when the first attorney gains the trust of families to have himself appointed guardian of incapacitated individuals. The second attorney supposedly keeps an eye on the first one. The probate judge approves it and the attorneys pilfer the poor soul's account."

Mark stated, "I think we should look into it. If it was my loved one being cleaned out, I'd be wild."

John agreed saying, "We can check the facts and if the attorney can prove he has the best interests of the person, we'll come home."

Ben and Tyler concurred and even though it wasn't going to be a dangerous investigation, we decided to see if Lady Justice needed help.

We phoned our loved ones to inform them of our plans. As we returned to the LP, we discussed what avenues we should explore.

Tyler suggested, "I think we should leave the attorney alone. We don't want to spook him."

Ben indicated, "Mark and I can weigh in at the county court house to see how many deaths have occurred recently and who the legal guardian was."

I added, "I could check my son's adult-care facility to see if any of his patients are being bamboozled."

However, the more I thought about our usual approach, I became convinced it probably wouldn't work. Before we stopped the vehicle at my son's house, I said, "I think we better try something different. In addition to what we're doing, what if we plant someone in an assisted living home and inform the director our decoy is very wealthy, but has no family and probably will need an attorney."

Right away, Mark retorted, "Oh, no. You're not doing that to me. I'm not going to a nursing home." The others tried to keep a straight face.

John said, "That will probably be our best bet. We have to lure the vermin to us. We could investigate every attorney in the county and we would still be at square one."

Ben concurred, "I'll bring you flowers every week."

Mark grimaced and repeated, "There's absolutely no way, you're going to put me in a home."

Driving through Midland, by now, had become comfortable. Ben and Mark dropped us at my son's to learn more about the dishonest attorney while the others began their quest.

Ben and Mark drove to the court house to uncover how many suspicious deaths occurred at the local nursing homes and who the legal guardians were.

Walking into the courthouse, Ben and Mark found the office that was responsible for recording deaths. The deceased would have an official place of residence and whoever signed the paperwork would be the guardian. After some smooth talking, they were granted access to the list.

Ben asked, "Is there a computer we could use?"

The clerk looked around and said, "I guess you can use Sue's. She's on her lunch hour right now."

Ben and Mark hurriedly started scanning the registry looking for deceased individuals that listed assisted living facilities as their residence.

By the time Sue returned from her lunch, Ben and Mark had over fifteen names with the same assisted living facility as well as the same attorney listed as the guardian. Ben and Mark thanked the clerks and left.

Armed with the list, John and Tyler drove to the suspected assisted living complex and prepared to pave the way for Mark.

John and Tyler entered and introduced themselves to the desk clerk.

John asked, "May we speak with the director?"

The clerk responded, "I'll page her, would you take a seat?"

It wasn't long before a professionally dressed woman appeared and whispered to the desk clerk. After hearing the clerk's response, she turned and gave John and Tyler a smile.

Both men stood and introduced themselves and the lady responded, "I'm Anne Hobbes. How may I help you?"

John responded, "My name is John Baldwin and this is my son, Tyler. We've been hired to find a suitable assisted living facility for a man. He's very wealthy but has no relatives. He's had 24/7 nursing, but now he has become confused. Do you have any available accommodations? Money is no object."

Mrs. Hobbes thought and said, "Not right now, but we have one resident that might be going to the memory care unit. Before we admit your employer, we will need all the necessary paperwork."

John responded, "That won't be a problem."

Mrs. Hobbes asked, "What is the gentleman's name?"

Tyler said, "Mark Kestila."

Mrs. Hobbes asked, "Does he have an attorney of record?"

John answered, "No, not anymore. We're hoping you might know one."

Mrs. Hobbes replied, "Yes, we have an attorney that we have worked with in the past."

Tyler gave the director his cell number and responded, "We'll wait to hear from you."

The two pseudo-detectives departed and Mrs. Hobbes tapped her cell phone. After the voice on the other end answered, she said, "We have another live one."

The voice jokingly replied, "At this rate, we'll be able to retire early."

They both chuckled and appreciated their good fortune.

Chapter Three

Meanwhile, as we were preparing to admit Mark into an assisted living facility, I returned home to spend a few days celebrating my wife's birthday, 29 again. The wind was howling and the coyotes were answering one another. Barb and I were snug in our beds enjoying the roaring fire. We had golfed all day and had enjoyed a wonderful meal complete with my wife's favorite wine, Stella Rosa. The world was miles away and we were planning to spend a week at our cottage.

This time of year, the Dead River was extremely quiet except for an occasional fisherman that floated by and waved. Our children and grandchildren were taking care of their own problems, leaving us to enjoy nirvana. No matter how much inclement weather we received, we knew we were only a few miles from civilization. In fact, I liked to think the remoteness kept society's problems away.

It was not unusual for us to enjoy watching a bull moose cross our property to get his drink. It was neat the way he waded in and drank his fill. Even the wolves knew enough not to take on a bull moose in his prime. When he was ready, he returned to the top of the hill and surveyed his domain. After all, we were only borrowing his land. I certainly wasn't going to argue.

Last week we saw some otters enjoying a playful day of sliding down a hill and returning to the top to repeat their frivolity. It was better than watching television. There was an occasional eagle flying majestically overhead to see if some small game or fish dared venture within sight.

Frequently, our neighbor, Burt Bengtson, would pay us a visit. I think he could tell when I had some wine chilled. He was probably the last homesteader on the Dead River. He had owned a parcel of land about a mile from us since the 1950s. Luckily, he was grandfathered in when the land became available in the 1990s.

We had helped each other numerous times repairing many mechanical beasts. I have to admit, Burt knew more than me and by helping, I mean I just handed him tools. As long as we had cold beverages and a warm meal, the two of us repaired many motorized pieces of equipment.

If Burt couldn't fix it, the engine didn't deserve to run. All in all, Burt was one heck of a mechanic. He lived off his wits his entire life. If he needed food, he would work a day for his meal. There were no hand-outs involved. His vehicle was probably a combination of twenty-seven engines and vehicle parts. I don't know how, but he kept it going year after year.

Unfortunately, time was catching up with him. He no longer had that spring in his step as when I first met him. He was now looking haggard and bent-over. I didn't want to think what was probably in store. The winter months were the worst as I would watch him try to split his wood for the fire. His firewood stacks became smaller and smaller each year. It was only a matter of time before he had to go to Plan B.

We were walking past Burt's house one day, and I noticed a deputy sheriff's cruiser parked in Burt's driveway. My wife and I had to see if he needed help. Looking through the front door window, I could see the deputy standing over Burt who was seated in a chair. There was a look of despair on Burt's face. Without knocking, I forced the old wood door open and stepped into the small dwelling. As I walked through the house, the top of my head barely missed the ceiling. I introduced myself to the deputy who seemed to be apologetic. I asked, "What's up, Burt? Trouble?"

He couldn't answer. The deputy stated," Mr. Bengtson has to vacate the premises within thirty days because of unpaid taxes over the past three years."

I knew the deputy was just doing his job, but it tore my heart out as I was powerless to help. I said, "Burt, you can stay at our cottage as long as you want. In fact, you can become the official caretaker. How does that sound?"

My wife, Barb, added, "We need so much repaired there, you won't have time to rest."

I'm not sure if that wasn't a back-handed compliment to Burt or a slap in the face to me.

Burt sat motionless for a long time and said, "No, I don't take hand-outs. I have a brother in Bay City. He's asked me to come and live with him."

"Are you sure you want to do this? You've lived here your whole life," I stated.

Burt said, "I'll start packing and be out of here by the end of the week. I'm not one to stay where I'm not wanted."

The deputy said, "Mr. Bengtson, there's no hurry. You can take all thirty days. If you need a ride to the bus station, I'll be glad to drive you."

I knew the deputy meant well, but it sounded so harsh. My wife and I left with a lump in our throats. The end of the week arrived and I returned to Burt's adobe to help him stow things in his bags. He didn't have much, but to him it was his entire life. I couldn't help but choke up as we had to discard old family photos and mementos that there just wasn't enough room for them in his bags.

Burt wasn't one to endure good-byes. He said, "My ride is coming at the top of the hour."

Looking at the cell phone, we only had a few minutes to finish. Burt was moving his bags outside and dropping them in the driveway. Burt looked at me and said, "Here's a pocket knife I used to field-dress my deer and clean my fish. I doubt if I'll be doing any hunting or fishing; take it but don't lose it. You hear!" I choked up with emotion and gave him a hug that I knew would upset him. I couldn't help it. In minutes, he'd be gone. The deputy arrived and placed Burt's few belongings in the cruiser's trunk. Burt walked out the door, taking one last look around and entered the deputy's vehicle. He never looked back. That was Burt.

Chapter Four

Spring turned into summer and the Dead River came alive. Boats were plentiful and every cottage opened with major excitement. Once my dock was in the water, it was easy to put the pontoon boat and jet skis alongside.

My thoughts turned to Burt, who I hadn't seen in months. I was feeling pretty melancholy so I tapped his name into the Tri-City Directory hoping a relative would be able to put me in contact with the old homesteader. Unfortunately, there was no one with that last name in the Three-City Area.

Being a private detective does have its perks. I had access to certain websites that are clandestine. They are used by highly sensitive security and the military. I was optimistic Burt would show up on their radar. At a minimum, perhaps a relative of his would. Spending hours scanning all of the available websites, I became frustrated turning up nothing. He had to be somewhere. Maybe, he was in a nursing home, hospital or even an assisted living facility; no luck.

I reluctantly tried one more website. It was a shared-site of mortuaries throughout the country. Even if he had passed, I wanted closure; still no luck. Where could he be? The only way a person falls off the radar is if they become homeless. That wasn't acceptable to me.

The weather was getting better by the day. All the animals and birds had returned to enjoy our Superior warmth and beauty. My wife could tell I was not as happy as I should have been. "What's the matter?" she asked one day.

"It's Burt. I don't know what happened to him. He was going to live with his brother in Lower Michigan and now he's nowhere to be found."

She asked, "Would it help, if you went there and looked?"

I thought for a moment and said, "It probably wouldn't hurt." She responded, "Go for it."

With that inspiration, I packed a few things and drove south across the Mighty Mac.

I felt I was getting on a first name basis with the longest suspension bridge in the Western Hemisphere.

I arrived in Midland and after spending time with my son Roy and his family, I started to explore the lesser-known parts of the Tri-Cities. Using an old photo taken years ago of Burt holding a beautiful mess of fish, I made it a point to stop at all the nursing homes, assisted living, and even funeral homes. Showing them the picture only brought negative answers.

The only places left were homeless shelters. I knew he originally hailed from this area and probably felt he could survive better here. Driving from one shelter to another brought the same response. Over the next few days, my stops included the shelters in Bay City and Saginaw. They gave me the same responses.

One sister from a Catholic Order did give me a glimmer of hope. She said, "Because the weather was warmer, he might have staked out an underpass or alley and was living there." The next step involved me searching such places and displaying his photo. I had to make it worthwhile, so I offered a reward if someone could tell me where he might be living.

After several more days of fruitless searching, I had one more idea. Maybe, he came in during the lunch hour and was missed in the confusion. I now started to stake out the missions that gave free lunches. I knew it was a longshot, but I was desperate. As each indigent walked through the lunch line, I showed them Burt's photo. Days passed, and the dog days of summer made their long-awaited arrival. It became that much harder to locate someone with the weather being warmer.

Phoning my wife, and after talking it over with her, I was ready to throw in the towel. *Could I think like Burt?*

He always said he wouldn't take a hand-out. Now, I had to think like Burt. *Where could he be?*

I checked my smartphone, but this time for Habitat for Humanity. Now we were cooking with gas. It was just a matter of searching the right place.

Early in the morning, I had a list of the places that built homes for people.

I drove to the first site in Bay City, and approached what appeared to be a foreman. I asked, "Do you know this man?" as I held the photo out to him. His response was, "Sure, that's Burt". "Hallelujah!" I almost jumped for joy. The foreman gave me a crazy look and I said, "I've been looking for him for weeks. He was my neighbor in the Superior Peninsula and I was worried about him since he moved here. Can you tell me where he is?"

The foreman responded, "He just left for the site. You can follow me if you want."

I replied, "That'd be great!"

Once the crew was loaded with everything they needed, they drove away with me following.

We arrived among the confusion, and I watched the men start. I scanned the roof trusts hoping I would see my old friend. There he was. Naturally, he had to be on the highest peak. I didn't want to shout for fear of startling him. I sat down and hoped a break would be in order. Coffee time arrived and the men didn't have to be told. I ambled over to the ladder and watched the old codger come down like a teenager. Once he was on the ground, I saw it was a different story. Burt was bent over and walked with a noticeable limp.

Trying not to scare him, I strode up behind him and asked, "Do you have a union card?"

Burt was preparing to give me an earful as he turned to face me. A giant smile covered his face from one ear to the other. We embraced and I said, "Burt, I thought you were living with your brother."

He answered, "No, my brother died some years ago. After I lost my home, I came here hoping I could start over."

I said, "I checked all of the homeless shelters, nursing homes, and even funeral homes, but you disappeared. I finally thought like you and I knew this would probably be the place to find you."

We sat on a stack of lumber and enjoyed our coffee. It was just like old times. I said, "The fish are biting at home. I've used your knife to clean several messes of pike and bass." He responded, "That's fine, but don't you lose that knife."

I replied, "I promise I won't." I wanted to know more about him, but I was reluctant to ask. Finally, my curiosity got the better of me and I asked, "Where do you sleep at night?"

He replied, "Some of us camp down by Saginaw Bay."

"Is it cold at night?" I asked.

"You get used to it. I have some blankets they gave me at the shelter," he answered.

"What about food? Are you eating?" I pushed.

"Of course, I am. Do you think I'm stupid?" he answered.

"I know you're working. How about if I take you out tonight to a nice restaurant?" I asked.

He replied, "I don't want a hand-out!"

I said, "This isn't a hand-out. Consider it payment for your knife."

He shook his head and said, "I guess I can do that. We're done here at 5:00 and it takes us an hour to clean up and go back to the supply shed."

I responded, "I'll be there, Burt."

The rest of the day couldn't go fast enough. I phoned my wife and told her the good news, "I'm taking him out to eat and then bringing him back to the beach where he and some friends are camping."

She responded, "That's great. Tell him I said hello."

Quitting time came, and sure enough, ole' Burt walked out of the shed waving good-bye to his buddies.

He stepped into my vehicle and said, "It's been a long time since I rode in something this nice."

I played it down and asked where he wanted to eat.

He said, "There's a nice country buffet, the fellows said over on the other side of town. If you don't want to drive that far, it's okay with me!"

I responded, "Are you kidding, I drove half way across the state to see you. I'll take you anyplace you want."

We arrived at the restaurant and I could tell Burt was looking forward to this. We entered and found a seat. The waitress said, "You can help yourself when you're ready." Burt took off like he was shot out of a canon. I was not completely innocent in this assault. Burt returned from the buffet table and commenced to eat. Several chicken breasts were devoured in seconds. Mashed potatoes, dressing, green beans, corn on the cobb and rolls were just his first course. He returned from the buffet table many times over the course of the evening, loaded with various portions of pasta, meat loaf, prime rib, turkey and soup. I didn't have the heart to ask him what kind of soup he was enjoying. It was gone in seconds. This went on forever.

I was casually consuming my morsels while Burt found the dessert table. The chocolate fountain almost ran dry. Slices of cheesecake, blueberry pie, carrot cake were all devoured in minutes. I didn't look at him for fear I might start laughing. He probably didn't care. Truth be told, I guess neither did I.

As I was paying the bill, I was afraid they were going to ask us not to come back. We entered the restaurant when the sun was high in the sky; when we exited, it was pitch black.

I asked, "Burt, where to now? Do you want to drive around the city and see the sites?"

He answered, "Hell no. It's my turn to collect the fire wood!"

I respected him for knowing he had an obligation and wasn't about to shirk his duties to his friends. I said, "Give me directions and I'll take you to the beach. Can we pick up some refreshments?"

He wanted to say no, but I knew he wouldn't turn down a chance to have some cold drinks.

Burt mumbled, "If you have time. I don't want to be a bother."

I responded, "It's no bother. I see a convenience store over there." I parked my vehicle and we entered the 7-Eleven. Burt made a bee-line for the beverage coolers. This wasn't his first rodeo.

I waited at the counter for Burt to retrieve his drinks of choice. I had to marvel, for an old man, he could sure carry a lot. The youth rang up the order and I slid my card through the machine. Burt seemed to be engrossed by the procedure. He said, "I guess people don't need money." I replied, "I suppose you're right. Money's becoming obsolete." He chuckled and said, "Like me!"

We loaded my back seat with Burt's sustenance. He gave me directions to the beach and after parking my vehicle, I gave him a hand unloading the drinks. Upon seeing Burt arriving with liquid nourishments, his friends ran to help. Burt's friends relieved us of our load and I extended my hand to Burt. He grabbed it and it felt like I was shaking a piece of steel. As usual, he turned and walked away without a word. I stood there with my eyes misty.

I had to tell myself, *Burt's okay. He's with friends and they would look after him.* I couldn't control the future. I wish I could. I shouted, "**I'll see you tomorrow morning, Burt!**" I don't know if he heard me.

Chapter Five

It was a restless night for yours truly. I told myself a thousand times Burt was going to be fine. By morning, I didn't think I slept more than a few minutes. The alarm was set early enough so I would be able to touch base with Burt before he went to work. I showered and inhaled a cup of coffee, making sure I wouldn't miss him.

The sun was just rising when I started to drive to the beach. As I pulled into the parking lot, there were several police cruisers and emergency vehicles parked. Something was wrong. I exited my vehicle and sprinted to the beach. An officer stopped me and said, "Nobody's allowed beyond this point!"

I screamed, "My friend, Burt, is down there. What happened?"

The officer answered, "We're not sure, but it looks like a simple case of robbery and murder. We found some empty bottles of beer and we think somebody wanted their beer and killed them for it."

I was in shock. *Could it have been the beer I innocently supplied Burt to enjoy with his friends? Are there individuals low enough to kill over that?*

Remembering the clothes, he wore yesterday; I could see Burt's body from a distance. The EMT's carefully placed Burt into a body bag and was removing it on a gurney. As it passed me, I said, "Could you wait minute?" I unzippered the bag and placed Burt's knife into his pants pocket and closed the bag.

One by one, the victims were brought to the waiting ambulances and left quietly.

A detective approached me and asked, "Did you know any of them?"

I replied, "Yes, I brought my friend Burt Bengtson here last night. I gave him and his friends the beer. It was my fault that they were murdered."

The detective replied, "You can't blame yourself. In this area, people kill over a cigarette. They have a hard life and it often ends up like this."

I asked, "Who found the bodies?"

The detective answered, "Some kids were going fishing and called it in. Lucky one of them had a cell phone."

I saw them standing over by the edge of the parking lot. I asked, "Those kids?"

The detectives said, "Yes, they're pretty shook up. Their parents are coming to get them."

I walked over to them and as I approached them, I asked, "What kind of fish do you guys catch here?"

The tallest boy responded "We like to catch walleye, but we've also caught gizzard shard, drum, bass, and perch; both white and yellow. Are you going fishing dressed like that?"

I answered, "No, I hear you boys found the dead guys. Was there anybody around?"

One of them responded, "No, nobody. In fact, it was so dark when we got here, Johnny tripped over one of the bodies."

"I'll give ten dollars to any of you that can give me information about the individuals that might have done this," I volunteered.

The biggest lad retorted, "Even if we knew, we wouldn't tell you. We'd be killed. You don't tell on anybody around here if you want to live."

I said, "I can understand that. I tell you what. I'll give each of you my phone number. If you want to call me later when nobody's around, we'll work out a deal to pay you secretly. Deal?"

Nobody responded as the boys' mothers started to arrive. One little fellow said, "I might know something." His older brother gave him nudge.

I whispered, "You call me later and nobody will know. I promise and I'll give you twenty dollars if it's legit. Okay?"

His mother took him under her arm and the two brothers and their mother walked to their vehicle.

My only lead was a little boy. Meanwhile, I decided to see if the troops wanted to help. I phoned John and told him about the bad news. John provided empathy and expressed his regrets. I laid it on him but I didn't want to pressure him. I said, "I'm going to investigate and see if I can learn anything. Don't laugh, but my only lead is a little boy. By the way, how's Mark doing with the idea of moving into an assisted living?"

John replied, "I'll talk to the guys over coffee this morning and see if they're interested in lending you a hand. Regarding Mark, we're still working on him and I think he's starting to accept it."

I murmured, "That's fine. This is my problem. I'll deal with it. Take care." We disconnected and I had to wait to see if the little fellow called.

I decided to walk along the beach hoping a clue might emerge. Perusing the shoreline, I found the usual cigarette butts and empty energy drink bottles in the river. I decided to go for it. I went to the local sporting goods store and bought some waders. If I was going to investigate, I might as well do it right.

Returning to the site, after putting the waders on, I walked into the water and began picking my way downstream. My assumption was the murderers probably killed the men and then went to the beach to enjoy their beer.

It was still early in the morning and I was only accompanied by some seagulls and egrets. My investigation led me down to the "man-made" island, as the locals call it, and I noticed a small pup tent pitched on a berm. I didn't want to scare the people inside the tent if they were still sleeping. As I got near, I shouted, **"Hello, to the pup tent. Is anybody in there?"**

There was some commotion and it was obvious it was occupied. I didn't venture any closer in case they didn't appreciate being bothered. A man's head popped out and the fellow asked, "What can I do for you?"

I said, "Some men were killed last night about a ¼ mile downstream. Did you see anybody come this way during the night?"

The fellow replied, "Yeah, we heard some shooting and then we saw some guys by the shore. They were drinking beer and shooting at the birds."

"How many were there?" I asked.

"I'd say about a dozen. They were getting pretty drunk so my girlfriend and I walked the other way. We didn't want any trouble."

"Would you recognize them if you saw them again?" I asked.

The young man replied, "No, I don't think so. As soon as they started getting wild, we left!"

By now, a young woman had crawled out of the tent wearing most of her clothes. She began, "They looked like they belonged to a gang, if you know what I mean."

I said, "You've been a big help." At least I had an idea of who was responsible for killing Burt.

Chapter Six

With Mark preparing to become embedded in the nursing home, I forgot about revenge for Burt's murder for a while. The senior sleuths and I reconvened at my son's house and together we developed a plan to thwart the assisted living murderers. Mark was still steadfast against the plan, but when I told him the nurses gave him a hot bath every day, he dropped his opposition.

My son promised he could provide the fake background information on Mark.

I said, "Let's make him a wealthy investor."

John said, "If I remember correctly, a lot of hedge fund managers made a fortune in the 80s."

We researched hedge funds on the internet. We knew we had to make Mark reasonably knowledgeable about them. We discovered hedge funds are alternative investments that don't have to play by the rules. They are not investigated as often as mutual funds or stocks.

Ben added, "Because Mark isn't supposed to be in his right mind, he can feign dementia and that should be easy."

Mark retorted, "Shut up!"

Smelling money, we thought we wouldn't have to wait long. We were right. The next day, Tyler's cell phone chimed while we were having breakfast.

Tapping his phone, Tyler said, "Hello?" He listened intently and after disconnecting said, "We can bring Mark there this afternoon, a room just became available." I guess money talks.

I said, "We have to get busy. We have to buy him some expensive clothes and rent a limousine."

We spent the rest of the morning getting Mark ready for his entry into his future home. John was responsible for getting a limo. I took Mark to a local men's haberdashery and bought him some expensive clothes so he could look the part. My son forwarded the forged papers to the assisted living home that included a fictitious attorney's signature. Tyler created a fake hedge fund company complete with non-existent CEO and officers. A photo of our office building was borrowed from a public domain site. We hoped it would work.

Arriving after lunch, Mark was wheeled into the assisted living building accompanied by his entourage. We hired a nurse to help transfer our boss into the facility to enhance the scam. Once inside, we had to assume every employee could be an accomplice.

Mrs. Hobbes was waiting at the door and after the introductions were completed, the rest of the pseudo-detectives and I were identified as his bodyguards. I wanted to make sure we would have access to Mark if needed.

As we made our introductions, the director stared at me and asked, "Haven't we met before?"

I replied, "As a matter of fact, yes. I was considering putting my uncle in an assisted living home but he passed before I had to make that decision."

She nodded her head and relayed, "Oh, yes, now I remember. I'm sorry for your loss."

With that we began the tour of the facility. As expected, Mrs. Hobbes showed us the amenities of the place. The entertainment, dining, and crafts rooms were predictable. We reached Mark's room and as expected; it was pretty stark. All during the tour, Mark pretended to be disinterested. When he did speak, he was nonsensical.

Mrs. Hobbes said, "We received the paper work and everything seems to be in order. Our resident doctor is here Monday and Thursday afternoons. One other thing I should tell you is that we insist on no visitors for the first 48 hours. Also, the resident is not allowed to have a cell phone. If he wants to make a call, an employee will be glad to loan him one of ours. Are there any questions?"

Mark asked, "When do I get my bath?"

Ben spoke saying, "Sometimes, he says things that don't make a lot of sense." When Mrs. Hobbes's attention was diverted, Ben poked Mark in the arm.

Mark's belongings were brought in and we stowed shirts in the closet, and toiletries in their place. When we had finished, Mrs. Hobbes said, "That will be fine gentlemen. It's time for our newest resident to get acquainted with us."

We were cordially led out of the room and Mark was left to his own devices.

As we were returning to our vehicle, Ben said, "I sure don't like leaving Mark in that place by himself."

I agreed saying, "Mark is resourceful. If he can persevere the first 48 hours, we can take turns protecting him."

Once we had departed, the smile on Mrs. Hobbes disappeared as well. She turned and glared at Mark saying, "Listen, you little twerp. You might have been something on the outside, but in here you belong to me. If you want to survive, you'd better behave."

Mark continued to act incoherent. The director looked at the orderlies and bellowed, "Stand the old man up." The orderlies each grabbed an arm and lifted Mark out of his wheelchair. As they did, Mark asked, "Is it time for my bath?" The female director struck Mark across the face and punched him several times in the stomach. Mark had to pretend he didn't feel anything. The woman stared at Mark to see if he reacted to the pain. Once, she felt he wasn't of sound mind, she motioned for the orderlies to dump him in the bed. She said, "When you're done with that, go through his things and make sure he doesn't have any electronic devices." Again, the orderlies did as they were told.

Once they left, Mark grimaced and swore under his breath to get that bitch. Not trusting the director, we had sewed a throwaway cell phone in his suitcase. Fortunately, the orderlies didn't find it. Satisfied, Mark didn't have any communicable devices; they shoved his clothes into his dresser drawers and tossed the suitcase in the closet before leaving.

As much as Mark wanted to phone us to come and rescue him, he laid down in the bed knowing a phone call to us would disrupt the plan.

Outside Mark's room, the orderlies conversed between themselves. The bigger orderly started, "I don't think we have to worry about that sawed-off runt. He seems pretty harmless. Especially when our doctor starts treating him."

The other orderly responded, "You're probably right, Sam, but there's something that bothers me about that new resident."

The bigger orderly asked, "What's that, Chip?"

"I just have a funny feeling about him. But, maybe, once he settles in, he'll be pretty tame. Like you say, once Dr. Medford starts giving him doses of Oxycodone, he'll be putty in our hands."

The two orderlies left feeling the new resident would be easy to control.

Once she was back in her office, Mrs. Hobbes phoned her business partner. She began, "Well, we admitted old man Kestila. I checked out his portfolio. He's worth a cool $5 million. You should be able to whittle that sum down."

The voice on the other end responded enthusiastically, "No problem. Just have Doc. Medford start giving the old man drugs. We can decide later when we want the old geezer to die."

The next two days went as the first afternoon. Mrs. Hobbes slapped Mark in the face accompanied by several thrusts to his stomach all the while Mark had to appear to be oblivious to it. Hobbes became satisfied he was suffering from dementia, and wouldn't be a problem. Mark laid in bed hoping for a chance for payback. His pride was hurt worse than his body, but he swore he would get redemption.

By the time 48 hours were up, we couldn't wait to see our partner. This time, Mrs. Hobbes, met us in the hallway and walked us to Mark's room. She stayed long enough to make sure Mark was not going to relay any information regarding the torture. After she left, Mark regained his composure. I asked him, "How's the food?"

He said, "Forget the food. That woman beat me to see if I'd respond. Fortunately, I was able to act as if I was oblivious to it.

Ben started for the door, but I shouted, "Not now! If Mark can take this abuse, we'll get these bastards, but in good time."

Ben punched the door and I was surprised his fist didn't go through it. I handed Mark a .38 special and I said, "Keep this under your mattress. If it gets too rough, use it and phone us. You don't have to be a martyr."

Mark whispered, "When this is over, that woman and I are going to have a talk and there won't be any witnesses."

All of us agreed. Ben asked, "That woman couldn't have done this by herself. Who helped her?"

Mark said, "Those two goons, Jenson and Kendell." That's all we had to know. Those two thugs now had a rendezvous with destiny.

We agreed to take turns staying with Mark. Since we were official bodyguards, we assumed the director wouldn't have a problem with that. Ben wanted to stay first. I think he wanted to learn more about the pain inflicted on his friend. We agreed to rotate every few hours in order to remain alert. Meanwhile, I wanted to check on the attorney. John and Tyler would research the assisted living home's doctor on staff. With our roles assigned, we dispersed to meet sometime later that week.

Upon hearing Mark had a bodyguard in his room, Mrs. Hobbes flew through the halls and upon entering Mark's room, abruptly ordered Ben to leave. After some disagreement, Ben said, "I'll go, but one of us will be checking him every hour."

Hobbes seemed to accept that and said, "That would be okay, as long as it's during visiting hours, which are from one o'clock until eight o'clock p.m."

Ben nodded and looked at Mark who pretended to be confused, saying, "I'll be back in an hour boss." Ben stared down the female director and departed.

Feeling she had won a moral victory, she looked at Mark and said, "Well, old man, I guess we're going to have to move your medical treatment ahead."

As she was leaving, she phoned Dr. Medford. Upon answering, he said, "Yes, Anne. I got the text to start treatment for Mr.

Kestila. I was going to begin Thursday, but I can be there later this afternoon." Hearing what she wanted; the female director disconnected.

Later that night, the two orderlies were making their way to their vehicles. They noticed the street light was not working. As they neared their vehicles, they could see individuals lurking in the shadows. Both men halted and strained to identify who they were. Jenson looked at Kendell and asked, "Are you expecting someone?" Jenson replied, "No, I was hoping you knew them." They started to back pedal when others approached them from behind. One of the shadows asked, "I hear you like to beat up old men!"

Jenson responded, "I don't know what you're talking about!"

Another voice responded, "I think you're going to enjoy our brand of payback!"

Both Jenson and Kendall now started to run, but it was too late. They were tackled unceremoniously, their hands tied, and heads covered.

"You're going to get some exercise!" Another voice scoffed, "Are you ready?"

Both men were tied to the back of our vehicle and without fanfare, I shouted, "Go ahead."

Ben started the vehicle and the two orderlies kept pace for a few feet, but then fell face first. Ben continued to drag them around the parking lot. Finally, after a few laps, I gave the signal to stop. Ben shut off his engine and exited. We gathered around the two battered men and I exclaimed, "If anything happens to Mark Kestila again, this will be like a Sunday picnic! Do you bums understand?"

Both men mumbled something that I took as a "yes". Ben untied them and we left them in their blood and urine. As we were leaving, Ben said, "They're lucky Mark wasn't here. You know they would have had their skin peeled." I smiled and said, "We're not through yet."

The next morning, I visited the attorney that Ben and Mark saw on many death certificates. I figured something was wrong because the poor souls were only in the facility a few weeks when they passed.

That day, I entered the attorney's office and was impressed with the décor. They didn't spare any expense to make a point that they were very successful.

I approached the administrative assistant and asked, "Is Mr. Dombrowski available?" She replied, "Who may I say is calling?" "I replied, "Just say it's an interested person from the assisted living facility." It wasn't long before a well-attired man walked into the entry way. I stood and he said, "My name is Mark Dombrowski. How may I be of service?"

I replied, "My friends and I are investigating a string of unusual deaths at some of the local assisted living homes. We noticed your name is listed as the executor on many of the death certificates. Doesn't that seem like a coincidence?"

Dombrowski quickly retorted, "Not at all, I do a lot of work with the local assisted living homes."

"I read in some of the probate court papers, your junior partner was listed as the guardian ad litem. That can't be a coincidence. How is he going to be neutral overseeing your executor position if he belongs to the same law firm?"

Dombrowski had a pat answer. He said, "It's simple. It's not a matter of him looking over my shoulder, but rather we work pretty much as partners to make sure the residents at the assistant living facilities get the best care."

I said, "Thanks for your time." It was clear I wasn't going to get anywhere with this legal beagle.

I returned to my hotel to see what the others were doing.

Meanwhile, John and Tyler were very successful investigating other nursing homes. The same names kept popping up as executor and guardian ad litem. There was definitely a picture forming. These two attorneys were making a fortune signing off on seniors who passed.

Back at the hotel, we compared notes and it seemed that we were on the right path. We just had to keep Mark alive.

The next morning at the assisted living facility, Mark's door opened. and two well-dressed gentlemen stepped inside. The older man approached Mark and said, "Mr. Kestila, my name is Mark Dombrowski. This is my associate, Henry Waters. I have been asked by Mrs. Hobbes to be your attorney of record. Mr. Waters has been asked to be, what we call in the legal field, your guardian ad litem. His job is to make sure you are treated fairly by me. You see, in a few weeks, the county probate judge will hear your case. If the judge agrees with us, I will become your legal guardian."

"Alright, let's begin," The attorney said as he removed a thick stack of papers from his briefcase while Mark continued to stare at the wall. The two attorneys signed and initialed the papers one after another. When it came time for Mark to sign, Dombrowski took Mark's hand and guided it as they mutually scribbled Mark's signature. When they were finished, Dombrowski said, "We'll leave copies of the papers with you. Good day, Mr. Kestila." With that the two men stood and left.

Mark, knowing he was alone, mumbled under his breath, "What a couple of crooks. Now, I see how it's done."

After the attorneys departed, Mrs. Hobbes entered and said, "Mr. Kestila, you have another visitor. This is Doctor Melbourne. He's going to give you a physical exam and then if you need any medication, he will prescribe that also."

Hobbes left the room and Dr. Melbourne began to examine Mark. He ignored the marks on the senior's face and torso since he had seen them countless times in the past. It was just a rite of passage as far as the doctor was concerned. When he had finished, the doctor said, "I'm going to give you a sleeping pill to help you tonight. I want you take it before bedtime every night. The nurse will administer it." The doctor, ignoring any concerns Mark might have, stood and left. He did stop at the nurses' station and whispered to the charge nurse. She nodded her head acknowledging the procedure.

Chapter Seven

It was late when we returned to our hotel room, thinking it would look less conspicuous if we stayed at one rather than at my son's house. As I laid down, my phone chimed, and I immediately grabbed it since I had set Mark's ringtone to Star Wars. Realizing it had to be important, I grabbed it and pressed the receiver. I could hear someone mumbling, "**Mark, is that you?**" I shouted.

The others stopped what they were doing and concentrated on my conversation. "**Mark, is that you?**" I repeated.

Not hearing anything, I said, "Let's go!"

The others were right with me as we made a quick exit and drove to the assisted living facility like the back of our car was on fire. Emerging from our vehicle, Ben was the first to reach the front door. Because it was afterhours, the doors were locked. Tyler rang the buzzer while the rest of us pounded on the door. Eventually, a voice was heard through the intercom, saying, "It's after visiting hours. You can come back tomorrow at 1:00 p.m."

Ben screamed, "Open this door or I'll break it down!" We heard the door latch open and we sprinted through the foyer and the hall. When we arrived, we flung open Mark's door and saw him lying in bed. Ben shouted, "What the hell is this?" We raised Mark to a sitting position, but he didn't respond. Ben felt for a pulse and found one, albeit barely. He reported, "His pulse feels weak. They must have given him something to put him to sleep." Without saying a word, Ben laid Mark gently down and strode to the nurses' station. There, an elderly nurse was typing into a computer. Ben shouted, "What did you give Mark Kestila? He's barely alive!"

The nurse said, "It's normal to prescribe a sedative if a patient is unable to sleep. He's okay. He'll be fine in the morning. You can come back tomorrow afternoon. You'll have to leave now; the residents need their rest."

Ben was trying to calm down when we led him outside. I could tell he was extremely upset about his good friend. Ben was composing himself when he said, "This whole plan is stupid. These people just want to murder the residents and collect their money."

I tried to placate him by saying, "We got Mark inside. Now, we have to protect him. We'll nail these people, but there are risks involved." That didn't seem to help Ben at all and I knew he would be vigilant about Mark's safety.

"Our next problem," I said, "was to replace whatever powerful meds they're giving Mark with placebos. Let's find those two idiots that helped rough Mark up and make them divulge what drugs they're giving our buddy. Then, we're going to sneak into the assisted living pharmacy and replace them."

Tyler interjected, "That sounds good, but they have monitors at the front desk. The charge nurse will see us."

I replied, "That's right, that's why we need a diversion to get her away from her desk."

We entered one of the orderly's' names into our smartphone and came up with an address for Sam Jenson. We drove to his ramshackle apartment complex and identified his residence. Ben said, "Let me take care of this."

I responded, "We'll come with you. I don't want you to kill him."

Ben smiled and said, "That'll come later."

We knocked on the injured orderly's door and heard some commotion. "Who is it?" asked Jenson.

Ben snarled and said, "Open up, or we'll break the door down and throw you out the window!"

After a lengthy waiting period, the door was opened and a bandaged Jenson recognized us and stepped backward. He said, through a bandaged face, "What do you want? I'm barely alive."

Ben growled, "We need some information and I personally hope you don't tell us. As far as I'm concerned this isn't over."

I stepped in front of Ben and asked, "We need to know what meds the nurses are giving our friend. Tell me or I'll turn this guy loose on you."

The orderly replied, "Medford gives them Oxycodone. There's no record, but the night nurse knows to give each patient one before they go to bed."

Ben said, "You better be telling the truth or I'll be back!"

We closed the door and left.

As we were driving, I said, "We better wait until evening when everything is quieter, but before they give them the meds."

We now had to come up with a deception. I looked at Tyler and asked, "Do you think you can divert the desk nurse with your charm? To enhance our ruse, Ben and I will create a stir to help get the nurse involved. While this is happening, John, do you think you could pick the pharmacy door lock, find the Oxycodone, and replace them with placebos?"

John replied, "It'll be child's play."

I said, "We have to stop at a drugstore first and find a suitable replacement for the Oxycodone."

We found a drugstore on Eastman Ave. and entered. It wasn't as easy as I thought it would be. We perused the drug section opening boxes to examine them. "Remember," I said, "We have to be able to fool the night nurse." Rummaging through the drugs, we finally hit pay dirt. We found an aspirin that closely resembled the real McCoy. We bought the entire supply and left for the assisted living home.

Before we entered, I asked, "Does everybody know their job?" To heighten the suspense, Ben and I were going to get into an argument to distract the nurse's attention while John picked the pharmacy's lock and replaced the Oxycodone with a placebo duplicate. The plan started well, we entered the facility and Tyler started to make small talk with the desk nurse, doing his best to flirt with her. Ben and I started to argue as we came through the entrance door. There were still a few residents, in wheel chairs, near the front desk. I shouted at Ben, "You're wrong. I paid you back the hundred dollars I borrowed from you!"

Ben retorted, "No, you didn't! You still owe me!"

I shoved Ben who returned the favor. Both of us increased our struggle all the while the residents were seated in their wheel chairs. I purposely pushed Ben extra hard and down he went. In a flash, he was off the floor and the flurry was on. The desk nurse shouted, "**Stop it, you're scaring the residents!**" Ignoring her demand to stop, we continued to scuffle on the floor. Tyler stepped over and pulled me from Ben. He grabbed me and dragged me toward the front door. The nurse, by now, was busy trying to calm some of the agitated residents. Ben continued to hurl insults at me and I returned the verbal assault.

Meanwhile, John found the dispensary, picked the lock, and entered. He scanned the shelves for the Oxycodone, and upon seeing it in a large container, picked the cupboard lock and removed the powerful barbiturates. He switched the aspirin for the Oxycodone and returned the placeboes to the shelf. He closed the cupboard door and exited the pharmacy making sure the door was locked as he walked away.

We left the home knowing Mark would be safer.

Chapter Eight

Returning to have my revenge for Burt's murder, I left Mark in the other guys' capable hands. My next mission was to find a waterhole where Burt's murderers might call home. I'm sure they had no worries about the police being interested in finding them. In an area like this, life was cheap. Six homeless men killed along the Saginaw River wasn't going to turn into a massive manhunt.

I drove through the streets of Saginaw looking for possible suspects or at least someplace where they might call home. I stopped my vehicle several times and sauntered into some establishments. After a while, I decided that these particular places weren't low enough for those low lives.

As I was visiting the bars, my cell phone rang and I finally got some good news. On the other end was the little boy's voice that quivered as he spoke. He began, "Sir, is this the man that offered money for information to help catch the men that killed his friend?"

I tried to sound as friendly as possible so I said, "You bet, whatever you can tell me, I'll appreciate it and I'll give you a reward."

There was a pause and I assumed the boy had to be extra careful. He finally continued saying, "I think the guys that were responsible are from the Tweeners."

Confused, "What do you mean by the Tweeners?" I asked.

He answered, "There are several dangerous areas in Saginaw, but the guys you're looking for live somewhere between 3rd and 10th streets on the East Side. We call that area the Tweeners. You don't want to go there if you don't have to."

I replied, "That's great, but how do you know the murderers are the Tweeners?"

They come to that beach lots of times to drink and party. They think it's theirs. If they catch anybody there at night, they hurt them bad. Sometimes, they have girls with them. They do stuff to the girls to make them cry. The guys just laugh when that happens. It's an initiation to get into their gang."

I wanted to be clear so I asked the youngster, "You're saying these guys come to the beach pretty often to drink and party."

The young boy said, "That's what I've been telling you. Now do I get my money?"

I said, "Absolutely, I'll put fifty dollars under the garbage receptacle in the park. I appreciate it a lot young man. Do you have a way to get to the park?"

"Yes, I can borrow my brother's bike."

With that, we disconnected and now I planned to wait for those hoodlums to come to me.

I returned to the local sport shop and outfitted myself with some heavy-duty weaponry. There was a three-day grace period to purchase a hand gun, but I didn't plan to use one anyway. If there were about a dozen gang members, I'd need some heavy fire power.

Leaving the store, my cell phone chimed and after connecting, I recognized it was John Baldwin's cell number.

I answered, "Hey, John, what's up?"

He replied, "Mark seems to be okay for now. The boys and I decided to give you a hand if you want us."

"Great," I said, "My snitch came through. He told me the gang bangers come to the beach fairly often to party. There's about a dozen, I guess. Sometimes, the lad said, they have girls with them."

I texted the location from my GPS where they could find me.

The sun was setting and there was no moon. It was dark and gloomy. I thought if they come tonight, it'll be perfect. I only hoped my reinforcements arrived in time.

At the river, I found a clump of small trees that would provide a good backdrop. If the shooting started, it would be hard for the ganstas to pick their target. I heard some loud ganstas music getting louder as the punks came nearer to the shore. They must have found some hard stuff as they were passing the bottles among them. I didn't see any girls, which would make my job easier.

My cell phone chimed and I had to retreat into the woods. Some of the hoods heard the chime and looked in my direction. Luckily, I was on the other side of the river and they weren't about to get wet.

I whispered to John, "Yeah, the punks are here and drinking heavy. I think we should wait and let them get as drunk as possible."

John said, "Roger that. Give me a location where you are!"

After giving him my coordinates and disconnecting my cell phone, I returned to the bushes to wait.

In the distance, I identified John and Tyler crawling toward them from the west while Ben was doing the same on the east side. We maintained our positions until the hoods were thoroughly intoxicated. Most of them had fallen asleep and only a few were able to move.

I stood and opened fire. My cohorts did the same. With a few quick bursts of our automatics, in seconds, our targets were motionless. We didn't bother to check for wounded. I knew their type of lifestyle wouldn't change. These people grew up in abject poverty knowing only violence as a way of life. Maybe, they didn't value an education or training.

It was with a heavy heart that the pseudo-detectives and I returned to help Mark in the assisted living facility. It was a hollow victory and we had degraded ourselves to their level, but we did obtain *Revenge for the Homeless.*

Chapter Nine

The next morning, attorney Mark Dombrowski entered the home and walked into Mrs. Hobbes's office. She looked at him and asked,

"To what do I owe the pleasure?"

Dombrowski retorted, "Good news, Kestila's papers were signed by Judge Patterson. The old man can pass anytime."

Hobbes answered, "That's good, but we're going to have to be careful. Kestila has a slew of bodyguards that are nosing around every day. We're going to have to take the slow drip approach. Every day he'll have to worsen a little."

Dombrowski responded, "Yes, I know, one visited me yesterday. We got that other old man in room 118. He can't be hanging on very well, can he?"

Hobbes agreed saying, "I suppose we could arrange a little help for Mr. Doppler to pass into the next world. My two orderlies have been calling in sick every day. I'm short-handed. Normally, I would have one of those clowns take a pillow to the old man, but I don't have anyone right now, unless you want to do the job."

He said, "That's not my forte. I simply set the table and you deliver."

"We'll have to wait until one of those buffoons come back," Dombrowski answered.

The two were interrupted by an, "Hello, top of the morning to both of you. Isn't it a beautiful day?" The two stopped their conversation and looked toward the door. There stood Mark, smiling and talking to everyone as he strode through the hallway. Dombrowski looked at Hobbes and said, "I thought you said Medford started him on Oxycodone?"

Hobbes answered, "Yes, we're giving him enough to knock a

horse unconscious. I'll have to check into this."

We entered the facility as Mark was passing the front door. Ben shouted, "What the hell is this?"

Mark was doing a jig in front of the nurse's station as they accompanied him by clapping in time."

Mark turned to engage Ben in a dance step, but Ben pushed him away saying, "I worried about you all night. I come here and you're entertaining everyone."

Mark smiled and said, "Follow me. We're having a dance contest later today and I'm in it!"

I stated, "I'm glad to see you're so chipper, but if you're entering a dance contest, they're going to slip you more powerful drugs."

Mark answered, "I never thought of that. I suppose you're right."

Tyler interjected, "Why don't you just go to your room and lie down?"

We got Mark back to the room and closed the door. I asked him, "Have you seen anything that's suspicious?"

Mark replied, "Look around you. Every resident is comatose. I'd consider that suspicious."

John said, "Last night, we replaced the Oxycodone with placebos. That's why you feel good. The other residents should start recuperating also."

Mark said, "I'll watch for that!"

We conversed some more, updating him on various sports team and the weather.

As we were leaving, I said, "After they give you the pill at night, you have to fall asleep and tomorrow don't call attention to yourself."

Mark answered, "Okay, I can do that."

Later that day, not satisfied with the effects on Mark, Hobbes entered the nurses' station and told the nurse to double Mark's dosage of Oxycodone." *That should do it.* She thought to herself as she left.

Anne Hobbes returned to her office to finish some paper work.

There was a slight knock on her door. She replied, "Come in." The door opened and in stepped Chip Kendell. He was walking, but only with the help of crutches, and was bandaged from head to toe. His face was scraped so bad it hurt just to look at him. The director exclaimed, "My God, what happened to you?"

Kendell hobbled in and threw himself in the chair in front of her desk. He started, "The other night, Sam and I were walking to our vehicle when we were attacked by a gang. They tied, blindfolded us and dragged us around the parking lot. After they were done, they told us to leave old man Kestila alone. I think the men who did this were his bodyguards. Sam is so scared; he won't leave his apartment. Somehow, Kestila must have told them and they came after Sam and me."

Hobbes listened intently and said, "You did the right thing. We're going to get rid of that old man once and for all. I'll call Medford and have him come now."

Kendell propped himself forward and using his crutches hoisted himself to an upright position. He started to leave, but he turned, and said, "Get those guys, will you?"

Anne Hobbes replied, "Count on it."

The boys and I had returned to our hotel hoping to get a good night's sleep. Meanwhile, back at the assisted living facility, Doctor Medford walked into the director's office and asked, "What's wrong? I got your text, but you didn't explain what happened!"

Hobbes stated, "Kendell was here about an hour ago. He's all banged up and on crutches. Sam Jenson is even worse. Apparently, those body guards grabbed them in the parking lot the other night and dragged them with a vehicle. They warned Jenson and Kendell not to harm Kestila again or they'd be in trouble. That old man has become a liability. I want you to give him something to finish him once and for all."

The doctor thought for a minute and said, "I can do that as long as I perform the autopsy. Don't let the M.E. take the body to the morgue. We'd be in big trouble. If I can conduct a cursory autopsy, there are a number of reasons that could be the cause. I'll do it tonight."

Hobbes smiled and replied, "The sooner the better." After the doctor left to prepare his deadly cocktail, Hobbes' land line rang. She answered, and said, "Mrs. Hobbes, Director." The voice on the other end said, "I hear you're having trouble."

She answered, "Nothing we can't handle."

The voice pursued the topic, asking, "Do I have to come there and fix it?"

By now, Hobbes was getting nervous. She knew fixing it meant getting rid of her. She replied, "It'll be taken care of tonight!"

The voice responded, "You better or have the doctor fix a potion for you too!"

Across town, I was lying in bed unable to sleep. Sometimes, fresh air helps me relax. I dressed and grabbed the keys from the dresser. I felt as long as I was driving, I might as well look in on our favorite senior.

Once I arrived at the home, it was a chore to get the evening nurse to buzz me inside. After several pleas, she opened the latch and I entered. As I approached her desk, she glared at me and said, "It's past visiting hours."

I answered, "I just want to look in on Mr. Kestila."

She said, "Hurry and don't wake anybody."

I nodded my head as I sauntered through the hall toward Mark's room.

Once there, I pushed on the door, but it wouldn't open. I never knew a resident's room to be locked. My mind soared into overdrive. I kicked the door in and saw a man in a white surgical coat standing over Mark. He was holding a syringe preparing to inject him. The noise of the door shattering startled him as he turned to face me. I drew my Glock and shouted, "**Drop it or die!**"

He took a step toward me as I prepared to fire. Just then, I felt something sharp shoved into my back. It was Hobbes holding a scalpel. She shouted, "Drop it mister or I'll shove this into your ribs!" I had to make an instant decision. If I dropped my gun, I knew both Mark and I would be dead. I tossed the handgun on the floor and as I did, I turned and threw a haymaker into her face. The force knocked her flat on her back and I retrieved my weapon. Looking at the attempted murderer, I said, "Now, drop that syringe doctor or I'll jam it into you!" Pondering the threat, the would-be murderer dropped it.

I ordered the doctor to sit and I wasn't too worried about the woman. Hobbes was still unconscious, but I wanted reinforcements so taking my cell phone, I dialed a familiar number. After John answered, I shouted, "**Get here now!**" He woke the other two and they borrowed my son's vehicle. Within minutes they rushed through the door and I was thrilled to see them. In the meantime, I phoned 9-1-1 to relay the pending crimes. Once the police arrived, we had hours of explaining. The pieces of the puzzle were starting to come together.

Needless to say, the commotion woke a certain senior sleuth from a sound sleep. He rolled over and saw the police escorting the doctor and the director away in hand-cuffs. He said, "I was really looking forward to squaring off with her for what she did to me."

I replied, "Well, if it's any consolation, I gave her a good smack that knocked her unconscious."

Mark grunted, "I wish I could have seen it."

"You should know you came pretty close to checking out permanently," Ben said.

"What are you talking about?" Mark asked.

"Bill broke in when the doctor was about to give you a lethal injection. If he hadn't come through the door when he did, you'd be leading the parade to the cemetery."

"Really?" Mark exclaimed, "I was that close to being killed?"

John said, "You owe Bill your life old man. It's that simple."

Mark smiled and said, "I want to thank all of you."

I replied, "That's nice, but we're not done."

The next morning, we found out how prophetic my words were.

The arraignment was set for 10:00, and the senior sleuths were in attendance. Naturally, Mark Dombrowski was the attorney of record for both the doctor and the assisted living director. We all rose as the probate judge entered and we sat down. After the charges were read, it seemed like an open and shut case. Fifteen charges of first-degree murder were read by the bailiff. Dombrowski argued the two were not flight risks. They had ties to the community. This was the first time either had been charged with a felony. Hearing all of this, the judge tapped a gavel and said, "Bail is set at $100,000." We were shocked. They were accused of murdering fifteen seniors at the nursing home. A light came on and I started to wonder, *why would a judge set bail at such a low figure?* Something wasn't right.

Chapter Ten

Outside of the courthouse, after we finished venting, I said, "There must be a reason why the judge set bail so low."

John suggested, "Maybe, he's in on the crimes?"

I wanted to say he was wrong, but the more I thought about it, collusion made sense.

"Let's find out if that judge has a connection to our murderers, and even to Dombrowski and Waters," I said.

Since we were at the courthouse, it was a simple matter to climb the steps and check into the judge's past. John said, "Tyler and I will visit the local coffee shops and see what we can divulge."

Ben said, "Mark and I can see what the court records show."

I said, "I'll check with the local sheriff. Maybe, he can provide some incite."

Once again, we dispersed on our separate ways searching for answers.

John and Tyler made a beeline to a local café and started picking the locals' brains. Ben and Mark found the courthouse records court convictions.

I had the dubious job of trying to delicately ask questions from the local law. My experience told me from the past that most law enforcement officers are protective of their judges. I hoped I was wrong.

John and Tyler started a conversation with some local hayseeds. The boys were careful to feel the locals out first. They didn't want to jump into a conversation and antagonize them. John started, "We just came from the courthouse and we were surprised the probate judge let the two accused murderers out on $100,000."

That was like throwing gas onto a fire. The whole counter lit up. It was clear, there was no love lost for that judge. One patron shouted, "Judge Patterson has got to go!"

John's ears bristled as he tried to remember where he heard that name before.

Tyler asked, "Is there another judge with that name?"

Another local said, "Sure there is, there are two brothers. Both are judges. One is the probate judge and the other is the circuit court judge. As you know, the probate judge sets the bail for all felony cases."

All of a sudden, things started to click for John and Tyler.

At the county courthouse, Ben and Mark were having a field day finding many cases that were decided by Circuit Court Judge Patterson. It wasn't unusual for Mark Dombrowski to be the attorney of record for the defendant. The conviction rate was very low or minimal at best. Ben and Mark kept calling attention to cases that resembled a travesty of justice.

Across the street, I was trying to pave my way into the sheriff's good graces by reminiscing. I introduced myself and he replied his name was Skip Canon. I informed the sheriff I once wore the same badge in the Superior Peninsula. His demeanor softened and we relaxed as we swapped stories for hours. Eventually, I steered him toward his opinion of Circuit Judge Patterson.

I said, "I was present when Probate Judge Patterson allowed the two accused murderers of killing fifteen residents a light bail."

Sheriff Canon recoiled and said, "I know, we bring a lot of criminals into his court only to have him make a mockery of everything. Between him and his brother they are an embarrassment."

Now I had him, "What do you mean an embarrassment?" I asked.

He said, "Since they were elected, they have done nothing but let criminals get probation or a minimal sentence. I'm thoroughly disgusted," responded the sheriff.

I replied, "I'm glad you said that. I was wondering if I was the only one that felt that way."

The sheriff answered, "No, together they have set jurisprudence back a hundred years."

I asked, "Can't something be done?"

The sheriff threw up his hands saying, "What can I do? Patterson's the judge."

Now my mind started racing. I said, "How about if we set a trap for them? I commit a crime and I hire Dombrowski to defend me. Hopefully, he wants a kickback to split with the judge?"

Sheriff Canon said, "I wouldn't do that. You're taking a big chance. If something happens, you could go to prison."

I suggested, "What about if we bring the state's attorney general in on it?"

Sheriff Canon replied, "I could make a call to the state capital tomorrow and see."

"All we have to do is create a crime that I didn't commit. By the way, I met Dombrowski earlier when I told him when I was investigating deaths at the assisted living facility. I don't think that will deter him from demanding a bribe knowing how greedy he is."

I shook his hand and waited to hear from him. The next afternoon, my cell phone rang and as I answered, I heard, "Guess what? The attorney general is on board. They've heard some rumblings in Lansing that the two brothers are taking some questionable legal actions."

I responded, "Great, now what crime could I have committed that would bring me in front of Circuit Court Judge Patterson?"

We thought for a long time before I suggested, "What about murder? I have some buddies that could help create the scenario. One of my friends could disappear with circumstantial evidence against me and you could arrest me. I could be accused of murdering him. We have to make sure Dombrowski takes the case. We'll see if he demands a bribe to help influence the judge."

After listening to my argument, Sheriff Canon said, "It just might work! Bring in your boys and we'll fine tune it."

Over dinner, that evening, our plan was hatched. It was daring and very risky. I felt as long as the state's attorney general was on board, I was safe.

Our plan originally called for one of my pseudo-detectives to be murdered. I would be arrested and I would retain Mark Dombrowski as my attorney. It was hoped, during the trial, Dombrowski would approach me and ask for money to sway the judge in our favor. Once that was proven, we'd have both Dombrowski and the judge dead to rights.

During our meeting, Sheriff Canon wanted the plan changed. He said, "How about if I talk to one of my deputies and arrange for her to be the victim. She has a cabin in the woods and could hide there indefinitely after you're accused. It would also make for more bad publicity. Dombrowski will be thrilled to take the case."

My pseudo-detective friends had grave reservations against that idea.

John said, "This could get very dicey. We don't know these people! Besides that, Dombrowski has already met you."

I answered, "I'm relying on his greed to be more important."

Ben added, "Once, you're accused of the crime, we can't undo it!"

Tyler spoke against it as well, but I trusted Sheriff Canon. I said, "The sheriff's points are well taken and I agree to go along with it."

The sheriff said, "Let's do it tonight. There's no time like the present. I'll talk to Laurie Smith, my deputy, and tell her what we're asking her to do."

Canon said, "Here are the directions to her cabin," as he handed them to me. "You plan to arrive about 9:00 and after it's over, you phone 9-1-1 with the tragic news. I'll bring my department up to speed and they'll cooperate. It'll be great. We'll catch Dombrowski and Judge Patterson in their own trap."

The boys and I went for dinner, and needless to say, they were all against the plan. I held steadfast, as I said, "This is the only way we're going to catch these bums. After I'm arrested, either the sheriff or I will call you from the jail."

That night, I arrived promptly at 9:00 and approached the

deputy's cabin. I peered through the window hoping to see our victim. I did, but it wasn't the way I wanted. She was lying almost naked on the floor. I opened the door and ran to her. I felt for a pulse, but there wasn't any. Her clothes were torn to shreds and her body was full of lacerations and bruises. I realized I had been set up by the sheriff. I called John and upon him answering, I shouted, "**I need help! I'm at the cabin and the deputy's been murdered! I've been set up by the sheriff!**"

John exclaimed, "We'll be right there. Don't touch anything!"

I gave them directions to the deputy's cabin and disconnected. My nerves were frayed and I didn't know what to do.

Nervous as hell, I returned to my vehicle and waited for the boys. It seemed like an eternity before they arrived.

Upon arriving, together, we slowly opened the cabin door and our eyes fell on the body. Tyler said, "I don't think she's more than 25 years old." We walked through the room careful not to touch anything. Mark said, "I knew this was a horrible idea. That sheriff had this planned all along."

Ben added, "It's possible someone else may have done this."

John retorted, "And there's a bridge north of here I want to sell you."

Examining the body closer, John said, "There's some skin scrapings under her nails. She probably fought hard. Her panties were down around her knees indicating there was probably sexual trauma." Tyler said, "I wish my wife, Carolyn, could examine this body. I'd feel a lot better."

We heard a vehicle's engine outside and it wasn't long before several deputies entered the cabin with their guns drawn. "Put your hands up. Don't move," one of them shouted.

Ben exclaimed, "Just great! Here we are in the middle of a murder scene!" The deputies ordered us to move to one side and lay down. We accommodated them, knowing they were as nervous as us. Our hands were cuffed behind our back and we lay motionless. The sheriff entered and looked at everything. He said, "Well, boys, I guess we caught you red handed. Folks don't take kindly to one of my deputies being murdered. Get 'em out of here. My poor Laurie never had a chance."

I had to admit it looked pretty incriminating. The question in my mind was: *how did the sheriff's deputies know to come here?* I pondered this as we were driven to the police station.

We were fingerprinted, photographed and jailed. We were told the arraignment would be in the morning. Mark mused, "I suppose we're going to be arraigned by Probate Judge Patterson. Isn't that ironic?"

John agreed, saying, "Yeah, we were going to trap him, but instead we're up on serious charges." We each got one phone call and rather than contact my wife, I made a special call to an old friend, John Crane. We had worked many cases together and had solved countless crimes. He was as tough as they came. His medals in combat were just the tip of the iceberg. He possessed a crusty outward appearance and didn't make friends easy. I assumed he learned that in combat. Once you gained his trust, he was your friend for life. Boy, did I need one now.

A deputy handed me my cell phone and I made a phone call I thought I'd never have to make. John answered with his usual cursory attitude, "I assume you're in a jam again. Where are you?"

I replied, "I'm in jail along with the others in Midland, Michigan."

"What are you idiots accused of now?" John asked.

"The worst," I replied. "We're accused of murdering a female deputy sheriff!"

There was a moment of silence and then John said, "When you fools screw up, you don't kid around! I'll pack some gear and be there as soon as I can." As usual, there were no congenial good-byes, just silence. That was John.

We had settled down for an evening in the slammer. It was hard to get comfortable on the hard bunks. Suddenly, in the front of the jail, we heard gasping and wheezing sounds. A smoke permeated under the door. Immediately, our eyes became watery. The door was kicked open and tear-gas masks were flung into our cells. A giant emerged through the door way and worked the combination opening the cells. We donned the masks and followed the behemoth. As we made our escape, we stepped over one guard that displayed a bloody face. I assumed he knew the combination to the cells and had to be persuaded to divulge it.

Once outside, our man-mountain savior raced to the Humvee parked in front. Like the Pied Piper's children, we dashed after him, diving into the vehicle. With the last one inside, we sped off to parts unknown. Since this happened so fast, I didn't have time to develop a plan to catch the rats responsible.

Upon arriving in the countryside, we removed our masks and we were grateful to our savior once again, John Crane. After thanking him profusely, he responded, "Now you're on your own! Get out!"

With that, we tumbled out of the Humvee and watched our rescuer disappear into the night.

Mark asked, "Well, what now?"

I said, "We have to find a place to lie low and stay off the main roads. Naturally, the sheriff and his deputies will have a BOLO out, with roadblocks on every main road."

Not sure where we were, we walked into the woods and continued until we found an abandoned farmhouse. It wasn't much, but it was a roof over our heads. Due to the sheriff deputy's forgetfulness, I still had my cell phone. I decided to put it to good use. Phoning my son, Roy, I brought him up to speed on our escape. I explained our predicament and our approximate location. I assumed he would be under surveillance so I told him to take an indirect route and make sure he wasn't being followed. After we disconnected, I regretted I had to get him involved.

Later that evening, a vehicle approached, and after making sure it was my son, we met him on the dirt road. As expected, he had ample amounts of food, water and money. Roy said, "Hop in and I'll give you a lift. Where do you want to go?"

After due deliberation, I said, "Let's start with the attorney, Mark Dombrowski. I think he's the weak link."

Scanning my smartphone for his residence, Roy dropped us off near Dombrowski's address and I said, "Go home and stay there. You've been a big help. We'll take it from here."

The boys and I approached Dombrowski's residence, and without fanfare, kicked the front door in. We liked to make an entrance. By now the litigator had heard about our escape. He retreated to a corner of his living room holding a hand gun. He murmured, "Don't come any closer or I'll shoot!"

John responded, "You better be able to get all four of us with one shot because that's all you're going to get. The rest of us will rip you apart."

He dropped the gun begging, "Don't hurt me. I just went along with the plan."

I wanted to hear from the horse's mouth, I bellowed, "What plan?"

The litigator whimpered, "We were having coffee one day and Sheriff Canon suggested, "It would be easy if we started to use our positions in the legal system to make some extra money."

Canon looked at the judge and said, "We could work together and along with Dombrowski make some serious money arranging kickbacks for lighter sentences."

Surprisingly, Judge Patterson seemed to like the idea. He replied, "I'm pretty sure my brother, the probate judge, would do the same in his court."

Anne Hobbes, added, "I could arrange untimely deaths in the assisted living home. I think I could persuade our doctor to cooperate."

She looked at me and said, "You could become the guardian for the senior wards." For several years, we had all the bases covered and it worked great. Then you bums had to come along and ruin it."

He had just finished divulging the plan when we heard, "It's still not over, Mark!" We turned and standing in the doorway was Sheriff Canon. He was pointing his weapon at us and he said, "Unlike Dombrowski, I'm pretty sure I could nail all of you before you get to me. Put your hands up and keep them where I can see them." As he was speaking, Judge Patterson entered and said, "What do we do with them?"

The sheriff exclaimed, "Are you kidding? We caught them breaking into Dombrowski's house. We had to shoot them."

I replied, "There's only one problem. We're not armed. How do you explain that?"

Canon rebuffed the argument and said, "I have some old pistols in my trunk that'll do nicely."

Trying to buy time, I asked, "I assume you murdered the deputy."

Sheriff Canon replied, "Yeah, we had some good times, but she didn't want to continue so when you suggested your plan, I just altered it."

I asked, "Are you the one that phoned 9-1-1?"

Canon laughed and said, "I even used her phone."

I have one more question. "Did you ever contact the state's attorney general?"

Canon became hysterical and said, "Sure, and I even called the governor. What'd you think?"

"You're pretty smart, aren't you? But you know eventually you're going to get caught!"

Canon laughed and said, "Maybe, but not by you guys!"

The words were barely out of his mouth when a look of anguish overcame him. He fell forward with a knife in his back. Immediately, I grabbed Canon's gun and John did the same with Dombrowski's. I motioned for both Patterson and Dombrowski to sit down. Neither man posed much of a threat. We all knew who threw the knife into Canon's back and I thought: *I'll thank him later.*

I tapped 9-1-1 into my cell phone and hoped everything would get sorted out, this time correctly.

Fortunately, the state sent in a special prosecutor and the trials, through a change in venue,

were moved to the next county. Luckily Dombrowski, with Canon dead, exchanged information in return for leniency. Nobody asked the fifteen residents that were murdered if it was alright.

Even though judges belong to a fraternal club they take a dim view when one of their own takes advantage of their authority. Both judges were found guilty of abusing their powers, and were given stiff sentences.

Anne Hobbes felt the weight of the legal system as did Henry Waters. His role as guardian ad litem was taken as a serious abuse of power. He was given a sentence that wouldn't allow him to be out of prison until he was middle-aged. As for Anne Hobbes, she would be released from prison in time to enter an assisted living facility. If there was justice, I hoped someone like her was waiting.

I was happy to have solved the crimes in *Double Trouble.*

Post Script

(Justice for the Homeless)

Chapter One

As we were driving to the facility to retrieve Mark, John found every driver's nemesis, black ice. He tried to maintain control of the wheel, but the vehicle went into a full-blown skid. The front end left the pavement and we started to do a 360, spinning out of control.

Try as hard as he could, he couldn't stop the vehicle from sliding into the other lane. Fortunately, because of the time of day, there was little traffic and nobody was in the oncoming lane. It was impossible to tell how many times we spiraled across the lane, coming to a rest under the overpass.

We were able to crawl out of the vehicle on the passenger side with the driver's side buried in the snow bank. I felt a helping hand pull me to my feet. I expected to see one of my compatriots, but instead I saw an older man wearing worn-out clothes. He helped me to the side of the road and asked, "Are you okay, buddy?"

I replied, "Yeah, I think so. Thanks, partner."

Other poorly dressed people helped my friends the same way. I didn't know who they were. Looking at the overpass, I realized they were homeless people that had sought shelter where they could.

Once, we realized we were uninjured, my buddies and I smiled in relief.

John started, "I can't believe nobody was hurt!"

Ben chimed in, "I think my life passed me by!"

I added, "We're lucky there weren't any vehicles in the other lane!"

Tyler said, "Let's see if we can get this thing out of the snow!" With a lot of effort pushing and John rocking the vehicle, we freed it from the frozen embankment. After examining the vehicle, there appeared to be minimal damage. Before we left, I wanted to show our appreciation to the homeless folks that assisted us.

Walking over to them huddled under the concrete viaduct, I handed one of them some money. I said, "Thanks, for helping us. We appreciate it a lot. You take care now."

One of them reached out and took the money and replied, "You're welcome. We'll see you down the road."

I re-entered our vehicle, but I couldn't get them out of my mind. There by the grace of God go I. Later that night, borrowing my son's vehicle, and unable to put them out of my mind, I stopped at a convenience store and bought some food for the homeless.

I arrived at the overpass only to see it vacated. Not sure what to do, I set the bag of groceries down and hoped the next group that happened along could use them.

That night, I was eager to find out how big of a problem homelessness in the greatest nation in the world was. The most recent government statistics stated that over ½ million Americans were **homeless**. In addition to that, 40 million **people** struggle with hunger and the same number live in poverty. I read where Volunteers of America try to prevent homelessness through a range of services including eviction prevention, emergency services, temporary housing and permanent affordable housing. But I knew that wasn't enough. How could I help? I felt so guilty. My family had everything we needed: a roof over our head, a warm bed, plenty of food, and good medical care. All my life I never knew anybody that was in dire need. At least, I didn't think I did. I had to plead ignorance to one of our country's biggest problems.

On researching further, I learned there are a variety of homeless assistance programs available depending on the type of assistance that is needed. HUD helps homeless people through its housing assistance programs.

The LGBT homeless are at increased risk of violence compared to other groups. Transgender people are also at danger of being placed into the incorrect shelters. In some cases, transgender women can be turned away from women's shelters.

I found in one survey where the findings showed that of the surveyed homeless, two-thirds are men and most likely to be single adults between the ages of 25 and 54.

One startling statistic was that one out of every four men experienced domestic violence in their youth. In addition, young men who have been abused as children are more likely to become homeless and are at risk of becoming chronically homeless if they are not living in a permanent situation by age 24.

I was hoping homelessness was better for women, but their plight consisted of different problems. Women are at great risk of both homelessness and poverty because they are most likely to bear child-rearing responsibilities and are vulnerable from family member or sexual partners.

Women seeking refuge from domestic violence are not always able to find rooms in shelters. Some women have been turned away from homeless shelters because shelter staff maintain that turning women away will stop people from having intercourse inside the shelter.

My next concern was what personal problems did the homeless have.> Reading closer, I found alcohol abuse was the most common health problem among the shelter's guests, with other drug abuse a close second--both problems seemed to appear among about half of the guests. As I suspected, chronic mental illness was only slightly less common, while only about one in three appeared to be physically ill.

Chapter Two

The next day, my first stop was at the Catholic Homeless Shelter. I wanted to help, but how? I also wanted to know what type of people could do this wonderful charitable work.

As I entered two nuns were stripping cots and carrying the bedding into what appeared to be the laundry room. I decided to continue into the kitchen. There I saw two young adults working a perfect assembly line. The young man rinsed a plate and handed it to his co-worker. She scrubbed it clean and placed it in a drying rack. They made a well-oiled machine. I didn't want to startle them so I casually approached them and asked, "Are you guests here or employees?"

The young man replied, "We're volunteers from the local university."

I replied, "You are well organized. I can tell you have done this before."

The young lady answered, "We come every morning before class and wash the breakfast dishes."

Answering, I said, "That's very commendable. By the way, who runs this shelter?"

The young girl replied, "There are two nuns, Sister Angelina and Sister Kate. You'll find them in the main room."

I strolled out to the cots and noticed one of the nuns had returned. She saw me and asked, "What's your story?"

I said, "I just saw the Shelter sign and thought I'd come in and see for myself."

She replied, "Breakfast is over. Do you have any skills?"

I said, "I'm a fair carpenter."

She said, "I'm Sister Angelina. Go to the back and in the shed you'll find a hammer, nails, and a ladder. The roof needs repairing. Don't fall off the roof. If you do, try to land in the street. The city has better insurance."

Following her directions, I stepped out the back door and after zipping my coat; I found the supplies she had mentioned. I started my ascent, not being overjoyed with the cold weather. Reaching the roof, I was a little nervous realizing how far up I was. The cold weather made the roof treacherous. I crawled along the shingles and it wasn't long before I found a loose one. I pried the nails off and replaced it. I continued for hours being careful not to slip.

I noticed it must have been getting later in the day as people were entering the shelter. I decided to skip lunch because I felt if I ever got down, I would not be able to screw up my courage to return to this icy slope. The day passed as I continued to find more and more loose shingles.

The sun was starting to recede and more guests were pouring into the safe haven. The last shingle was put in place and I felt that was enough. The whole roof should be replaced, but I'm sure money was the controlling factor. I climbed down the ladder and replaced the tools.

Walking into the main room, I was impressed with the number of guests. Some had staked out their cot and the rest were lining up for the evening meal. My stomach was calling for attention and I ambled over to the end of the line. I picked up my dinnerware and asked the person ahead of me, "What's for dinner?"

Without moving, the man asked, "What day is it?"

I answered, "Tuesday."

The fellow replied, "Then it's stew."

I realized everyday was designated a certain meal. I asked the fellow, "What's the schedule for food?"

He replied, "Meat loaf on Monday, stew on Tuesday, pasta on Wednesday, shepherds' pie Thursday, fish on Friday, hamburgers on Saturday, and leftovers on Sunday."

The line was getting shorter and my mouth was starting to drool. As I slid through the line, Sister Angelina said, "Thanks for repairing the roof. Are you going to be here tomorrow?"

I answered, "I could. What do you need done?"

She answered, "The steps leading to the basement are worn and we need some dry walling in the back room."

I replied, "I think I can do that."

After my plate was filled, I turned to find a seat. That was going to be a challenge. Apparently, the guests wanted to sit next to their friends. I felt like I was back in grade school trying to find a place to sit. A few times I saw an open seat only to be told it was taken.

Finally, I saw a fellow wave to me and motion to an empty seat. I was glad to finally sit and as I did, he asked, "What's your name?"

I answered, "Bill Bennett. How about you?"

He replied, "Tom Simmons."

He asked, "What's your story?"

I answered, "I'm originally from the Superior Peninsula."

He said, "Our parents used to take us there when we were kids. I really like the Tahquamenon Falls."

I said, "Maybe, someday you can go back."

He answered, "Right now, there seems to be a monetary shortage."

We both chuckled.

I asked, "Are you from the area?"

He looked down and said, "Yes, I'm an accountant, but my firm said I wasn't doing a good job anymore so they fired me. I started to drink too much and my wife ordered me to leave. The hardest thing was leaving with my two girls crying."

I replied, "Yeah, that's got to be tough."

He asked, "Are you spending the night?"

I answered, "If there's a cot available."

He said, "I'll take care of that." He removed my hat and walked over to a pair of unclaimed cots. He placed mine on one and his hat on the other.

We continued to discuss sports and anything else. I told Tom my favorite team is the Green Bay Packers. I was used to disappointment. He laughed and said, "You'll never guess. My favorite football team is the New Orleans Saints." After we returned our dirty dishes and dinnerware, I told Tom I was going outside for a smoke. Once there, I tapped my cell phone. John answered and I heard, "Where the hell are you? We've been worried about you!"

I said, "I'm fine. I'm at the Catholic Homeless Shelter in Bay City!"

"What are you doing there?" asked John.

"Remember those homeless people we saw yesterday. I just wanted to do something to help."

John said, "Okay, we're here if you need us."

I disconnected and slid my cell phone into one of my socks. I assumed it would be a hot commodity for someone to steal. I returned to the main room and Tom and I continued to converse about politics and anything else that interested us. At eleven 'o clock, Sister Angelina said loudly, **"Lights Out!"** The room went dark except for the flashing lights from outside. Needless to say, I was a little apprehensive sleeping in a homeless shelter for the first time. I think Tom realized it and said, "Just go to sleep. I'll keep an eye on your cell phone."

I wondered how he knew, but thinking about it, there were only a few places to hide your valuables.

Working all day on the roof and enjoying a delicious home-cooked meal did the rest. I fell asleep and when I opened my eyes, Sister Angelina was standing over me. She said, "You missed breakfast. Get up! I want to strip your cot, lazy bones."

I couldn't argue with her. Standing, I realized Mother Nature was calling. She pointed and said, "It's that way." I was starting to think maybe, she did have a connection to the Big Fellow.

All of the other guests had eaten and left. When I returned to the main room, Sister Angelina said, "You know where the tool shed is. Get some lumber out back and start replacing the steps. When you finish that, I'll show you where the drywall supplies are. You're not going to eat free as long as I'm here. Get moving!"

I had to like her. She had a big heart and I knew she was just trying to get the most out of me.

I looked for an electric saw, but I only found a hand saw in the shed. I didn't have the courage to ask Sister Angelina if she had a circular or a table saw.

Removing the old boards was more of a chore than I imagined. They had been installed when Moses was young. The boards split and cracked as I pulled on them. I hadn't used a hand saw since I was in high school. Blisters developed right on cue. Again, I was afraid to ask her for Band-Aids for fear of arousing her wrath. By lunch time the stairs were finished. I sought out Sister Angelina to seek her approval. Upon finding her, I explained the stairs were finished.

She exclaimed, "Well, it's about time!"

Nothing I did seemed to please her.

She continued, "I'd thought you'd be done a long time ago. Was the circular saw broke?"

I said, "You have a circular saw?"

"Of course. We're not in the Dark Ages, you know. Why didn't you come and ask me? I can see you're a little on the slow side. I'll have to give you easier jobs I guess."

I got in line for my lunch and ate my tomato soup and sandwich. I wanted to argue with Sister Angelina, but I was raised Catholic and I didn't want the wrath of God down on me.

Sister Angelina looked at me and said, "When you're finished, see if you can do the drywall in the backroom. I've had one of the boys bring everything there for you. Do you think you can handle that?"

I shook my head, and like a school boy, returned my dishes and dinnerware to the kitchen and sauntered into the back room.

Stepping into the room, I counted fifteen sheets of drywall. I had my work ahead of me. Placing the first drywall piece in place I wondered if I dared ask Sister Angelina if she had a power drill. I thought better of it and used a screwdriver.

Chapter Three

Later that day, since I had met my match in Sister Angelina, I wasn't looking forward to meeting her pastoral partner, Sister Kate. As I was finishing my meal in the dining hall, I noticed occasionally women and children would emerge from a doorway to receive a meal and then promptly returned the same way.

Being curious, I had to see what was on the other side. When nobody was looking, I slid the door open and was amazed. There was a smaller room with cots, but these were being used by women and children. I assumed they were families that had to use the shelter to escape a dangerous situation.

No sooner was the door opened than I was chastised by the other nun. She sprang into action and was reprimanding me when her counterpart appeared out of nowhere and picked up the gauntlet. Now I was being castigated by both nuns for committing one of the seven deadly sins (or so I thought). Closing the door did reduce the reprimanding by half. Sister Angelina said, "You have no business on the other side of that door. Do you understand?" As least she didn't have me hold out one of my hands to have my knuckles rapped.

Eventually, the other sister emerged and made her way to the coffee table. This was my moment. I casually made my way across the room and pretended I was waiting to refill mine. As I casually stepped next to her, I could see she was much younger than Sister Angelina. She could have been accused of being an Anne Hathaway look-alike.

I said, "First of all, I want to apologize for opening the door. I was just curious and I didn't know the rules. My name is Bill Bennett."

The sister blushed and said, "I think I over-reacted. My name is Sister Kate. Sister Angelina takes care of the men on this side and I work with the domestic violence survivors in the other room. We separate the men from the women, otherwise, it just creates problems. As hard as it is to conceptualize, once our guests have a meal, shower and a warm place to stay, they think about other needs. To avoid trouble, we keep men and women in different rooms.

I asked, "What are the rules for families to stay here?"

She replied, "Everyone is welcome unless a child is over sixteen. Then we have to find a home for that young person."

I replied, "You and Sister Angelina perform a great service for these people."

"A lot of people don't know that hundreds of homeless individuals die each year from diseases, untreated medical conditions, lack of nutrition, starvation, and freezing to death. Twenty years ago, homeless people were more likely to die than the general population. In New Orleans, approximately 10,000 homeless people were unaccounted for after the hurricane in 2005. The reason we wash the bedding every night is to prevent bed bugs. It's a constant challenge to keep the cots sanitized."

She informed me, "Homeless individuals in the United States are subject to being arrested and held in jail for disturbing the peace or for drinking in public. In some communities, businesses have petitioned their city council to have homeless people banned from lying on the streets. Panhandling is always a problem."

Sister Kate looked at me and asked, "And what may I ask brings you to our humble place?"

I asked, "Can you keep a secret?"

She smiled and said, "After all these years of being a nun, I'm pretty good at keeping secrets."

I whispered, "I'm really not an indigent. I'm with my friends and I'm just trying to do something nice for the homeless."

She covered her face and stifled a laugh. She answered, "My, are your friends here now? I think I see one of them over there talking to himself. What about the fellow next to me? Is he a millionaire incognito?"

I could see she was having some fun at my expense. Rather

than continue to try to prove my real identity, I just capitulated and said, "I guess you got me, Sister."

She tapped my hand and said, "I always appreciate a good story. I haven't heard anything like that in a long time. I think I'll return to my space machine and go back in time. It was nice to meet you Mr. Bennett." She continued to giggle as she left.

Before I bedded down for the night, I broke the cardinal rule again and chanced to return through the door leading to the domestic abuse survivors. By now, the women and children were long asleep and I scoured the area for Sister Kate.

There was noise coming from the back room and I continued walking toward it. I could see Sister Kate wrestling with a man that looked down on his luck.

I immediately jumped into action. Racing into the kitchen, grabbed the tattered looking man and pulled him from her. I struck him several times and that seemed to persuade him from his quest. Getting to his feet, he leaped out the back door and ran into the night. I thought about giving chase, but thought Sister Kate needed my help.

She was getting to her knees and I helped her stand. She said, "Thank you. You never know what's going to happen here!"

I said, "First thing in the morning, I'll fix that lock."

She answered, "That would be swell. Sister Angelina said you were handy. We could sure use a man with your skills here, that is, when you're not saving the world."

I bit my tongue realizing she had just suffered a terrible ordeal and it was good she could still have a sense of humor.

I said, "You should call the police and report it."

She replied, "Oh, that's just Andy."

I asked, "You know that guy? Is he a regular?"

She answered, "Yes, he's been through a rough patch. His wife left him last year and he's found solace in alcohol."

I said, "That's no excuse. The next time you see him, point him out to me and I'll have a talk with him. In the future, it might be one of the women staying here that gets attacked."

Sister Kate said, "It's God's will that you intervened. Let it go at that. It's time for Vespers. Good night Mr. Bennett and thank you again."

She left to say her prayers in the small chapel attached to the back of the shelter. I returned to my cot, determined to have a talk with Andy.

Chapter Four

The next day, I was awakened by men in the chow line. I was able to strip my bed and bring the bedding to the laundry area. Sister Angelina even smiled as I handed them to her. I was making progress.

After breakfast, I was enjoying one of the few pleasures in life, my morning coffee. To my surprise, Sister Angelina took a break and sat next to me. I felt honored she would take a minute out of her busy day to commiserate. She stated, "One of the women told me how you helped Sister Kate last night. I want to thank you."

I replied, "Don't mention it. I was glad to be in the right place at the right time. How is it the two of you landed here?"

She pondered the question and answered. "Our order is in Baltimore and we were cloistered. However, one of the priests saw us as easy pickings. I was able to fend off his advances, but Sister Kate wasn't strong enough."

I asked, "You mean she was taken advantage of by a priest?" She said, "We don't talk about it, but yes. When we complained to the bishop, his solution was to send us here. As least I feel we're making a difference. I deal with the men and Sister Kate cares for the families."

"How long do you think you'll stay here," I asked.

"It's up to our order and the bishop," answered Sister Angelina.

With that, she stood and returned to her chores of stripping the beds and doing the laundry. I had a whole new respect for the dutiful ladies. They wanted to serve God and mankind despite the inhumanity they faced. When I saw Sister Kate exit her door, I made sure I was next to her as she filled her coffee. If I didn't know what occurred last night, nobody would even conceptualize it. "Good morning," I said. "I see you're up bright and early."

"Good day to you too, Mr. Bennett. Do you have plans to stop any alien invasions today?" Sister Kate asked playfully. Going along with her humor, I said, "I just got a call from the White House, they want me to investigate your order," I replied. Sister Kate grinned and said, "Well, you've got a full day ahead of you, don't you?"

I retaliated, "People are saying you and Sister Angelina have been heard whispering after dark." She smiled and chirped, "They're probably right. We like to huddle in the church and ponder dastardly deeds. I guess you're on to us. You're quite the detective."

"A little bird told me you were taken advantage of while you were cloistered," I began.

"That little bird better be careful or she'll get her wings clipped," Sister Kate responded.

"My wife says it's therapeutic to discuss painful experiences," I answered.

"I'm sure your wife is very wise, but this time she's wrong," replied Sister Kate.

"Why don't you try me and see? After all, you'll probably never see me again. I'm not affiliated with the Church," I retorted.

"Sometimes, I blame myself," she stated.

"Come on, you can't blame yourself. You know as well as well as I do, the Catholic Church has played a shell game with pedophiles as well as turning a deaf ear to priests' inappropriate behavior," I argued.

"After the first attack, I didn't repel him, but allowed him to continue. He came almost nightly while I was there. I wanted to go to the bishop, but my attacker told me the bishop wouldn't believe me," she stated.

I wasn't able to respond satisfactorily, but I just thought the best thing I could do was continue listening. She continued, "I even thought of leaving the Church, but I gave myself to Christ in my vows," she admitted.

I could tell I was getting somewhere. I stated, "Is the bum still in the church?"

"Yes, he's still a priest. When other nuns brought the allegations to the bishop's attention, he just responded by moving the priest to another parish. At least his new responsibility doesn't have any nuns for him to assault. I pray every day to forgive him," she murmured.

"I hope the Pope does something to help the victims," I interjected.

"I don't think even he can solve the problems in the Church, but he can help the victims heal. I'm finding solace here at the shelter helping families," she responded.

"You are making a tremendous influence on the needy. Just think, if you and Sister Angelina weren't here, these homeless people would really suffer. You should feel great regarding the contribution you're making."

"Are you still sticking to your story that you and your friends are trying to help the needy?" she asked.

"As a matter of fact, I am," I answered.

"Well thanks for listening to me. It doesn't solve the injustice or help me sleep at night, but it was good to talk about it. For that, I thank you," Sister Kate said as she rose and returned to her duties.

Just then a fracas started by the doorway. In a flash, both Sisters Angelina and Kate sprang into action. They approached two disheveled men that appeared to be in a scuffle. Suddenly, one man brandished a knife and swung wildly at the other. Angelina stepped between the two men and said sternly, "We'll have none of this in the shelter. If you want to fight, take it outside!" By the time I got to the quarrel, Sister Angelina had the situation well in hand. She wasn't finished. She stared the one man down and ordered, "Give me the knife!" Looking at his feet, the combatant looked sheepish and held the weapon out for her to take. Sister Angelina spoke sternly again saying, "Now both of you get out and I don't want to see you until tonight. If you come back, you'll behave yourself. Understand?" Both men nodded and ambled toward the door.

I couldn't help myself. I said, "Sister, that was very

impressive."

Sister Angelina replied, "It's nothing. I grew up with four brothers."

"Both of you do a fantastic job keeping this place going. I'm very impressed," I relayed.

Sister Kate responded, "And coming from a secret Good Samaritan, that means a lot." I shrugged my shoulders and said, "All in a day's work."

Sister Angelina had a puzzled look and asked, "Am I missing something?" Sister Kate looked at me and answered, "It's a secret between Mr. Bennet and me."

Chapter Five

Drywalling was not my specialty, but I could handle a trawl. Stepping back, the room looked pretty good. I cleaned the utensils and returned to the main room daring Sister Angelina to challenge my workmanship. Seeing me, she strode toward me and looked in the room. She said, "Not bad for an amateur. Tomorrow, I assume you'll start with the first coat of primer."

I could only nod my head and say, "That sounds good. I'll start tomorrow."

She said, "Get in line and don't spill."

My return to grade school was complete.

After dinner, I looked around for my new cot mate, Tom. He was nowhere to be found. I asked a few men if they saw him on the streets, but they shook their heads negatively. I now became worried, and putting my coat on, I walked out to join the smokers. Once again, I asked, "Has anybody seen Tom Simmons?"

One of them replied, "No, not since this morning."

"Do you know where he goes?" I asked.

One of them answered, "He likes to go to the alley behind the bakery. Sometimes, they throw the stale bakery in the dumpster and he brings them back for us."

Before I started to look for Tom, I asked directions to the alley. After walking a few streets, I could see the bright lights of the bakery. Ducking into the alley, I perused both sides. There were several dumpsters and I checked each one.

I opened the one directly behind the bakery not knowing what to expect. There was my worst nightmare. Tom was lying among the bags of garbage covered in blood.

I dived in and tried to prop him to a sitting position. I checked my cell phone and I only had one bar left. I hoped it was enough as I tapped 9-1-1. The dispatcher answered and I relayed the horrible news. He told me to stay on the line but I informed him that wasn't possible. My cell phone was about to expire and I had to make one more call. I finished saying, "Come as soon as you can!" I disconnected and I again tapped my lifeline. John answered and I repeated the news to him. He replied, "I'm having trouble hearing you. Is this Bill?"

I jumped out of the dumpster and ran to the main avenue hoping it would give me better reception. This time John could hear me, but my cell phone battery was dying fast. I was able to shout out the street address before it died.

I waited for the EMTs and police to arrive. No luck. I marched into the street and waited for a patrol car to come into sight. Seeing one in the distance, I stepped in front of the vehicle. They immediately turned on their flashing lights. I didn't have time to explain. Both officers jumped out of their cruiser and body-slammed me against the hood. Unceremoniously, I was handcuffed and thrown in the backseat. They drove to the station house where I would have to explain my dilemma.

Upon arriving, the officers didn't care to hear my story. Dragging me inside, they threw me in front of the desk sergeant.

One of the officers began, "This homeless guy stepped in front of our cruiser. He probably just wants a hot meal and a cot. What's the problem, buddy, are the shelters filled up already?"

I wanted to smash the officer, but I had more important problems than my pride. I shouted, "I was trying to get your attention! My friend is in the dumpster and is hurt bad! I phoned 9-1-1 but they didn't respond!"

The desk sergeant was anything but apologetic. He said, "We get these calls every day. Your friend probably ran into somebody that wanted something of his. Where did this happen?"

I answered, "Behind the bakery. Someone told me they occasionally throw out old food and I suppose someone might have wanted his. That still doesn't excuse the emergency people not responding!"

The sergeant, still uncaring, replied, "The EMTs will get there eventually, but they have so many calls, they have to prioritize them."

That answer didn't sit well with me. I retaliated, "It shouldn't matter who calls, they should be answered in the order they are received."

The sergeant now got testy. He said, "Do you want someone's child to die because the EMTs were dragging a homeless guy out of a dumpster?" I was now furious. I said, "Take these handcuffs off me. For one thing, I'm not a homeless person. Even if I was, what difference should that make?"

The desk sergeant chuckled and asked, "Do you have any identification?"

I said, "In my sock you'll find my driver's license, cell phone and some cash. I know how much is there, so don't steal it."

He pulled my ID and cell phone from my sock and said, "I guess you're not homeless after all. You're from the Superior Peninsula. I used to snowmobile there years ago. Nice place."

I said, "I don't give a hoot and a damn about you, my friend has been injured and he's lying in a dumpster. Send someone to get him!"

The desk sergeant motioned for the two patrol officers to remove the handcuffs. Neither one apologized. I guess good manners were in short supply around there.

The sarge talked into his radio and gave the address of the alley in question. Without fanfare, I followed the patrol officers to their vehicle. I calmed myself enough to ask, "Are you officers returning to the same area?"

One of them nodded their head. I asked, "Could you give me a ride back there?"

The other officer replied curtly, "Get in!"

With that warm treatment, they drove me back to the alley that contained my friend, Tom.

They slowed down enough for me to exit and then sped on their way. I thought: *they must not teach human decency anymore.*

I waited at the entrance of the alley for fear the ambulance might miss it. After a long-extended period, one finally arrived. Being totally oblivious to a homeless person, The EMTs exited and slowly walked to the dumpster. One of them lifted the lid, looked inside, and asked, "What body?"

I blew a gasket as I jumped inside. I crawled through the smelly debris feeling for his body. He wasn't there. I jumped out of the first dumpster and raced to the next one. I threw up the lid and scanned the contents. It was empty.

I stood dumbfounded. I said, "I don't know what to say. He was in that dumpster an hour ago."

The EMTs returned to their ambulance, stepped inside and drove away.

I didn't know what to do. I returned to the homeless shelter and retold my story to Sister Angelina. She stated, "I suppose someone, feeling sorry for him, took him someplace."

Sister Angelina may have been on to something. *Maybe, someone removed the body, but not for good intentions. What if it was a set up?*

I asked, "Sister, is it okay if I use your land- line?"

She replied, "I assume it's in connection with your friend's disappearance?"

I said, "Yes, I want to call my buddies and have them pick me up."

She seemed surprised by my answer. "Aren't you an indigent?"

I said, "No, my friends and I are here trying to solve some crimes in the tri-city area."

She said, "I thought I was doing such a good job saving you."

I smiled and said, "I appreciated your efforts."

Tapping John's cell number into Sister's landline, I was glad to hear a friendly voice. I said, "Could you bring everyone? A fellow I met yesterday was murdered and I found him in a dumpster in an alley." I gave John the address of the homeless shelter and I couldn't wait to see them.

Soon, they arrived and entered the shelter. Sister Angelina approached them and said, "Welcome, get in line and wait your turn. We're having pasta. If you want to wash your hands, the restroom is in the back."

John said, "No thanks. We're looking for an old tired-looking man."

Sister Angelina replied, "Look around!"

Seeing my buddies, I walked to them with a look of relief. As I got closer, I said, "Am I glad to see you guys. A new friend was murdered and tossed in the dumpster behind the bakery. The police don't seem too concerned. Sister Angelina thinks a Good Samaritan may have removed the body and brought him to a hospital, but I doubt it."

John asked, "What do you know about the guy?"

"He only told me a snippet last night. I know he was an accountant for a company in Bay City. He was married, but his wife kicked him out because he was drinking too much."

The pseudo-detectives talked me into returning to our hotel for a shower, clean clothes and to re-think everything.

Chapter Six

Later that day, after I got control of my feelings, I checked my smartphone for Tom Simmons' home address. Upon arriving, I couldn't help noticing two small bicycles leaning against the front porch.

As I rang the doorbell, emotions ran through me about how sad the girls will be when they find out their father is dead.

The door opened and I introduced myself and the lady did likewise. Her name was Alice Simmons. I stated, "Yesterday, I spent some time at the Catholic Homeless Shelter and I got to meet your husband, Tom. He was a very nice man. We talked about sports and his family."

She said, "I didn't know Tom volunteered at the homeless shelter. I can see him doing that. He's such a dear."

I was a little confused and I said, "He wasn't volunteering, he was staying there."

Mrs. Simmons snickered and said, "There must be some mistake. Tom was here last night, wasn't he girls?" She looked at the two tykes and they both shook their heads. "You must have him confused with someone else. I'm sorry for your trouble," she said. "Oh, here he comes now," as she pointed to a vehicle pulling into the driveway.

A tall handsome man stepped out of the vehicle, and both little girls ran to him calling, "Daddy, Daddy!" Now I was really confused. The man approached me and Mrs. Simmons said, "This man said he saw you yesterday at the Catholic Homeless Relief Shelter. I didn't know you were volunteering there."

The man replied, "I'm not. You must have me confused with someone else. Maybe, you heard the name wrong. Anyway, as you can see, I'm here and very hungry. If you don't mind, I would like to eat. It's nice to meet you."

The Simmons family entered the house and left me standing on the front porch with egg on my face. *Did I hear the guy's name wrong? Am I losing my marbles? I have to get a hold of myself.*

Back at the hotel, I explained my problem. Most of the guys assured me that I just heard the name incorrectly. John said, "Just forget it. We have other problems to deal with!"

The others reinforced that concept and told me to blow it off as a case of mistaken identity. It's not like I could go to the shelter and get a few of the men that knew Tom Simmons and bring them to the police station. It's safe to say, the homeless guys would have no credibility.

Was there a cover-up? My detective juices were flowing and I owed it to Tom Simmons, or whoever he was, to find out what happened. I went to bed and tried to sleep, but that was impossible.

The next morning, I was up early and parked down the street from the Simmons' residence. The new Tom Simmons stepped out of his house and gave his wife a peck on the cheek. The two little girls clung to their mother's legs as she waved good-bye. Simmons backed out and I assumed he proceeded to his work place. For good measure, I followed him. Sure enough, it was a large business complex with multiple buildings. There's no way this guy, if he was an imposter, could fool all of these employees. Where was the weak link? I had to determine if this man and his family were lying.

I returned to the hotel and the guys were just having breakfast. They ordered coffee for me, but I ignored it. John said, "I can tell by that far-away look you have this thing is eating you alive. Forget it!"

I answered, "I can't let it go. That man described everything to me the other night."

Mark asked, "Could he have been a little touched in the head? Maybe, he just thought he was Tom Simmons. He might have had a crush on the wife at one time."

I said, "That's possible, but he sure seemed lucid."

The next morning, I decided to stake out the Simmons' house, hoping there would be an opportunity to talk to the girls when the mother wasn't present. *Maybe, I can talk to the girls and find out if that man was their real father.*

For days, ignoring my comrade's wishes, I continued to park down the street from the Simmons' residence. Days passed until one day, Mrs. Simmons finally exited with her girls. After strapping them in the back seat she drove onto I-75 with me following at a distance. She took an exit, and after a few turns, arrived in front of a day-care. The girls exited their vehicle, and together, they entered the center. After a few minutes, the mother left and I assumed she had a commitment. I had to think, what would encourage little children to entice them out of a day-care? I took a trip to the local Wal-Mart and I returned with helium-filled balloons. Realizing this would appear to be weird to the daycare employees, I pressed the buzzer on their front door and waited for a reply. Realizing security of the children was critical in this day and age, I heard a muffled voice ask, "Yes, what can we do for you?" I answered, "I was told to deliver these balloons for one of the children's birthdays."

I was skeptical that would work, but to my surprise, the door popped open and I was overrun by a dozen urchins screaming and jumping for a balloon. I held the balloons up as high as I could and speaking in a loud voice, I asked, "Who wants a balloon?"

That was followed by a chorus of more screams.

I continued, "Everyone gets a free balloon and all you have to do is tell me who your father's favorite football team is. Okay? Who wants to go first?"

Many tykes shouted different team names and I started handing out the balloons purposely waiting to ask the Simmons girls last. Finally, it was their turn and I asked them, "What's your daddy's favorite team. They both responded in unison, "It's used to be New Orleans, but now it's the Detroit Lions."

I asked, "Did your daddy switch teams?"

One of the girls said, "No, we got a new daddy. I miss my old daddy."

I gave the girls their balloons and now I knew I wasn't hallucinating.

Needless to say, I received many skeptical looks from the adults as I left and drove back to the hotel. Now I could enlist the help of my cohorts and get this straightened out. In our hotel room, I explained what the young Simmons girls told me. The boys seemed to come around. Mark said, "Supposing you're right, what do we do now?"

I said, "We have to get inside that company and see what's happening."

That night, we did a dry run to the company headquarters. Once we arrived, we could see it was lit up like Rockefeller Plaza. As we approached, John said under his breath, "My God, how are we going to get in there?"

I answered, "We're going to be invited!"

Chapter Seven

Obviously, we weren't going to break into that fortress. We had to do our research. After reading about the company on the internet, we discovered the company dealt with gold investments.

In researching gold speculation, it showed with the rise in the value of gold due to a financial crisis, there has been a surge in companies that will buy personal gold in exchange for cash, or sell investments in gold bullion and coins.

Many of these companies are under investigation for a variety of security fraud, including laundering money for terrorist organizations. Was that possible?

It seemed this company sold gold for cash. As we were enjoying a cup of coffee, I pondered: *what if they were going to be investigated by the Securities and Exchange Agency. Would the leadership of an entire company pool together and allow one of their accountants to disappear to avoid legal problems?* We knew the answer to that.

That morning, I contacted the company and let it be known that our gold brokerage firm was in town. Would they be interested in doing business?

Within the hour, our appointment was confirmed. Since the new Simmons would probably be there, I could not participate. The others would have to attend and act the part of wealthy gold financiers.

The boys had to visit a men's haberdashery and get outfitted in expensive suits. When the store employees finished, the boys were decked out with diamond stick pins and expensive suits.

My job was to get a limo and impersonate a chauffeur. By mid-afternoon, the boys were ready to swindle the best. We arrived fashionably late due to a last-minute call from London, or at least that's what John told the thieves upon their arrival. The neophyte gold traders were introduced to the CEO of Brinks, Inc. His name was Herman Schuyler. The president of the board was Carter Rutherford, the vice president was Brock Van Cort, and the chief accountant was Tom Simmons.

It took a long time to exchange introductions and pleasantries. John explained, "We were on our way to Detroit for a Gold Symposium sponsored by the Federal Reserve System. The only reason we're attending is after the symposium is over, we're going to lobby the Feds to do away with Form 8300.

"After all, under current law, we are free to buy as much gold as we want in any form, including bars, bullion coins, collectible coins and jewelry. No federal law or regulation oversees individuals trading in the metal. Furthermore, there are no reporting requirements on the purchase of gold, whatever the quantity, with one exception. A seller must notify the government when he uses more than $10,000 in cash to buy gold. With today's purchases, that's an antiquated law. Don't you boys agree?"

CEO Schuyler cleared his throat and agreed, saying, "Absolutely, we deal in millions of gold bullion bought and sold every day and to think the Federal Trade Commission has to examine everyone one of our sales is ridiculous."

John related, "I'm glad to see we're on the same page. Now gentlemen, let's get down to business. We understand you have some gold you're going to sell on the open market. What if we play a shell game?"

Carter Rutherford asked, "What do you mean?"

Ben, trying to sound like a true financier, replied, "It's simple, you sell us the gold and we hide it from the Federal Reserve. You have all your documents showing you sold it to our hedge fund. We then hide it in a Cayman Island account and we then sell it on the open market in Russia for twice what it's worth. You make millions and we take a small commission."

Brock Van Cort hesitated and said, "How do we know you will sell?"

Tyler replied, "Here comes the perfect answer. We have your accountant hand deliver it to the Cayman Islands. It's guaranteed foolproof."

The boys sat quietly while Schuyler, Rutherford, Van Cort, and Simmons discussed it among themselves. After conferring, Schuyler said, "We have a deal!"

Everyone shook hands and the trap was set

Schuyler asked, "When do you want this to occur?"

This time the pseudo-detectives conferred, and after a few minutes, John responded, "How about the day after tomorrow? That way, it'll give you fellows time to prepare the shipment." The boys smiled and left the board room believing they were going to swindle the thieves.

Upon entering the limo, each of the guys couldn't help but laugh hysterically over the whole scam. As we were driving away from the complex, Rutherford asked, Schuyler, "Are you sure, you want to do this?"

Schuyler asked, "Are you nuts? Of course not. I could see right through them. Simmons, you set everything up. We make a big show of carting the gold to an armored car. We'll have another armored car waiting in our garage. We'll delay those chumps from leaving. We load our armored car into a semi and the other armored car continues on its way.

"At the airport, those fools watch the plane leave for the Cayman Islands. Meanwhile, we hide our gold until the IRS is satisfied. Those idiots are on the hook for millions of dollars.

They toasted a glass of champagne and were ready to fool us.

Chapter Eight

We were feeling pretty smug about the whole scam. I said, "These guys are very shifty. I think I'm going to investigate and see what I can uncover."

"Somewhere along the trail they're going to switch armored cars. As far as I can tell looking at the map, once they're on the road, it's a pretty clear shot to the airport. I think they're going to switch vehicles in the garage," I stated.

The guys agreed and since the others had to be there, I was the only one that could foil their plot

There were many armored car companies in South East Michigan. I gambled that they were going to switch armored vehicles. Since the gold's weight was so great, there would be no way they could unload it.

I phoned each of the armored car companies in the area and pretending I was the contact person for the gold investment company and was in charge of lining up the armored vehicles. After finding the company that had scheduled an armored car for the gold company, I said, "I just want to double check what time the vehicle will be ready."

The dispatcher said, "We have you down for two vehicles."

I quickly corrected myself and said, "That's right, we want both of them for ten o'clock a.m. Thanks," as I disconnected.

I looked at my cohorts and said, "We're not as smart as we think. They have two armored vehicles ordered for that day."

Mark bellowed, "Well, I'll be a monkey's uncle. We have to fix that."

John said, "We don't drive in until the armored car is loaded and ready to leave. They're probably going to do something to distract us and switch vehicles."

I said, "I can hide under the limo with a 4-wheeler under me.

If you go slow enough, I will slide out from underneath at the right time."

It was another hair-brained scheme that had to work or else we'd owe the IRS millions.

That morning, nervous as hell, we drove to the gold investment firm. Before entering the complex, John pulled to the side of the road and I slid under the limo lying on a 4-wheeler. We entered the complex and proceeded to the underground garage. We assumed they had closed- circuit cameras everywhere, so we had to be quick. At one point, John slowed to a crawl and I slid out from under the limo and beneath the 18-wheeler.

By now, the driver was relaxing in his cab waiting for the ruse to start. I emerged on the passenger side of the truck and opened the cab door. The thug was caught completely off-guard. I tasered him and relegated him to the trailer.

Now the real trick would start. Ben, John and the others had gathered along with CEO Schuyler and his cronies to watch the gold be loaded into the first armored car. Upon wheeling the last of it inside the heavy plated vehicle, both limos and the armored vehicle started to accelerate. Then, all of a sudden Schuyler's limo stopped and an angry CEO exited and shouted, "**I forgot my cell phone!**" Naturally, the pseudo-detectives waited patiently while the CEO retrieved it. After a few minutes lapsed, the two limos began their journey. By this time, the first armored vehicle had driven into the back of the semi. I slid the ramp into its place under the cargo area and locked the doors. I returned to the cab and sat nonchalantly as the second armored car appeared from its hiding place and left the premises. Within few minutes, both limos maneuvered past me.

To complete the plan, both vehicles accelerated and fell in closely behind the second armored vehicle.

Once the convoy reached the airport both sides were positive that they had fooled the other. Both entourages watched as the valuable cargo was loaded onto the specially-equipped airplane that was designated to fly non-stop to the Cayman Islands.

With the last of the gold loaded onto the plane, both sides shook hands and prepared to watch the plane depart. To complete the subterfuge, Simmons boarded the plane to guarantee its arrival.

Both sides watched with apprehension as the plane taxied to the runway, and with final take-off approval, soared into the sky.

The plane was just gaining altitude when suddenly it exploded in mid-air. Both sides stood staring as the wreckage plummeted to earth. John and the pseudo-detectives were speechless. Schuyler turned and said, "You didn't think I'd let you steal the gold that easy, did you?" The high establishment gold financiers drew their weapons and Schuyler said, "If you please, phone your associate and tell him to bring the gold."

John tapped his cell phone and relayed the message. I had to make a decision, should I bring it back to them or disappear with millions in gold. There wasn't much of a decision to make. The two groups were standing on the runway when I appeared with the semi. Schuyler said, "If you don't mind, please step out and join your business associates." I obliged and threw my hands in the air and shouted, "Sorry guys, we almost pulled it off."

Chortling, Brock Van Cort stepped into the semi cab and proceeded to drive away. Schuyler looked at us and said, "I would like to shoot all of you, but then we'd have some explaining to do to the authorities. I'll leave you with your lives such as they are. I trust we won't see you again." With that he stepped into the limo and followed the semi. All of the guys were down in the mouth, with Mark saying, "Now, what do we do? Should we return to the Superior Peninsula or turn ourselves in and beg for mercy?"

I replied, "I don't know about you, but I'm going to Disney World!"

They all shouted in unison, **"What are you talking about?"**

I replied, "I drove to the Simmons residence and parked the armored car. "I gave the two drivers the choice to die or make a run for it. They chose the latter. Using a pre-arranged rented fork lift I offloaded the gold from the first armored vehicle. As I was doing it, Mrs. Simmons told me the gold investment company threatened to kill her little girls if she didn't go along with the deception.

We never found Tom Simmons' body. The gold investment firm was charged with many felonies relating to the disappearance of millions in gold bullion. Mrs. Simmons got a good investor of her own. We were satisfied to have achieved *Justice for the Homeless.*

Made in the USA
Monee, IL
30 August 2020